AUG 1 2 2010

P9-DNO-104

MURDER IN THE AIR

▼

MURDER
IN
THE AIR

BILL CRIDER

MINOTAUR BOOKS

A THOMAS DUNNE BOOK

NEW YORK

A THOMAS DUNNE BOOK FOR MINOTAUR BOOKS.
An imprint of St. Martin's Publishing Group.

MURDER IN THE AIR. Copyright © 2010 by Bill Crider. All rights reserved. Printed in the United States of America. For information, address St. Martin's Press, 175 Fifth Avenue, New York, N.Y. 10010.

www.thomasdunnebooks.com

www.minotaurbooks.com

Library of Congress Cataloging-in-Publication Data

Crider, Bill, 1944–
    Murder in the air / Bill Crider.—1st ed.
      p. cm.
    ISBN 978-0-312-38695-5
    1. Rhodes, Dan (Fictitious character)—Fiction. 2. Sheriffs—Fiction.
3. Farmers—Crimes against—Fiction. 4. Agricultural pollution—Texas—
Fiction. 5. Texas—Fiction.
I. Title.
  PS3553.R497M856 2010
  813'.54—dc22

                                                   2009047488

First Edition: August 2010

10 9 8 7 6 5 4 3 2 1

For Judy

Author's Note

▼

THIS BOOK IS A WORK OF FICTION AND AS SUCH IS NOT BASED ON any actual events or persons. However, the negative impact of factory farms on rural living is real.

MURDER IN THE AIR

▼

1

▼

SHERIFF DAN RHODES WASN'T SURE JUST WHY THE BLACKLIN County Sheriff's Department needed an M-16.

Commissioner Mikey Burns was happy to explain. "Firepower," he said. His eyes gleamed. "Nine hundred and fifty rounds a minute. The bullets travel at twenty-nine hundred feet per second. Can you believe that? Punch a hole in a tank with something like that."

Burns didn't look like a man who'd be so interested in so much firepower. He was the most informal of the county commissioners and always wore an aloha shirt to work. The one he wore today had a navy blue background decorated with red and white airplanes, some of which appeared to be flying upside down, and palm trees with waving green leaves. Some of the palm trees were upside down, too.

Even Burns's name was informal. He was actually Michael Burns, but his brother had tagged him Mikey because, unlike some child actor in a nearly forgotten TV commercial, he'd eat anything, even, according to one account, a piece of bicycle tire.

Rhodes wasn't sure if that was true, but he had to admit that it made a good story.

"Firepower for what?" Rhodes asked. "I can't remember a single time we've had to take out a tank."

"There are other things to worry about," Burns said.

"Water moccasins?" Rhodes asked. "They're about the most dangerous things in the county, but I don't think we'd need nine hundred and fifty rounds a minute at nearly three thousand feet per second for a snake."

"Not water moccasins," Burns said. "Something a lot worse. Terrorists."

Burns and Rhodes were in Burns's office at the precinct barn. It was a bare-bones place, with a couple of wooden folding chairs, an old desk, and two dark green metal filing cabinets with long scratches on the sides. They looked as if they came from an army surplus store.

"Terrorists?" Rhodes asked. "You think they'd consider Blacklin County a prime target?"

He tried to think of what the terrorists would hit. The only thing that came to mind was the coal-powered electricity plant on the far eastern side of the county, and even if that were to be destroyed, it wouldn't exactly cripple the United States.

"Maybe we're not a prime target," Burns said. He crossed his arms and leaned back in his desk chair. "Think of it like this, though. We have a highway passing right through Clearview."

Clearview was the largest town in the county, but the highway wasn't a main thoroughfare. It didn't connect to any of the state's large cities.

"So much the better for the terrorists," Burns said when Rhodes brought up the point. "Let's say they come into the country from the south. It'd be easy. They'd go to somewhere like Cuba, take a boat to Mexico, and come up through Texas. They'd use the less-traveled highways because that way they wouldn't be as likely to get caught. Check with Clyde Ballinger. He could tell you all about it."

"Clyde Ballinger?" Rhodes asked. "He's a funeral director. What does he know about terrorism?"

"It's all in a book he read. He told me about it yesterday. You'll have to ask him."

Rhodes knew what kind of books Ballinger read: old paperback crime novels that he picked up at garage sales or thrift stores. He'd probably never read a book less than twenty-five years old. Certainly he wasn't likely to have read anything about terrorism. Not anything factual, anyway.

Rhodes must have looked skeptical because Burns said, "I'm not kidding, Sheriff. You ask Clyde. You'll see."

"All right," Rhodes said. "I'll ask him if I think of it, but I still don't think we need an M-16. Even if we needed one, I don't think the county could afford it."

"We can use drug seizure money," Burns said.

Rhodes's department had closed down a few dozen meth labs, but the labs had all been in dilapidated trailers and tumbledown shacks that lumped all together wouldn't have sold for enough to buy an M-16.

"Or we can get a grant," Burns said. "The Feds know that small-town law enforcement teams are the eyes and ears of the country in these troubled times."

Burns must have read that somewhere, Rhodes thought. It wasn't the kind of thing that anybody in Clearview or the surrounding area would have come up with.

"Yes, sir," Burns said. "You don't have to worry about the Feds. They'll come through for us."

The Feds, as Rhodes recalled, hadn't come through on Burns's previous grant request. The commissioner had hoped to get the county a really up-to-date crime lab, state of the art, something on a par with the one on some TV show that he watched. It hadn't worked out.

"Or if they don't come through," Burns continued, "we'll find some way to put it into the county budget. You'll need special training to use an automatic rifle, but you'll catch on quick, I'll bet."

One thing Rhodes knew for sure, and that was if the county really did get an M-16, he wouldn't be the one to use it. That would be Deputy Ruth Grady's job. She was a good shot with a pistol, and Rhodes knew she'd be good with an automatic rifle, too. Even if she wasn't a crack shot, she'd be better than he would.

Not that you'd have to be a crack shot with an M-16. If you were firing off nine hundred and fifty rounds in under a minute, you were bound to hit something or other. Maybe you'd even hit what you were aiming at. Or maybe not.

"Anyway," Burns said, "we can use a rifle like that. If you don't believe what Ballinger has to say, you can talk to those two women who write those books about you."

Rhodes repressed a sigh. Two women named Claudia and Jan had come to the county to attend a writing workshop held on an old college campus in the little town of Obert. Their plan had been to write nonfiction articles, but after they'd met Rhodes, they'd changed their minds. Instead of nonfiction, they wrote a novel about a handsome, crime-busting sheriff named Sage Barton, a former Navy SEAL who'd retired to a small town and entered law enforcement. Sage Barton was a two-fisted action hero about as different from Rhodes as a hamburger patty was from prime rib. To Rhodes's surprise, the book had been a success, and the happy authors had recently followed it with a sequel called *The Doomsday Plan,* in which Sage Barton, armed with a pair of Colt .45

revolvers, and maybe even an M-16, had single-handedly foiled a terrorist plot to blow up a nuclear power plant.

"Those books aren't about me," Rhodes said. "That sheriff is nothing like me, and there's no nuclear power plant within two hundred miles of here."

"Sage Barton has a cat," Burns said. "A black one. So do you."

That was a pretty slim connection if you asked Rhodes.

"I don't own the cat by choice," he said. "Ivy took him in, not me. I'm allergic to him."

Burns smiled and said nothing. He rocked a little in his chair.

"We don't have a nuclear plant around here," Rhodes said, "and I don't have any .45 revolvers. I've never been a Navy SEAL, and I've never fired an M-16."

"I'll take care of the M-16," Burns said. "You can see about getting yourself some revolvers."

Even if he'd had the revolvers, Rhodes couldn't have fired them both at the same time the way Sage Barton did. Nobody could have, but that didn't seem to bother the people who read *The Doomsday Plan*. It was selling even better than Claudia and Jan's first book.

"Think about this," Burns said. "A nice photo spread in the *Clearview Herald*, you standing in front of an American flag, holding an M-16. You'll be a shoo-in at the election this fall."

Rhodes was about to remind Burns that he didn't have an opponent in the upcoming election, so he was a shoo-in even without any photo. He didn't get a chance to say anything because the phone on Burns's desk rang.

"I'll let Mrs. Wilkie take it," Burns said. "We don't need to be interrupted when we're talking about the security of the nation."

Mrs. Wilkie was Burns's secretary, or executive assistant. Rhodes wasn't sure of the proper term these days. For a good while, Mrs. Wilkie had had a crush on Rhodes, and his marriage to Ivy Daniel hadn't entirely discouraged her. Lately, however, she and Burns appeared to have developed a relationship that extended beyond the office and into the social area. Rhodes didn't know any more about it than that, and he didn't want to know.

He could hear Mrs. Wilkie's voice through the hollow-core door between the offices. Then it stopped, and the phone on Burns's desk buzzed.

"Must be pretty important for her to interrupt us," Burns said. "I'd better take it."

He learned forward, picked up the phone, and listened. After a second, he glanced at Rhodes. He listened some more, then offered the phone to Rhodes. "It's for you."

Rhodes got up and took the phone. "Hello, this is Sheriff Rhodes."

"I know who it is," Hack Jensen said. Hack was the dispatcher at the jail. "You think I don't know your voice after all these years?"

Hack and his friend Lawton, the jailer, weren't fond of getting to the point. Even when the matter was urgent, they liked to take the long way around, so conversations with them could occasionally be aggravating. That was one of the reasons the county paid Rhodes the big bucks, he supposed.

"What's up?" Rhodes asked, ignoring Hack's gambit in hopes that he would get to the point quickly, though Rhodes knew the chances of that were slim.

"Nothin' much," Hack said. "Just the usual this and that. Miz Stubbs called about somebody's hog bein' loose. I sent Alton Boyd over to her house to see about it."

Boyd was the county's animal control officer. He could handle an alligator, as Rhodes knew from experience, so he should be able to handle a hog with ease.

"Might not be a loose hog," Hack said. "Might be one of those feral hogs that wandered onto her place."

Feral hogs were a plague on much of Texas. They roamed the farms and ranches, churning up the soil, scattering weed and brush seeds in their profuse droppings, and generally wreaking havoc. Rhodes didn't think they'd be on Mrs. Stubbs's place, however. They hadn't gotten into town. Not yet.

"You didn't call me about a hog," he said.

"Nope."

"What did you call about, then?"

"Lester Hamilton. You been lookin' for him for a day or so."

"I know I have. What about him?"

"Somebody's found him."

"Good," Rhodes said. "Where is he?"

"Murdock's rock pit. You know where that is?"

Rhodes knew. Long ago he'd done some fishing there, but he hadn't visited it in years.

"It's on County Road 36," Hack said, before Rhodes could answer. "That's the one with the old wooden bridge that crosses the river."

There was only one river that flowed through Blacklin County, and it fed all three of the county's man-made lakes. It was about a quarter of a mile down the road from the rock pit. Rhodes wondered what Les had been doing at the rock pit, but then it occurred to him.

"They catch him noodling?" he asked.

"Nope," Hack said. "They caught him dead."

"Dead?"

"That's right," Hack said. "Dead. No Les, no more."

2

▼

LESTER HAMILTON WAS, OR HAD BEEN IF HE WAS REALLY THE one who'd been found in Murdock's rock pit, the most hated man in Blacklin County. He'd claimed it was because of his success, but everyone knew better than that.

His success, and all that went with it, had to do with chickens.

Before Lester had come on the scene, there had already been some chicken trouble in Clearview. Some people in town had objected to the keeping of chickens within the city limits, saying they were a health hazard. They complained that the roosters crowed early in the morning and woke people up. The chickens clucked and scratched all day.

After a while, however, things had calmed down. The complaints stopped, and people pretty much forgot about the problem. No one had expected what was about to happen thanks to Lester Hamilton.

Hamilton owned some land east of Clearview in a small community called Mount Industry. Rhodes had no idea where the name had come from. Lester's land was on a little rise, hardly even enough of a rise to be called a hill, but it was the closest thing to a mountain in sight. As for the industry, Rhodes didn't recall that there had ever been an industry of any kind around the place until Lester got his big idea, not unless you counted orchards of peaches and persimmons, and Rhodes didn't think you could call orchards an industry.

Lester's big idea was chickens. Not just a few of them, like the numbers kept in town. Lester thought bigger than that. His chickens numbered in the thousands, so many thousands that Rhodes had trouble thinking about that many chickens.

Hamilton had thirty long metal buildings full of them, twenty-five thousand chickens in each one. Seven hundred and fifty thousand chickens, give or take. That was a lot of chickens, all right, but Hamilton already had plans to build a dozen or so more houses and supply even more chickens to a country that thought of grilled chicken breast as a healthy alternative to red meat.

Empty trucks came down the highway to Clearview and drove on out to Mount Industry five or six times a year. After they were loaded, the trucks drove away, taking their cackling burden to the big chicken-processing plant in East Texas, trailing chicken feathers and a powerful stink in their wakes.

Nobody objected to the feathers, as far as Rhodes knew. It was aggravating to find them on the lawn or to have them waft into the house through an open window, but that was the kind of thing that people could put up with.

What folks living in Mount Industry couldn't stand was the odor. It wasn't just a smell. It was a potent stench, an almost physical thing that hung in the air like a mist that had to be brushed aside when you walked, or so the nearby residents claimed. Depending on the direction and strength of the wind, the smell could sometimes even make its way into Clearview, three miles away.

The stink didn't bother Lester, though, or that's what he told everyone. "Smells like money," he said when people complained. Then he'd laugh, a hearty, openmouthed bellow. The laugh didn't make anyone feel any better, except maybe Lester.

Of course, Lester didn't live in Mount Industry. He'd inherited his land there from his grandfather, and he'd lived there for years while he tried a little farming and a little cattle raising, none of which paid off for him.

As soon as the chicken farm became a reality, he moved away. He lived now just outside Clearview on the opposite side of town in a big new house that he'd built with what just about everyone in Mount Industry considered to be his ill-gotten gains.

There was more to the problem than just the smell and Lester's being an absentee landlord, however. A lot of the nearby residents complained that the chicken houses posed a serious health hazard, and some people were irate because they believed Hamilton had destroyed not just the air quality but their entire reason for living in Mount Industry. They'd escaped the smells and pollution of the city, and now they were suffering from something just as bad, if not worse.

So as a result of his thousands of chickens and their by-product, Lester had many enemies. His chickens were the talk of the county, but the fact that he had broken no laws made it impossible for anyone to do anything about them other than to complain.

Ten or twelve people, not quite the entire population of Mount Industry, but most of it, had written scalding letters to the *Clearview Herald* about the problem. Rhodes averaged a couple of calls of complaint every week, usually from the same people, who nearly always wound up yelling at him as if everything were his fault when he explained for the second or third time that there was nothing he could do. It was a good thing he was running for office unopposed this year. Otherwise, Lester's chickens might have been the issue that defeated him, though Rhodes didn't know what anyone could have done about them, short of getting rid of their owner.

Maybe someone else had come up with the same idea, Rhodes thought as he drove along the gravel road that passed by the land where the rock pit was located. It was mid-October, and the trees that grew along each side of the road had begun to lose their leaves, but on most days the weather was still warm enough for short sleeves.

Rhodes spotted a mailbox ahead on his right. It sat on a tilt atop a rusty pipe and indicated the spot where Rhodes had to turn off the road and enter Murdock's property. There was a gap in the fence but no gate. A sign on the fence instructed people who wanted to fish in the rock pit to put a five-dollar bill in the mailbox. It was a fairly new sign, and Rhodes remembered that the last time he'd fished there, he'd had to pay only a dollar.

Rhodes drove through the gate and down the hard-packed dirt road that led to the rock pit. The county car, a new Dodge Charger, handled well, but Rhodes was having a little trouble getting used to it. He felt like he should be driving in a NASCAR race.

In the past, the county had always bought Ford Crown Victorias, but the commissioners, like those in a lot of other counties around the state, had decided to switch to Chargers. Rhodes wasn't against change, but he was used to the Fords.

He couldn't see the rock pit from the road because it was surrounded by willow trees, most of which hadn't been there the last time Rhodes had visited.

A battered Chrysler dating from sometime during the Carter administration sat near the willows. It had once been black, but the paint had faded badly. The right front fender had been replaced with a red one after some long-ago collision, and the red was faded even more than the black. About half of one big round bull's-eye taillight was missing, and the vacant space was covered by opaque red tape.

Sitting on the trunk of the Chrysler, smoking a cigarette, was Hal Gillis, a well-known local character. He was a short, wiry man, eighty-five if he was a day and an erratic driver at best. People knew to steer well away from his old car when they sighted it on the road, and Hal was on the road frequently. He liked to fish, and he traveled all over the county in search of the place where the fish were biting best. He must have thought that today that place was the rock pit.

Another car was half hidden in the willows near where Gillis had parked. It was black and shiny, and Rhodes saw the stylized chrome *L* encircled on the trunk. Lester Hamilton was the only man in Clearview who drove a Lexus. He must not have wanted anyone to know he was there, which was logical if he'd been doing some noodling.

Noodling was a type of fishing that was illegal in Texas, though it was considered quite a sport in the neighboring state of Oklahoma.

Rhodes didn't know if he approved of noodling or not. It was dangerous, that was for sure, and while Rhodes enjoyed casting a lure for the wily bass if he ever got the chance, which he seldom did anymore, he didn't much like the idea of having a big flathead catfish clamp onto his hand while he was partially or fully submerged.

That was what noodling was all about. Flatheads liked to live quietly in holes in the bank, in underwater brush piles, or concealed in a pile of submerged rocks. A noodler would locate a fish and stick his hand in front of it in hopes that it would take the bait.

If it did, it would usually hold on for a long time. The noodler would try to pull it out of its hiding place and get it up onto the bank, which was easy enough if the fish was a small one. If it wasn't, then getting it onto the bank could become a problem. If the fish was in deep water, if the noodler got hurt, if the noodler got hung in brush, or if the fish was an especially big one, things could even get dangerous.

Rhodes had heard of flathead cats that weighed over a hundred pounds, though nobody in Blacklin County had ever caught one anywhere nearly that big, not as far as he knew. A man who got hold of a fish that size would have a heck of a time dragging it out of a deep hole, a hollow log, or a rock pile.

Rhodes parked his car and walked over to Hal Gillis.

"Hey, Sheriff," Gillis said.

He slid off the car and pinched off the end of his cigarette. He put the butt into the bib pocket of the faded blue overalls he wore and walked over to Rhodes. He put out a skinny hand. Rhodes shook it.

"Hack tell you I called?" Gillis asked.

Rhodes nodded. "He said you'd found a body in the rock pit. He said you think it's Lester Hamilton. What makes you think so?"

Gillis took off his grimy red Texas Rangers baseball cap and ran a hand through his thin white hair. He put the cap back on and said, "I looked at his driver's license."

"Where'd you find that?"

"In his britches," Hal said. "I'll show you."

He turned and led Rhodes through a gap in the willows to the edge of the rock pit.

"There," Hal said, pointing to a neat pile of clothes that lay folded on a nearby rock. "Billfold was in the pants pocket. 'Course those clothes there might not belong to whoever's floatin' in the water over there, but I figger the odds are good they do. Found the billfold in the clothes and took a look. Then I called Hack on my cell phone."

Gillis didn't look like a man who'd be acquainted with the latest technology, but Rhodes had long ago decided that everyone in Blacklin County had a cell phone.

"I didn't call an ambulance or anything," Hal said. "I figured you'd be the one to do that."

"I'll take care of it," Rhodes said.

He'd call the justice of the peace and the ambulance after he looked things over.

"You want me to go on home now?" Gillis asked. He seemed eager to get away. " 'Cause I will if you say so."

"I have a few questions first," Rhodes said.

Gillis didn't look too happy about that, and Rhodes remembered another drowning he'd handled, one that had appeared to be an accident until he'd done a little investigating. Then it had turned out to be something else entirely.

"You don't think I killed Les, do you?" Gillis asked.

"That's what I want to find out," Rhodes said.

3

▼

MURDOCK'S ROCK PIT HAD BEEN THERE LONGER THAN RHODES could remember. He doubted that anyone in the county, even Hal Gillis, remembered why rock had once been quarried from it or what the rock had been used for.

After the pit was abandoned, it had eventually filled up with rainwater, and someone, maybe Murdock, who had been dead for years now, had stocked it with catfish and bass. It had been Murdock's idea to charge people to fish there, taking the money on the honor system, and whoever now owned the land had followed his lead.

Rhodes didn't know who the current owner was. The land had been in the Murdock family for so long that nobody ever called it anything but Murdock's place, and the rock pit was Murdock's, too.

Hal Gillis said he'd been fishing there off and on for twenty or thirty years.

"That's what I was plannin' to do today. Put my five dollars in and everything. Looky there." Gillis pointed to a willow tree.

A long cane pole leaned against it, and a gray metal minnow bucket sat close by. "Got me some of them big shiners, thought I'd catch a couple of bass, or maybe even one of those big cats that hide in the rocks. Take 'em home, clean 'em, and cook 'em up for supper. Could be Les Hamilton had the same idea. I'll bet he don't eat chicken. Anyway, he was in the water when I got here. I didn't touch him. See? My clothes are dry as a bone."

That was true, but Gillis could have taken off his clothes before he got in the water.

"Besides," Gillis said, "I'm too little to do anything to Les. He was twice my size. You better have a look at him."

Rhodes hadn't caught a glimpse of the body yet. The rock pit was roughly circular, the bank about ten feet above the water. The willows shaded the eastern side at the moment, but before long the sun would be overhead and the shade would be gone.

"It's right over here," Gillis said.

He walked along the edge of the bank for about five yards. There was hardly room for him because of the willow branches. Rhodes followed him, making sure he got each foot planted before taking a step. He didn't want to fall in the water.

"Here he is," Gillis said, coming to a stop.

Below him a large chunk of white stone poked out from the bank. Sticking out from beneath the stone was about half of someone's torso. Black bathing suit, white legs, black and white athletic shoes on the feet.

"Sure enough looks like an accident to me," Gillis said. He pulled a package of cigarettes from his overalls. "You care if I smoke?"

Rhodes said he didn't care, and Gillis lit up.

"Probably *was* an accident," Gillis said after taking a puff.

"Sure are a lot of people who don't like Hamilton, though, and I guess I'm one of 'em. But that don't mean I killed him."

Rhodes looked down at the body. A slight breeze riffled the water and moved the leaves of the willows. The sun sparkled off the ripples. The body didn't move at all.

"You want to know what I think?" Gillis asked, but he didn't wait for an answer. "I think it was water moccasins killed him. I heard once about a fella got into a whole big nest of 'em right in this very spot, back when the swimming pools were still pretty much in one piece and people used to come out for a dip. Had a hundred bites on him when they fished him out, and he was swole up like a poisoned dog."

Rhodes had heard the same story any number of times, including the last time there'd been a drowning, but the location of the supposed incident was always different, depending on who was telling it. Sometimes the snake-bitten man was in a creek somewhere, but other times he might be in one of the county's big lakes or the river that fed them.

Nobody who told the story had ever witnessed the bitten body firsthand. They'd always heard about it from someone who saw it, though, or so they said.

Rhodes wondered if an M-16 would be effective against a big nest of water moccasins. He supposed it would if there weren't more than nine hundred and fifty of them.

"Might've been a snappin' turtle, though," Gillis said, exhaling smoke. "There's an old mossy-back living in this rock pit. I've seen him four or five times. Probably moved in when it started filling up. Sixty years ago. Seventy, maybe. Big as a washtub. Looks downright prehistoric. He got hold of a man's hand, he could bite it right off."

"Whatever got Hamilton," Rhodes said, "it's too bad."

"Not ever'body would agree with that," Gillis said. "You gonna take a better look at him?" .

Rhodes looked at the dark green water. The willow-lined bank was steep, and the only way to get to the water was to climb down the rocky sides. The remains of what might have been Lester Hamilton weren't going anywhere.

"I'll wait for my deputy to get here," Rhodes said.

He'd called Ruth Grady on his way to the rock pit. She'd work the scene with him.

"Let's go back to the cars," Rhodes said.

When they got back, Gillis was finished with his cigarette, and he disposed of it the same way he'd done the first one.

"What're you lookin' for?" he asked Rhodes, who had walked out to the rutted road that led to the pit.

Rhodes didn't answer until he'd walked back to the cars.

"You find anything?" Gillis asked.

It was what Rhodes hadn't found that interested him. The grass was crushed where Hamilton had driven his car off the road, and Gillis and Rhodes had left clear paths as well. There was no other path to be seen, which meant that no other cars had been there. It was looking like an accident investigation for sure.

Unless, of course, Gillis had killed Hamilton. Or unless Hamilton had been in the water a day or so.

"How long had you been here when you called?" Rhodes asked.

Gillis gave it a little thought. "'Bout fifteen minutes. Long enough to get my pole and minnow bucket out of the car and walk to the bank."

"How long before you saw the body?"

"Not long. I was lookin' for a good place to fish, and I've caught a couple of big ones by that rock before. I checked it out, and there old Les was."

Rhodes wasn't a hundred percent sure the body was Hamilton, but there was nothing to be gained by saying so.

"Nobody else was around?"

"Not a soul. That's what I like about comin' here. There's hardly ever anybody to bother me."

"Makes it a good place for noodling," Rhodes said.

"Sure enough. Les liked to do that, I hear. All those rocks make a lot of good places for catfish to hide, and there's more rocks under the water where you can't see 'em. Les would be able to find 'em, though."

"He could've gotten hold of a big catfish," Rhodes said.

"Sure could. They're in here, like I said. I hooked one once, a couple of years back. Must've weighed fifty pounds or more. Broke my pole and carried off my line. Take a mighty big fish to do that."

If the story was true, and Rhodes wasn't sure he believed it, a fish that big could have grabbed onto Hamilton's hand and held him under the rock long enough to drown him. It wouldn't have taken long. Hamilton was no athlete. He couldn't have held his breath for much more than a minute, if that long.

Rhodes saw a white Dodge Charger turn into the gate from the county road.

"Here comes my deputy," he said.

Ruth Grady stopped her car beside the one Rhodes had driven and got out. She was short and a little stout. Her dark hair was pulled back in a short ponytail that she'd pulled through the back of her baseball cap with the badge on the front. She was the best deputy Rhodes had, and she did most of the crime-scene and lab work for the county.

"Howdy, Deputy," Gillis said when she joined them. "I'm Hal Gillis."

Ruth shook hands and said she was glad to meet him, and Rhodes filled her in on the situation.

"Accident?" she asked, looking at Gillis.

"Looks like it to me," he said. "'Course, I wasn't here when it happened. I just found the body." He paused. "Am I gonna get arrested?"

"Not now," Rhodes told him. "You can go on home."

"Let me get my pole and minnow bucket," Gillis said.

He left Rhodes and Ruth standing by his old Chrysler.

"You think he had anything to do with this?" Ruth asked, keeping her voice low.

"I don't know. Doesn't seem likely, but I want to keep an open mind."

Rhodes didn't know why he felt so uneasy about the situation, but he did. The whole thing just seemed wrong to him, though he couldn't explain why, not even to himself.

"Probably just an accident," Ruth said.

Rhodes wanted to agree with her, but he couldn't quite bring himself to do it. Gillis could, however, and did.

"That's what I told him," the old fisherman said, emerging from the willows with his bucket and pole. "Just an accident. Any way you look at it, though, there's one thing for certain and sure."

Rhodes had a sinking feeling he knew what was coming. Even a man like Hamilton, who was so widely despised, deserved a little dignity in death, but it didn't appear that he was going to have it. Being found dead in the water wearing only swimming trunks and athletic shoes was bad enough without the jokes.

"What's so certain?" Ruth asked.

Gillis didn't answer at first. He opened the back door of his

Chrysler and set the minnow bucket on the floor. He closed the door and slid his fishing pole through the open back window.

"Well?" Ruth said.

Gillis turned to her. "No Les, no more," he said.

Rhodes sighed.

4

▼

RHODES HAD BEEN LOOKING FOR HAMILTON A COUPLE OF DAYS before the call from Hack came in. Nobody Rhodes talked to would admit to knowing where Hamilton was, and nobody would admit to having seen him recently, not even his employees who looked after the chicken houses at the factory farm.

It wasn't surprising that no one would talk to Rhodes, especially not Hamilton. Rhodes had called Hamilton about a complaint. He'd been doing that a lot lately, and Hamilton had stopped taking his calls. As Hack had said, "That's what caller ID is for."

Of course, none of Hamilton's employees would admit that they knew where their boss was. They'd probably been told that if they did, they'd no longer be his employees, so Rhodes hadn't been alarmed that he hadn't been able to get in touch with Hamilton.

Now, however, it appeared that maybe everyone had been telling the truth. They really hadn't known where Hamilton was because he'd been dead all the time.

Ruth Grady didn't think so.

"I don't believe he's been in the water more than a few hours," she told Rhodes.

They stood on the edge of the pit, looking down at the body below. They could see only the legs and bathing trunks since the rest of the body was still hidden by the jutting rock.

"Look at his legs," Ruth went on. "Do you see any marks on them?"

The wind had picked up a little, and it pushed the water toward the side of the pit. The chubby white legs bumped the rocks. As far as Rhodes could tell from where he stood, the legs were unmarked.

"They don't look touched to me," Rhodes said.

"Fish and turtles would have been at him if he'd been dead for long," Ruth said.

"Why didn't he sink?"

"Body fat. Maybe he doesn't have much water in his lungs. Or maybe he didn't drown. Maybe he jumped in, hit his head on the rock, and died of a concussion before he could inhale any water."

She had a point. It wasn't a certainty that Hamilton had drowned, no matter what it looked like. One of the biggest mistakes you could make was to come to a conclusion before you had the facts.

"Or maybe water moccasins bit him," Rhodes said.

"Always a possibility," Ruth said. "Did you hear about the guy who jumped into a whole nest of them a few years ago?"

"Not more than a hundred times. Gillis had the same thought."

"Hey, it could happen."

"Sure it could," Rhodes said.

They'd worked the scene carefully. Ruth had examined the car and the field, and Rhodes had gone over the clothes and the bank of the pit. He'd found nothing in the clothing other than the billfold Gillis had mentioned, some change, a folding knife, and some lint in the pants. The shirt pocket held a ballpoint. The billfold contained nothing other than a driver's license, a couple of credit cards, and two hundred dollars in cash, all twenties.

Of course there was a cell phone. Rhodes had checked it and found no calls in or out. Hamilton must have carried the phone only for emergencies. Rhodes couldn't blame him for not wanting to be bothered by calls all the time.

"Find anything in the car?" he asked Ruth.

"That's one clean car," Ruth said. "Nothing in it at all. So we're clueless."

Rhodes grinned. "We usually are. In this case, that just makes it look more and more like an accidental death."

"Time to call in the EMTs, then?"

"And the justice of the peace. You make the calls. I'll stay here with Hamilton, or whoever that is down there."

Ruth went back to her car, and Rhodes sat on a rock near the pile of clothes. He wasn't about to try to get the body out of the water and up the rocky bank, not even with Ruth's help. That was a job for someone who knew what he was doing, and Rhodes wasn't that person.

He looked down at the body. As he watched, something rose from the depths of the rock pit. At first it was just a dark shadow, but then Rhodes saw that it was the snapping turtle that Gillis had told him about or one equally large. Maybe it wasn't quite as big as a washtub, but it was big enough, at least the size of a garbage can lid.

It stopped a little below the surface and stretched out its long neck, which looked as thick as a python. Its beak looked strong enough to slice through bone. The dark shell was covered with slimy algae.

The turtle looked at Rhodes with its hard, beady eyes, giving him a little chill, though the sun was warm. Then it sank back down into the water. It had just disappeared from sight when Ruth came back.

"I made the calls," she said. "They should be here pretty soon."

Rhodes told her about the turtle.

"When they grab hold," she said, "they don't let go till it thunders."

"This one wouldn't have to let go," Rhodes said. "It would just bite a chunk out of you and move on."

"I've heard they aren't aggressive," Ruth said. "If you fell in, you'd probably scare him worse than he scared you."

Rhodes wasn't sure that was possible. He didn't like to think about it, and he didn't like to think about Hamilton's body being in there with that monster. He hoped the EMTs would hurry up.

The EMTs got there in about fifteen minutes, followed closely by the JP, who had to wait with Ruth and Rhodes until the EMTs got the body out of the rock pit. When that was done, they could all see that it was Lester Hamilton, all right. The JP declared him dead, and the EMTs put him in the ambulance and hauled him away.

"Autopsy?" Ruth asked when she and Rhodes were alone again.

"Routine in this case."

They'd had a look at the body. There was no sign that Hamilton had hit his head, but that still didn't rule out a heart attack.

"You saw his hand and wrist, right?" Ruth asked.

Rhodes nodded. Hamilton's right hand and wrist had been red and abraded, especially the wrist.

"If he was noodling, a catfish could have left marks like that," Ruth said. "A big one. It could have held him under long enough to drown him. Three minutes, five tops with a man like Hamilton. He wasn't in great shape. He never should have been in the water in the first place, especially not without someone to watch out for him."

Rhodes nodded, wondering who might have watched out for Les Hamilton. Who liked him enough to go noodling with him? Rhodes couldn't think of anyone.

"You think you might dive down there and look for a giant catfish?" Ruth asked.

Rhodes thought about the turtle. "Not a chance," he said.

"You don't seem satisfied about this," Ruth said. "Do you know something you aren't telling me?"

Rhodes shook his head. "Just a feeling."

"As in 'Trust your feelings, Luke'?"

"Not that kind of feeling."

"We've looked all around. There's no sign that anybody else has been here. No other car drove over the grass today, and it's a cinch Hamilton died this morning."

"Hal Gillis was here," Rhodes said.

"I don't want to sound prejudiced against old people," Ruth said, "but I just don't think he could have drowned a man like Hamilton."

Rhodes didn't think so, either, but that didn't change that feeling he had. He hoped it would go away by the time he got back to town, but he knew he couldn't count on that.

When Rhodes was called in to investigate a death, it usually fell to him to notify the next of kin. It was a job he didn't like, but he did it. Sometimes, if he could, he put it off a bit, and this time it was easy enough to do, mainly because as far as Rhodes knew, Lester Hamilton didn't have any kin living in Blacklin County.

Rhodes would have to let the people who worked for Hamilton know, however, and after that he'd find out if there was anyone else who should be told. Maybe there were some relatives living elsewhere. The chicken houses and the estate would be their problem, and maybe a lawyer's.

Before he went to Mount Industry to let Hamilton's employees know about their boss's death, Rhodes wanted to stop at the jail so he could find out what other excitement was going on around the county. The excitement would include, of course, the hog at Mrs. Stubbs's house.

Hack and Lawton were ready for him when he got to the jail, eager to hear all about Lester Hamilton's demise but just as eager to tell Rhodes about the hog, in their own good time, and in their own way. Rhodes wasn't even going to ask about it.

Hack was lean and had a thin, unfashionable mustache, almost completely gray, as was the thick hair combed across the top of his head. He was well past retirement age, but as far as Rhodes could determine, the dispatcher had no plans to quit his job. In fact, he'd once told Rhodes that when he died, the county could just stuff him and leave him at his desk.

"Just like Roy Rogers did with Trigger," he'd said.

"Trigger's not at a desk," Rhodes had told him.

"Same difference. Get Jody Tinkle to do the work. He's good at it."

Tinkle was the local taxidermist. Rhodes was pretty sure he'd never worked on a human before.

Hack didn't care. "Don't matter. He's worked on enough animals to know what he's doin'."

"The county commissioners might not like the idea of a stuffed dispatcher."

"You can convince 'em."

Rhodes had given up the argument at that point. He figured Hack would change his mind eventually.

Lawton, the jailer, was as round as Hack was lean and probably just as old, though he didn't look it. He liked to play the comedian to Hack's straight man, which often angered Hack, who would have preferred to play both parts himself.

Together the two men had a common goal in life: to drive Rhodes crazy. They would never have admitted it, and they might not even have been conscious of it, but the end result was the same.

This time, Rhodes planned to turn their own tactics against them. He'd done it before, with some success.

"What about Les Hamilton?" Hack asked as soon as Rhodes was inside the door.

"You were right," Rhodes said.

"Right about what?" Lawton asked.

Hack was at the dispatcher's desk, while Lawton stood across the big room beside the door that led to the cellblock.

"Right about Hamilton," Rhodes said.

"How was I right?" Hack asked.

"He's dead, just like you told me," Rhodes said. He walked over to his desk, sat down, and turned on the new laptop computer the county had bought for him. He liked it much better than an M-16. "I have to fill out my report."

"Wait a minute," Hack said. "What about Hamilton? Did he drown? Did a catfish get him?"

"I'm bettin' on water moccasins myself," Lawton said. "I heard about a fella dived off into a whole tangle of 'em in Buck's Creek one time. Fella told me about it, he said—"

"He said he'd seen it with his own eyes," Hack said. "I heard that same whopper a dozen times, and it ain't ever been true."

"You callin' Bradley Doakes a liar? 'Cause that's who told it to me, Bradley Doakes, and his granddaddy was a Babtist preacher over in Obert for a lot of years."

"Havin' a granddaddy that's a preacher don't mean your mouth is a prayer book," Hack said.

Rhodes smiled at the laptop screen as the computer booted up. It was a lot more fun when Hack and Lawton were going at each other than when they were going at him.

"You wouldn't say that if Bradley Doakes was in the room," Lawton said.

"Sure I would," Hack said, " 'cause he couldn't hear a word I said. Bradley Doakes's been dead five or six years, just like ever'body else that ever passed that story along. Dead or moved off to California without leavin' a forwardin' address or a phone number."

Lawton opened his mouth, but nothing came out. After a couple of seconds, he leaned back against the wall, shoulders slumped.

"Now, then," Hack said to Rhodes, "what about Hamilton?"

Rhodes pretended to be typing. He'd never had a typing course, so he banged out his reports with two fingers. The good thing about a computer was how forgiving it was of his mistakes.

"He's dead," Rhodes said.

"Dadgum it, you said that already. What I mean is, how'd he die?"

Rhodes stopped hitting the computer keys and swiveled in his chair. He'd won the round. Hack had asked a specific question.

"I don't know," Rhodes said. "Autopsy's not done yet. Probably be tomorrow before we hear anything. He was in the water, he was dead, that's it."

He turned back to the computer. Nobody said anything for a minute or so.

"Ain't you gonna ask about the hog?" Lawton asked, breaking the silence.

Rhodes swiveled back around. "What hog?"

"The one at Miz Stubbs's place," Hack said. "The one I told you about."

"Oh, that hog," Rhodes said. "I'd forgotten about it."

"No, you didn't." Hack had caught on. "You never forget anything. You're just messin' with us."

"Maybe a little bit," Rhodes admitted. "Tell me about the hog."

He knew as soon as he said it that he shouldn't have. It was just the opening they'd been waiting for.

"It was a big 'un," Hack said.

Rhodes was supposed to ask how big, but he didn't.

"Real big," Lawton said, after a few seconds went by.

Rhodes gave in. "How big was it?"

"Too big for Alton," Hack said.

Rhodes was almost afraid to ask what that meant, but he did.

Hack laughed. "All I know for sure is, I wish someone had put it on video. It'd be big on YouTube."

Rhodes had only a vague idea of what YouTube was, but he knew that whatever Hack was leading up to couldn't be good news.

"You'd better explain that," he said, hoping that Hack wouldn't evade answering this time.

He did, though. "You know Alf Eakin, lives about a quarter mile out of town on the road to Milsby?"

Rhodes nodded.

"Got him a few hogs. Sells a few ever' year."

Rhodes recalled a few complaints about the smell of Eakin's hog pen, but not nearly as many as he'd had about Hamilton's chickens.

"One of 'em got out," Lawton said, earning a hard look from Hack, who didn't like for Lawton to take over the story.

Lawton wasn't bothered. "Wandered down the road a little piece and paid Miz Stubbs a visit. Got into her flowers, and so Alton went out to see about it."

"He knows that," Hack said, taking back control. "I told him. What happened was that Alton didn't know how big that hog was."

"'Bout the size of a VW," Lawton said, "and it came right after him."

Hack didn't bother to glare. He just picked up the narrative.

"That hog ran flat over him. Miz Stubbs came out with a shotgun and was gonna kill it, but Alton wasn't hurt, so he stopped her."

"Hold it," Rhodes said. "Are you sure Alton's all right?"

"Sure I'm sure. Might have a hoof mark on him somewhere, but other than that he's fine."

"You don't need to worry about Alton," Lawton added. "He's tough as whet leather."

"Good thing he is, too," Hack said. "Otherwise, Miz Stubbs would've blowed that hog's brains out. Anyway, Eakin showed up about then. He had a trailer hooked onto his truck, and he and Alton got the hog into it. Miz Stubbs helped."

"With the shotgun?" Rhodes asked.

"Pitchfork," Lawton said.

"She has a pitchfork?"

"Don't ever'body?" Hack asked.

Rhodes finished his report and was on his way out of the jail when Jennifer Loam got there. She was a reporter for the *Clearview Herald*, and she had a knack for hearing about things Rhodes would rather have kept under wraps for a while.

"What's this about Lester Hamilton drowning?" she asked as she breezed in.

"Who said he drowned?" Hack asked.

"Don't start," Rhodes told him, and Jennifer gave him a quizzical look.

"Hamilton's dead," Rhodes said. "The body was found in Murdock's rock pit by Hal Gillis."

Jennifer moved to a chair by Rhodes's desk and pulled a digital recorder from her purse.

"Would you mind repeating that?" she asked after she turned on the recorder.

Rhodes repeated it. Loam could have looked at his report, but he supposed telling it worked just as well.

"Did he drown?" she asked when he was finished.

"That's the way it looks," Rhodes said, "but we don't know for sure. Dr. White will do an autopsy. We'll know more after that."

"He had a lot of enemies," Jennifer said.

She was young, smart, and ambitious. Or maybe she was just young and smart. Rhodes thought she'd have left Clearview by now if she'd wanted a job on a bigger paper. She was good enough to get one, but she might not have thought she was ready.

On the other hand, considering that all the big-city papers in the state were losing circulation and getting rid of staff, maybe not.

"Everybody has enemies," Rhodes said.

"Not you. Nobody's even bothered to run against you this year."

"And a lucky thing, too," Hack said. "He wouldn't join the barbershop chorus to get votes."

Rhodes didn't like campaigning, but he had to do a certain bit of it anyway. That bit didn't include singing.

"I'm doing a series of stories on Hamilton's farm," Jennifer said, getting back to the subject at hand. "The first one will be in the paper this afternoon. I might know a few things that would help you in your investigation."

"I'm not doing an investigation," Rhodes said, wondering if Jennifer had the same kind of hunch he did about Hamilton's death.

"I didn't say you were. If you start one, though, you might want to talk to me."

Rhodes grinned. "I can be pretty sure I won't have to go far to look for you."

"That's right. I'll be with you every step of the way."

She was only halfway joking. Rhodes had trouble avoiding her whenever he was working on a case of any importance.

"You'll let me know the results of the autopsy, won't you?" she continued.

"You can count on it," Rhodes lied.

"I'll bet." Jennifer stood up. "I'll be seeing you, and you can count on that."

Rhodes didn't have any doubts about it.

Rhodes almost got out the door before the phone rang.

"Better hang on," Hack said.

Rhodes stopped, and Hack answered the phone. After he'd talked for a second, he turned to Rhodes.

"It's Robin Hood again."

Rhodes went back to his chair and sat down.

5

▼

THE PERSON CALLED ROBIN HOOD HADN'T STRUCK IN MORE THAN
a week, and Rhodes had been hoping that he (or she, nobody knew
for sure) had given up his hobby, or left the county. The second
option would have been the better one from Rhodes's point of view.
Neither of those things had happened, it seemed, and now Robin
Hood was back in action.

This particular Robin Hood didn't steal from the rich and give
to the poor. He didn't steal from anyone, for that matter, but he did
use a bow and arrow. Jennifer Loam had used the name of Robin
Hood in her newspaper story about the goings-on, and it had stuck.

No one had a good idea what the rogue bowman, or bowperson,
looked like. Up until now, he'd worked at night, and it was a surprise to Rhodes that he'd done something during the daylight hours.

So far, the bowman's activities had been harmless but annoy-
ing. He'd put arrows into wooden fences, utility poles, and advertising signs. The arrows always had a message attached, usually a
political comment of some kind.

One of the arrows had even carried a message that said, "Re-elect Sheriff Dan Rhodes." Hard to argue with that one, Rhodes thought, but Mikey Burns had objected loudly to the one that said, "Commissioner Burns is a lazy lout."

"What did Robin Hood do this time?" Rhodes asked after Hack had hung up the phone.

"He shot an arrow into the air," Hack said.

Rhodes wasn't in any mood for the runaround. He said, "Just tell me."

Hack gave in. Almost. "He shot an arrow into somebody's car tire."

"Somebody's. Now who would that somebody be?"

Hack grinned. "It would be the commissioner's."

"Which commissioner?"

"Mikey Burns."

"Uh-oh," Rhodes said.

On his return trip to the commissioner's office, Rhodes went through the downtown area, or what had been the downtown years before. There wasn't much of it left. Many of the buildings were deserted. Some had collapsed and been razed. The only real sign of life on any given day was around what Rhodes referred to as the Lawj Mahal, a new building so white that it almost shone. Randy Lawless, an attorney with whom Rhodes had often had dealings, owned the building and used it as his office and base of operations. The building, along with its paved parking lot, occupied the spot where a number of stores had once stood. It took up an entire block of the old downtown.

As Rhodes drove by, he thought about Lawless. It was a cinch that Lawless was Hamilton's lawyer. A man with Hamilton's money would want the best, and in Blacklin County, Lawless was the best. Rhodes hoped that Hamilton's death wouldn't lead to any complications that would involve Lawless, that is, not if Rhodes was involved, too.

Rhodes's Charger was the only car moving on the streets. He passed an empty building that had once held a department store. The windows were dusty, and one of them was cracked.

Clearview was still lively in some places, but not downtown. All the activity now was out on the highway around the big Walmart store. A new motel stood nearby, and a couple of small strip centers had located not far away, along with a big grocery store. The area on the highway wasn't anything like the downtown Rhodes remembered from his childhood, but it was proof that Clearview was still alive and well.

Rhodes parked in front of the precinct barn where Mikey Burns had his office and went inside. Mrs. Wilkie was at her desk, and Rhodes noticed that she was wearing new glasses, the rimless glasses of the kind popularized by a recent vice-presidential candidate.

"Mr. Burns is a little upset," she said.

"I heard he was a *lot* upset."

"That's probably more like. You may go on in."

Rhodes went through the door into Burns's office. The commissioner sat in his leather chair, looking out the window. He didn't turn around when Rhodes came in.

"You wanted to talk to me," Rhodes said.

"That's right," Burns said. He still didn't turn. "I want this Robin Hood stopped. Now."

As sheriff, Rhodes worked for both the county and the city of Clearview. His major employer was the county, but the town of Clearview, which didn't have its own police force, contracted with the county for law enforcement. In some ways, it wasn't a good situation. Rhodes answered to the county commissioners and to the Clearview city council, usually in the person of the mayor, and every council member, every commissioner, and the mayor thought he was Rhodes's boss. In a way that was true, but Burns really didn't have the right to direct Rhodes's investigations. Not that Rhodes planned to mention it.

"We've been after him for a while," Rhodes said. "Nobody ever sees him."

The truth was that Robin Hood hadn't appeared to be much of a threat, and while the investigation was ongoing, it wasn't a priority. Rhodes didn't plan to mention that, either.

Burns spun his chair around and leaned forward onto his desk. He didn't ask Rhodes to sit down.

"You have evidence," he said. "Why don't you use it?"

"You mean the arrows?"

"Damn right I mean the arrows, and the notes, too. Get some fingerprints. Catch that bastard."

Burns was worked up more than a flat tire should have warranted.

"We haven't been able to get any fingerprints," Rhodes said.

"Why not?"

Rhodes knew what Burns was thinking. Like most of the population of Clearview, Burns probably watched one of the *CSI* shows, or all of them, and believed that law enforcement forensics in Blacklin County matched those on television. They didn't. Rhodes would have been willing to bet that even the forensic techniques in New York City didn't match those on television.

"Robin Hood must be wearing gloves," Rhodes said. "Even if we could get fingerprints, we'd have to find a match."

"What about that thing the Feds have? I can't remember the initials."

"That would be the FBI's Integrated Automated Fingerprint Identification System," Rhodes said. "IAFIS. Sure, we could use that, but if the prints aren't in the system, they wouldn't help even if we had them."

"Bow hunters have to be licensed."

The key word there was "have." The law required a bow hunter to have a license, but that didn't mean everybody with a bow was a hunter, and not all the hunters bothered with a license.

"We've checked out all the hunters with licenses," Rhodes said. "They're all alibied."

Burns stood up. "Maybe there's some fingerprints this time. Come on."

Rhodes followed Burns out the back door of the office, thinking that it might be handy for a commissioner to have a back door now and then. He could leave without his secretary even knowing he was gone.

Burns led Rhodes past a couple of road graders and county trucks to where his car was parked. The precinct barn was on a main road but at the outskirts of town. The side on which Burns parked was partially concealed from the road by trees. A couple of other cars were parked beside Burns's, a bright red Pontiac Solstice convertible.

Now Rhodes knew why Burns was so upset. The convertible was Burns's midlife toy. The commissioner usually drove an old pickup.

Robin Hood couldn't use the excuse that he was aiming for someone else's car. Nobody else in the county had a car like that one.

"Truck's in the shop," Burns said, before Rhodes could ask. "I never drive the Solstice to work. I wish I hadn't today. I should've walked."

The little two-seater sagged to one side, and Rhodes saw the arrow sticking out of the left rear tire. It looked like the other arrows Robin Hood had used, with red and black fletching. Though Rhodes hadn't mentioned it to Burns, the arrows weren't likely to be a clue. They had medium-weight aluminum shafts and broadhead tips. Both shafts and tips were popular brands, easy to obtain at sporting goods stores. If you didn't want to buy them in Clearview, you could drive to Houston or Dallas. You could even order them on the Internet. They were next to impossible to trace.

"I came out to go to lunch and saw it like that," Burns said. "It almost made me cry."

Rhodes was reminded that he'd missed lunch. Again. It was an all too common occurrence when he was on the job.

"I haven't touched the arrow," Burns said. "I know better than that."

TV again. Rhodes didn't think there would be any fingerprints, but it was good that Burns was being careful.

"It might be hard to get the arrow out of the tire," Rhodes said.

"Cut it out. It doesn't matter. The tire's ruined."

"Is there a note?"

"Come on," Burns said.

He walked over to the car and knelt down by the flat tire. Rhodes knelt beside him and saw the paper tied to the arrow with two pieces of monofilament fishing line. Both the line and the paper were common and easy to obtain if they were the same kind that Robin Hood had used previously.

Rhodes took out his pocketknife and slipped it under the monofilament at one end of the paper. He cut the line and removed the paper. Holding it by the edges, he unrolled it.

Burns stood up, and Rhodes rose as well.

"What does it say?" Burns asked.

Rhodes read the note. "What do you get when you cross a rooster with a razor?"

"A riddle?" Burns asked. "Are you joking?"

"I'm not joking."

"Is the answer on there?"

"Yes."

"Well, what is it?"

"A chicken Schick," Rhodes said. "Or a county commissioner."

Rhodes didn't smile when he read it, and Burns didn't laugh.

"Is that a clue?" Burns asked. "Or is it just a nasty joke?"

"Could be both," Rhodes said.

It might be even more than Burns thought it was, and Rhodes didn't like the implications. Hamilton's farm was in Burns's precinct, and Burns had received the bulk of the complaints about it, not that there was anything he could do. Since one of the earlier messages had also criticized Burns, Rhodes wondered if Robin Hood might be one of the Mount Industry residents. He also wondered if the arrow and the message had any connection to Hamilton's death, which was beginning to seem more suspicious than ever.

"Is it going to help you catch Robin Hood?" Burns asked.

Rhodes didn't think so, but he said, "You never can tell."

Burns looked at his little car. "You'd better catch him, and catch him quick. First it was telephone poles, and now it's cars. Next it might be people."

"I'll do what I can," Rhodes said.

Rhodes left the precinct barn without removing the arrow from the tire. He called Hack and asked who was on patrol duty nearby.

"Buddy," Hack said. "You need him?"

Rhodes told Hack to have Buddy remove the tire and take it to the jail.

"We'll let Ruth get the arrow out and go over it for prints," Rhodes said, though he didn't think it would do any good.

"Was there a note?"

"I have it bagged and tagged."

"What'd it say?"

Rhodes told him. Hack thought it was funny.

"And it's about chickens," Hack said. "You think it has anything to do with Hamilton?"

Rhodes wasn't ready to commit himself. "Maybe. Maybe not."

"It's really too bad you don't have anybody runnin' against you," Hack said. "You're a perfect politician."

"That's not a compliment."

"I guess not, but I didn't mean it ugly."

"Thanks. I'm going to Mount Industry to let the people who work for Hamilton know the situation. Don't mention the note to anybody."

"By 'anybody,' you mean that reporter," Hack said.

"I mean anybody," Rhodes said, "and that would include Jennifer Loam."

"Can I tell Lawton?"

"If you think he can keep his mouth shut."

"You don't have to worry about him. Nobody can get anything out of Lawton."

That was the truth, Rhodes thought, not unless they had a month or two to spare for questioning.

"Go ahead and tell him," he said.

6

▼

MOUNT INDUSTRY JUST ABOUT DIDN'T EXIST ANYMORE. RHODES couldn't remember when it ever had. Oh, at one time there had been a little more to the place than there was now, a church or two, a little grocery store, and a school. The churches and the school were gone now. The store was still there, but it didn't carry a full line of groceries, hardly anything more than cold drinks, bread, candy, and chips. The owner kept it open because he wanted to have something to do. There was a cemetery near where the church had stood, and enough houses were around to give the idea of a community, but that was all.

Rhodes drove past the cemetery and saw flowers, probably artificial, on some of the graves. He rounded a couple of curves and saw the chicken farm at the top of a low hill.

An expensive iron fence ran along the side of the road, and Rhodes wondered what it was for. It certainly wasn't needed to keep in the chickens. They never left the buildings they were kept in, never saw the light of day until they were hauled off to be processed.

The smell when Rhodes got out of the car was real and tangible, like worms crawling up his nostrils as he walked to the red metal building that served as the headquarters of Hamilton Farms.

Behind the headquarters, the long chicken houses covered the land, each of them almost as long as two football fields. Their silver metal roofs spakled in the sun. The canvas curtains along the sides were rolled up so the insides of the buildings could get a little sunlight, but the openings also made the smell worse than if the curtains had been closed. Rhodes heard the raucous noise of thousands of chickens. The stink clogged his nose, and he coughed.

As Rhodes approached the headquarters, he saw a pickup parked behind the building with a flat-bottomed aluminum boat in the bed. A chicken sat on the end of the boat, and Rhodes wondered if it had escaped from one of the farm buildings. More power to it if that was the case.

The headquarters door opened and a man came outside. It was Jared Crockett, Hamilton's supervisor, a rangy man who wore jeans, boots, and a cowboy hat. He looked more like a wrangler about to go off on a cattle roundup than a man in charge of chickens. He'd been known to claim that he was related to Davy Crockett, and Rhodes was surprised he didn't wear a coonskin cap.

No one knew where Crockett had come from or what his qualifications for running a chicken farm were. Hamilton had hired him from somewhere, and he'd showed up and taken charge of the operation. He lived in the old oak-shaded farmhouse that the original owners of the property had built sometime in the 1930s. It had been restored to something like respectability, and it was even air-conditioned. Rhodes didn't think that would help with the odor. He wondered how Crockett liked living there.

"Thought I saw you drive up, Sheriff," Crockett said as he walked to greet Rhodes. He had a big nose, a wide mouth, and small, hard eyes. "You here on business or pleasure?"

Crockett smiled, showing big white teeth. It was as if he couldn't smell a thing. All Rhodes could figure was that he must have gotten used to the stink.

"Business," Rhodes said, his throat constricted. He'd been there a couple of times before, and Crockett knew he wouldn't have come for the fun of it. "Can we go inside?"

"Sure thing." Crockett made a broad gesture. "Come on ahead."

Rhodes walked in front of him and went into the metal building. He'd hoped the smell there wouldn't be as bad as it had been outside, but he couldn't tell much difference.

The office was furnished with a gray metal desk, a matching file cabinet, and a couple of gray metal folding chairs. Hamilton hadn't gone in much for extravagance or comfort.

A photo of Hamilton and the current governor hung on the wall behind the desk. The governor had his arm across Hamilton's shoulders.

"Take a seat, Sheriff," Crockett said, and instead of going behind the desk, he sat in one of the folding chairs.

Rhodes took the other chair and said, "I have some bad news for you, Crockett."

"Let me guess. Another complaint about the way this place smells. I tell you, Sheriff, I just don't get it. People just like to complain, I guess. I don't smell a thing."

Either Crockett was an expert liar or he had something seriously wrong with his smeller.

"This isn't about the smell," Rhodes said. "It's about Lester Hamilton."

"What's that rascal gotten himself into now? I haven't seen him for a couple of days, and we need to be making arrangements for a shipment."

"You'll have to take care of that yourself," Rhodes said. "Lester's dead."

Crockett slumped and rubbed a hand across his face. "You sure about that?"

"I'm sure."

"What was it? Car wreck?"

"He drowned."

"Damn." Crockett paused and looked off, as if he might be thinking about his deceased boss. "Was he out noodling again? I've told him over and over how dangerous that is."

"It looks like that's what he was doing." Rhodes explained the circumstances. "He should've listened to you."

"He sure should've. What's happened is a damn shame, and not just because he's dead. I need to know what'll happen to my job. I can handle this place myself for a while, but I like to know who I'm working for and who's paying my salary. I can't work for nothing."

"You wouldn't just walk away, would you?" Rhodes asked, knowing that a lot of people in the county would hope the answer was yes.

"Not for a while. Too many other people working here that have to be taken care of. This is a big shock, Sheriff."

"You've been running the place without much help."

"Yeah, but Hamilton was the boss. He kept the books. He made a lot of the deals."

"Who gets the business now that he's gone?" Rhodes said. "Did Lester have any heirs?"

"Maybe nobody. Lester's got a cousin down in Houston. That's the only one I know about. I guess I'd better let him know."

"Good idea. Have him get in touch with Clyde Ballinger about funeral arrangements."

"I'll do that," Crockett said.

They talked for a while longer, but there was nothing Rhodes could do for Crockett. Crockett didn't have any helpful information for Rhodes, either, so Rhodes left and started back to Clearview.

Almost as soon as he left Hamilton's property, he saw a car behind him. There were two men inside. Just as he got to the cemetery, the driver started honking. Rhodes pulled over and got out of the Charger. The driver behind got out, too, as did the passenger.

At first glance the men looked like aliens from an old black-and-white science fiction movie, but then Rhodes realized it was just a couple of ordinary citizens, one of whom wore a half-face respirator mask with replaceable filters.

The other man had on a white particulate breathing mask, not quite as much protection against the smell as the more expensive respirator, but it would do the job. It was also a good bit cheaper.

"Sheriff Rhodes?" the driver asked.

His voice was tinny, and Rhodes saw that he had a little amplifier affixed to the respirator mask.

"That's me," Rhodes said.

The mask was attached to the man's head by rubber straps that went around the back and across the top. Wild gray hair stuck up around the straps.

"I'm Dr. William Qualls," the man said, as if he expected Rhodes to know who he was. He didn't offer to shake hands.

Rhodes knew him, all right, not that they'd ever met. Qualls was a retired university professor from Houston. He taught a couple of literature classes as a part-time instructor at the local community college, and he'd written numerous letters to the *Clearview*

Herald, all of them complaining about air pollution in Mount Industry.

According to his letters, Qualls had moved to the little community for his health. He'd left the frightening pollution spewed into the skies by the chemical plants and refineries of the Texas Gulf Coast for the pristine air of rural Texas, only to find that he was choking on the fowl (as Qualls put it in the letters, with a pun definitely intended) stink of Hamilton's chicken farm, which Qualls contended was even more of a danger to his health than the pollution he'd fled.

"I've heard of you," Rhodes said. He looked at the other man. "I know Dr. Benton, too."

C. P. Benton, known as Seepy, was a math instructor at the community college. He claimed extensive experience in criminal investigation on the amateur level, and he'd been tangentially involved in a couple of Rhodes's cases in the past.

Benton also claimed to be musically talented, and while Rhodes had heard him play guitar and sing, the sheriff wasn't convinced of Benton's talent. Currently, Benton was at work on his magnum opus, a book entitled *The Unreality of Reality,* which he'd described to Rhodes as "Castaneda without drugs." Rhodes wasn't at all sure what that meant. He supposed he'd have to read the book and find out, if it was ever published.

"Hey, Sheriff," Benton said, his voice muffled by the mask. "How's Deputy Grady?"

For reasons that weren't clear to Rhodes, Ruth Grady seemed attracted to Benton, who reciprocated her feelings.

"She's fine. What are you two fellas dressed up for? Halloween's not until the end of the month."

"You know why we're forced to wear these apparatuses," Qualls said. "I don't see how you can stand to breathe without one."

"We professional lawmen are fearless," Rhodes said, looking at Benton, who liked to talk about how many push-ups he could do.

"We're teachers," Benton said. "We're not supposed to be fearless. Except in the classroom."

"Bravery has nothing to do with it," Qualls said. "There's no way to fight the kind of pollution you're breathing in, Sheriff, without wearing a mask. You ought to know that by now. How often do you think they change the litter in those chicken houses?"

Rhodes started to answer, but Qualls held up a hand to stop him.

"I'll tell you how often," Qualls continued. "Once a year. Think about it. And do you know what happens then?"

Rhodes knew the answer to that one, too. He'd read Qualls's letters, and he'd heard from more than one person in town. He didn't answer, though, because he knew Qualls was going to tell him anyway.

"They have to rototill it after each batch of chickens leaves, but after a year or so they take it out and spread it around as fertilizer. To make the grass grow. Out in the open like that, it just stinks more, and it's even more damaging to our health when the wind picks up the parasites and germs and spreads them all over the county and beyond."

"Does that explain why you're here, Seepy?" Rhodes asked.

Benton, who lived on the side of Clearview directly opposite from Mount Industry, nodded.

"The smell even gets out to my house sometimes," he said. "So the germs and parasites must get out there, too. They don't use all that soiled litter for fertilizer, you know."

Rhodes knew. He didn't want Benton to say more, but Benton went right ahead.

"They put it in cattle feed, too," Benton said. "Think about that the next time you eat a hamburger."

Rhodes didn't want to think about it.

"I don't eat much meat myself," Benton said. "Thinking about those chickens and thinking about what goes into a steak has pretty much turned me vegetarian."

Rhodes didn't think that would happen to him.

"I've been working with William on the situation at Hamilton's," Benton said. "Something really should be done."

"Something's been done already," Rhodes said.

"What's been done?" Qualls asked. "Don't tell me the state's finally taken action. If so, I'm surprised and gratified. Is that why you were up there at the farm? Is the state going to shut it down? Please tell me that's what it is."

"That's not what it is," Rhodes said.

"Darn," Benton said.

"What has been done, then?" Qualls asked.

"Lester Hamilton's dead," Rhodes told them.

Rhodes couldn't really tell because of the mask, but Qualls didn't appear too saddened by the news.

"What happened to him?" Benton asked.

Rhodes gave them a quick summary.

"That's too bad," Benton said, though he didn't sound sincere. He must have realized it because he added, "It's always sad when someone dies. Some good will come of it, though, if they have to shut down that farm. Is that what you were talking to them about up there?"

"Not really," Rhodes said. "I talked to Crockett, but he didn't have any idea what would happen to the farm. It's too soon."

"I'm sorry the man's dead," Qualls said, but the tinny voice coming from the speaker didn't sound sad at all. "I'm glad there's a chance it's the end of the chicken farm, however. Thanks for letting us know, Sheriff."

"Glad to help out," Rhodes said.

"See you, Sheriff," Benton said, and the two men got back into Qualls's car.

Rhodes watched them drive away. He couldn't blame them for not being upset about Hamilton's death, and he hoped they wouldn't blame him for wondering if they might have had something to do with it.

Not that they could have. It was just an accident.

Rhodes repeated that to himself as he got into the county car. *It was just an accident.*

Still, he couldn't help thinking that he'd overlooked something obvious already, something that was wrong with the whole thing.

7

BECAUSE HE'D MISSED LUNCH, RHODES DECIDED TO STOP AT THE grocery store before he went back to Clearview. Not many stores like it were left in the county, though at one time there had been many of the small mom-and-pop operations spread around in little communities that had almost disappeared themselves.

Tall oak trees shaded the old wooden building, and the leaves littered the sandy ground around it. The porch sagged to the left, and the store needed a fresh coat of paint. Its tin roof was covered with large rust spots.

A fat black-and-white cat slept on the porch. It opened its eyes and looked at Rhodes when he got out of the car, but it must not have seen anything of interest. It stretched without getting up and went right back to sleep.

Rhodes went up the steps. The screen door was rusty. It hung a little askew, and the hinges squealed when Rhodes pulled it open.

The store's owner, Mitch Garrett, lived in back in a little house that was attached to the building. It was as old and rickety as the store.

Garrett was known to some of the residents of the community as Snuffy. Rhodes had never called him that, however. He sat behind the counter of the store, leaning back in a metal lawn chair. His feet were propped up on the counter. Rhodes saw the worn soles of an old pair of cowboy boots.

Garrett was small, dried up, and tobacco colored. In the dim light of the store, he looked a little like a mummy. Rhodes had no idea how old Garrett was, but he'd owned the store for all of Rhodes's life.

"Hey, Sheriff," Garrett said. He didn't get up. The shelves behind him held a few canned goods. The cans looked dusty to Rhodes. "What can I do you for?"

"How about a candy bar and a Dr Pepper?"

Garrett waved a hand. "Help yourself."

Rhodes walked past the counter to the back of the store where an old Frigidaire stood beside a red-and-white Coke box that was as old as the refrigerator. Rhodes got a paper towel from the roll that sat on one side of the Coke box. Then he opened the door of the box and pulled a Dr Pepper from the icy water that was circulated by a little pump in the corner. After he wrapped the dripping bottle in the paper towel, he popped the cap with the opener on the box's side.

He found a box of Zero candy bars in the Frigidaire. As far as Rhodes knew, Garrett's store was the only place in the county where he could get a cold Zero. He reached inside and took one. The bar's wrapper didn't have a polar bear on it as it had when Rhodes was a kid, but it would taste the same. An ice-cold Zero and Dr Pepper in a bottle. Two of life's real pleasures.

"You been up to the chicken farm?" Garrett said while Rhodes removed the candy wrapper.

Rhodes took a bite of the Zero. It would have tasted better if the smell of the chickens hadn't still been in his nose and everywhere else.

"That's where I was," Rhodes said.

"Stinks up there, don't it."

It wasn't a question, but Rhodes nodded anyway. He drank some Dr Pepper. It was so cold it almost made his teeth hurt.

"Stinks here, too," Garrett said. "You're the only customer I've had all day. Not that this place has ever been a gold mine, but I used to sell some candy bars and a little bread and milk. Not so much these days. People don't want to buy anything to eat in a place that smells like this. I'm surprised somebody hasn't snuck up there some night and burned those chicken houses to the ground."

Rhodes remembered visiting his grandfather many years ago. One Sunday they'd gone out to the chicken yard and picked out a hen for Sunday dinner. His grandfather had wrung the chicken's neck, whirling the clumsy bird around and around in his big hand, and when the neck and chicken had parted company, the chicken's body hit the ground running. It had run in a circle for what had seemed to Rhodes a long time before bumping into a tree and falling and twitching a time or two before becoming still. Rhodes had a feeling that if his grandfather did anything like that today, he'd be the subject of protests from all kinds of groups that would regard the action as extreme cruelty to animals. It had even seemed cruel to Rhodes at the time, but he'd thought it wouldn't have mattered much to the chicken whether it had had its neck wrung or its head chopped off with his grandfather's hatchet.

As memorable as that part of the experience had been, what had stuck with Rhodes even more than the flailing chicken was the smell when his grandfather had plunged the chicken into boiling water before plucking it. It was a smell of dampness and singeing, a scorching odor that seemed as if it would never go away.

Rhodes had helped with the plucking, and he could still feel the damp feathers as they stuck to his hands, but it was the smell that had capped the whole epsiode.

"You don't want burning chickens," he said. He wondered if he could eat the rest of the Zero. "It's a worse smell than what you have now."

"Don't I know it," Garrett said. "I smell burning all the time."

Rhodes had heard about this smell, too, but he hadn't experienced it. Not all the chickens in the long houses survived to be taken away and processed. Some of them died. The bodies were disposed of in "pathological incinerators" with two-stage burners that supposedly turned the chickens into inorganic ash very quickly and destroyed any pathogens. Qualls had written letters to the paper implying that as a cost-cutting measure someone wasn't following the proper procedures.

"I'd be about broke if it wasn't for all the Asians," Garrett said.

Jennifer Loam had done an article about the Asians who came from all over Texas to visit the persimmon orchards on Calvin Terrall's place at Mount Industry. Terrall had grown peaches for years, but the peach crop had become an unreliable moneymaker because of drought and hard winters. Persimmons were resistant to those things. Chinese, Koreans, and Japanese living in big cities like Dallas and Houston drove to Mount Industry to get the fruit that was an important part of their cultures but that was hard to find in American cities.

"They mostly come on weekends," Garrett said. "If they'd come every day and stop in for a Coke and a candy bar, I'd be doing fine. Trouble is, there's not as many of them coming as there was a year ago." He paused and sniffed. "Not near as many. It's the smell.

They don't like it any more than you and me do. Maybe less. Hamilton and Terrall have gone round and round about it."

Terrall had written nearly as many letters to the *Herald* as Qualls had. Rhodes had read all of them, and he'd taken a few calls from Terrall as well.

Rhodes managed to finish his candy bar and wash it down with the Dr Pepper. He paid Garrett for them.

"People around here sure do have it in for Lester," Garrett said. He swung his legs down from the counter and stood up to put the money in his old-fashioned cash register. After he counted out the change, he said, "Tell you the truth, I don't like him much myself."

"He's not going to bother you anymore," Rhodes said.

"Who's that? Lester?"

Rhodes pocketed his change and nodded. "Lester's dead."

Garrett didn't seem surprised. "Too bad, I guess. How'd it happen? Old man Terrall take an axe to him?"

"Nothing like that. He had an accident. He drowned."

"Noodling, I'll bet."

"You'd win that bet," Rhodes said.

"He should've had somebody with him, but who'd go? Nobody could stand him except those he paid, and they all have work to do. 'Sides, they didn't like him any better than anybody else around here."

Rhodes was beginning to think that instead of going to Lester's funeral, people would throw a wingding of a celebration.

"Why didn't they like him?" Rhodes asked.

"'Cause he worked 'em long hours and didn't pay 'em much. People need a job these days or he couldn't have got anybody to work at that place unless he paid double what he's paying now. The ones that work there resent it."

"Was there anybody in this county that liked him?"

56

"Just one fella, so I hear."

"Who?"

"Harvey Stoneman. You know him?"

"The preacher at First Baptist."

"That's him. 'Course since he's a preacher, he has to like every-body. It's in his job description. That's not why he likes Lester, or *liked* him if old Lester's dead like you say."

"He's dead all right."

"Harvey'll be sad about that, maybe the only one who will. He liked Lester, and you better bet he liked Lester's contributions to the church. Lester never showed a sign he felt guilty about all the trouble he caused around here, but he gave heavy to the church. I think he was making up for his sins, or trying to."

Rhodes supposed that meant there'd be a funeral after all, and not a celebration. Stoneman wouldn't be the only one who appreciated Hamilton's contributions to the church.

"I'll kinda miss old Lester myself," Garrett said. "Now and then he'd stop in and buy a Coke. Little friendly gesture, I guess you'd call it." He paused. "Didn't help the smell any that I could tell."

Rhodes said he had to get on back to Clearview. Garrett followed him out onto the porch.

"You don't have anybody running against you this year, do you, Sheriff."

"No. I guess nobody had the energy."

"I just wanted you to know I appreciated you stopping in and spending a little money since it wasn't because you wanted my vote."

"I was glad to do it. I needed a candy bar."

"We all do from time to time," Garrett said. "You come back now, you hear?"

"I'll do that," Rhodes said.

* * *

Back at the jail, Rhodes heard about the usual assortment of petty crimes that went on in Clearview, including a prank call to the jail from some youngster who thought it would be funny to order a burger and fries.

Hack hadn't found it funny. "I asked the little scallywag if he wanted cheese with that. He said he did, and I told him to come by and pick it up. Told him we'd check him into the Graybar Hotel for free and provide him with first-class accommodations and some free clothes besides."

"I hope he shows up," Lawton said. "Hope he likes orange, too."

The county's jail jumpsuits were a particularly awful shade of orange. Lawton hated them almost as much as the prisoners did. They were the Lester Hamilton of jumpsuits.

"You find out anything in Mount Industry?" Hack asked Rhodes.

"Not a thing. Somebody will have to take charge of those chickens, and for now that's Jared Crockett. If Hamilton left a will, that might change."

"A man like Hamilton always leaves a will," Hack said. "It'll be on file at the courthouse."

"None of my business, though," Rhodes said.

"Not yet, you mean."

"It was just an accident."

"Right," Hack said.

"Right," Lawton said.

Rhodes figured he might as well join in.

"Right," he said.

8

▼

RHODES WENT HOME EARLY BECAUSE HE KNEW HE'D HAVE TO GO out again later when he had a look at Dr. White's autopsy report on Lester Hamilton.

Rhodes's wife, Ivy, was still at work, but when Rhodes went into the house, he was greeted by Yancey, a little Pomeranian, who gave the impression that no dog had ever been so excited to see a human being in the entire existence of dogs and humans. He yipped and yapped and hopped around as if he'd been injected with the blood of the Energizer Bunny.

Yancey followed along as Rhodes walked on back to the kitchen, where the black cat, Sam, lay in his usual place by the refrigerator. Sam wasn't nearly as energetic as Yancey. In fact, he was the very model of energy conservation. He opened his yellow eyes and looked at Yancey, who immediately turned and ran off to the bedroom. If Rhodes knew Yancey, he was under the bed, doing an imitation of a quivering dust mop.

"You ought not to scare the dog," Rhodes said.

Sam yawned, showing a pink tongue and fangs that a vampire would have envied.

Rhodes sneezed. He was allergic to the cat, though Ivy wouldn't admit it. She said the sneezing was psychosomatic. Little did she know.

"Come on, Yancey," Rhodes called.

He waited a few seconds and saw the Pomeranian poke his head around the doorjamb.

"It's safe," Rhodes said. He went to the door to the little back porch and opened it. "Let's go outside."

Yancey shot across the room and through the door like he'd been scalded. When he reached the enclosed porch, he threw on the brakes and slid across the hardwood floor, coming to a halt only when he hit the door. Luckily, he didn't hit it hard enough to hurt himself.

Rhodes looked at Sam. "I guess you're happy."

Sam didn't even bother to open his eyes, but Rhodes thought he looked smug anyway.

Rhodes closed the door to the kitchen and opened the screen. Yancey dashed outside, where the much bigger dog, Speedo, waited. Speedo was more or less a border collie. Like Sam and Yancey, he'd become part of the Rhodes household in the course of an investigation Rhodes was pursuing. It seemed as if Rhodes had a knack for accumulating animals, even when, as was the case with Sam, he was allergic to them.

Rhodes sat on the back step and watched Speedo and Yancey cavort around the yard. Yancey appeared to have no idea that Speedo was about twenty times his size, and he barked and nipped at the larger dog as if they were equals.

Eventually, Yancey found Speedo's chew toy, grabbed it, and ran off with it. Speedo went after him to recover it.

While they worked it out, Rhodes thought about Lester Hamilton. He did some of his best thinking while he sat on the step, or so he told himself, and this was a good day both for sitting and for thinking. The early October air was soft and warm with just a hint of fall as the afternoon wound down. A faint smokey smell from somewhere helped Rhodes forget the stink of Mount Industry.

Speedo snatched the chew toy from Yancey and sped away with Yancey in close pursuit, yipping all the way, momentarily distracting Rhodes, but then his thoughts turned back to Hamilton, whose death was so convenient for so many people, or would be if the chicken farm shut down. Certainly motive enough for murder, not that Hamilton had been murdered.

Rhodes thought about William Qualls and Calvin Terrall. Their motives were stronger than those of a lot of others, but even someone like Mitch Garrett had reason to be glad that Hamilton was no longer around.

"What are you thinking?" Ivy asked, coming out the door behind Rhodes.

"Lester Hamilton," Rhodes told her.

Ivy sat on the step beside him. They watched Speedo and Yancey for a while.

"Those dogs are crazy," Ivy said.

"They're just dogs."

"All dogs are crazy. Why are you thinking about Lester Hamilton, of all people?"

Rhodes told her.

"That's sad," she said.

"You're about the only one who feels that way."

"That's what's so sad."

It was hard to feel sad while the dogs were having such a good time, and Ivy laughed when Speedo ran up and dropped the chew toy at Rhodes's feet. Rhodes snatched it up before Speedo could grab it again and threw it where Yancey could snap it up and run away with it. Speedo went after him.

"Are you hungry?" Ivy asked Rhodes.

"I didn't have a lot of lunch," he said, neglecting to mention what he'd eaten. Ivy occasionally lectured him on his poor eating habits and was trying to change them, without any notable success.

"We're having vegetarian lasagna for supper," she said.

Rhodes had suspected that might be it. She'd made the lasagna a while back and frozen it.

"That sounds fine," he said, and he meant it. "I've been out to Mount Industry, and I'm not in the mood for chicken. Or even beef."

"When do you want to eat?"

"We might as well eat early. I have to go to Ballinger's tonight."

"To see Hamilton's autopsy?"

Rhodes had no desire to watch an autopsy, much less right after he'd eaten. He'd seen more than enough of them.

"Just to get the results."

"All right." Ivy stood up. "I'll go heat it up. You can stay out here with your buddies. I'll call you when it's ready."

She went inside. Rhodes watched the dogs and thought about Lester Hamilton. After a minute or two, his thoughts drifted to the mysterious Robin Hood.

So far whoever was going around shooting arrows into the air hadn't been a danger to anyone, but Mikey Burns had a point about the possibility of worse things happening. Up until now, there hadn't been any destruction of property unless you counted holes in utility poles. The destruction of Burns's tire changed that. It was a step in the wrong direction.

Why hadn't anyone seen the bowman, or bowperson, if that was a word? He'd been careful to do his work during the night until now, and then he'd gone to a place where concealment was easy. That explained it, Rhodes supposed.

He'd meant to ask Hack if Ruth had brought in the arrow, but he could go by the jail on his way to Ballinger's and find out. Not that he expected they'd learn anything from it. It would be just as clean as the others that Robin Hood had used.

Ivy called Rhodes from inside the house, and he whistled for Yancey. Both dogs came over, and Rhodes roughhoused Speedo for a couple of seconds. Speedo grinned with pleasure, and then Rhodes went inside with Yancey at his heels.

"Yeah, she brought that arrow in," Hack said when Rhodes stopped by the jail. "Didn't do much with it, though. No time, and she's not gonna find any prints on it anyway. You on your way to Ballinger's?"

"That's right."

"You find out anything, you be sure to let us know."

"Tomorrow," Rhodes said.

Hack didn't like being out of the loop. "You can't come by tonight?"

"Tomorrow's soon enough."

"Okay, if that's the way you feel."

Rhodes didn't respond to that. "Anything else going on that I need to know about?"

"Nope."

The way he said it made Rhodes think he wouldn't have been told even if there had been.

"Good," Rhodes said. "I like it quiet."

He started to leave and had his hand on the doorknob when Hack said, "There might be one little thing."

Rhodes turned around.

"You read the paper yet?"

Rhodes hadn't even thought about it. Now he remembered that Jennifer Loam was supposed to have a story about the chicken farm in it.

"No," he said. "I didn't even see it."

Hack picked up the copy that he had on his desk. "You might want to take a look. That reporter really lays it on the line, and she says there's more to come."

"I'll read it when I get home," Rhodes said, turning again to leave.

"One more little thing," Hack said.

Rhodes sighed and turned around. "What?"

"Deputy Grady says she might get you a witness on that tire shootin'. She says there's bound to've been somebody around there, and she'll do some askin' tomorrow."

"Good idea," Rhodes said. "I hope she finds somebody."

"She's good," Hack said. "If there's a witness, she'll find him."

"We'll see," Rhodes said.

Ballinger's Funeral Home had once been a private mansion, or what passed for one in Clearview. Now it served the dead instead of the living.

Ballinger had his private office in the back of the building in a little brick house that had been the servants' quarters long ago.

Rhodes had called from his home to let Ballinger know he was coming, so he went inside the office without knocking. Ballinger sat behind his desk, which as usual was littered with old paperback books, Ballinger's preferred reading material. He bought them at garage sales for a nickel or a dime. Sometimes for a quarter if it was one he really wanted.

"Good to see you, Sheriff," Ballinger said. "Have a seat. Did you talk to Mikey Burns today?"

What with everything else that had happened, Rhodes had forgotten Burns's mention of Ballinger as a source of knowledge about terrorism in Blacklin County.

"I talked to him," Rhodes said, sitting on the couch that faced the desk. "He mentioned something about a book you'd read."

"That's right." Ballinger pulled a book out of a small pile to his right. "This one."

He held it up so Rhodes could see the cover. The title was *The Coyote Connection,* and the illustration depicted a young man with black hair and long sideburns. In one hand he held a knife. A woman in a low-cut dress reclined in his other arm. Rhodes supposed he was protecting her. The author's name was Nick Carter.

"I can't find any really old books anymore," Ballinger said, "so I've started reading these Nick Carter books. There must be hundreds of them. This one's set in Texas. It was published in 1981, and do you know what it's about?"

"Terrorism?" Rhodes asked, taking a wild guess.

"That's right, and it's scary stuff. Take a look at the back cover."

He tossed the book to Rhodes, who caught it and turned it over. According to material on the back cover, the book was about Middle Eastern terrorists slipping into the United States along with Mexican nationals coming across the Texas border from Mexico at Matamoros and Brownsville.

"It could happen just the same way right now," Ballinger said. "Nothing's changed. The terrorists could come over from some-

where like Cuba, cross the border at Brownsville with some smug-
gler, and work their way to Washington."

"It says here that the goal of the terrorists is assassination."

"Right. They'd go to the Capitol and kill all the congressmen
they could," Ballinger went on. "That's the plan in the book, I
mean. Probably they'd avoid the big main highways and maybe
even come through a little county like this one. Are you ready for
something like that?"

"From the looks of things," Rhodes said, turning the book
around so he could see the front again, "I don't have to be ready.
Nick Carter would take care of them."

"He's not real," Ballinger said, "and neither is that supersecret
agency he's supposed to be working for. His methods aren't exactly the kind of thing the current administration would approve
of, either. You're real. You're what stands between us and the terrorists."

"If they ever get across the border, that is."

"They could do it." Ballinger put the book back on his pile of
similar books. "Which is why we need that M-16."

Rhodes held the book so that Ballinger could see the cover.

"Nick Carter just has a knife," Rhodes said

"And a Luger and a gas bomb, but like I told you, he's not real.
We need real protection."

"If we can get any Homeland Security money, I'd rather use it
to get some other equipment. Something a little more practical.
More computers, video for all the county cars, that kind of thing."

"You can't shoot terrorists with computers," Ballinger said.

"Maybe we'd use arrows."

Ballinger got the reference. "Robin Hood up to mischief again,
huh?"

"He's more the kind of thing we have to deal with around here than any terrorists," Rhodes said, and he told Ballinger about Burns's tire.

"Mikey loves that little red car," Ballinger said. "I'll bet that flat tire got him plenty upset."

"It did," Rhodes said.

He didn't mention the note, which had upset Burns even more.

"You think you'll catch who did it?" Ballinger said.

"We're working on it. If we catch him, we wouldn't want to use an M-16 on him."

"I guess not. Tear him up too bad. You don't want to use it unless you got terrorists in your sights." Ballinger shifted in his chair. "You want to see that autopsy report on Lester Hamilton?"

"That's what I came for."

"Here it is," Ballinger said, getting it out of a drawer.

Rhodes got up and handed the book back to Ballinger, taking the report from him in exchange.

"You won't like it," Ballinger said.

"I was afraid of that," Rhodes said, and he started to read.

Dr. White's conclusion was that Lester Hamilton had died by drowning. Rhodes had expected that. What he hadn't expected was the discovery that the marks on Hamilton's right wrist weren't made by a catfish.

That wasn't true. He'd expected it. He just hadn't wanted to admit it. He'd spent most of the day denying it, but there it was, right there in the report.

In layman's terms, what Dr. White said was that the marks weren't consistent with the bite of a catfish, or any other kind of fish for that matter. They'd been made, he suspected, by a rope.

He'd found no trace of fibers, so he couldn't prove his suspicions, but he was certain that there was no catfish involved. That pretty much settled it, Rhodes thought.

Even though there wasn't any proof of it, Lester Hamilton had been murdered.

9

▼

"MURDERED?" IVY ASKED. "ISN'T THAT PRETTY MUCH JUST AN assumption?"

"It's more than that," Rhodes said. "Somebody got a rope around Hamilton's wrist and held him under the water."

"Who?"

"Well, that's the problem. There was nobody else there, and it didn't look like anybody else had been there."

Rhodes and Ivy sat at the kitchen table with the *Clearview Herald* between them. Rhodes hadn't looked at Jennifer Loam's article yet. Sam lay by the refrigerator, and Yancey was nowhere to be seen. Cowering under the bed, most likely.

"What about Hal Gillis? Didn't you say he was there?"

"He was, but it's hard to think of him as somebody who'd kill Hamilton."

"Has anybody you've ever arrested for murder looked like a killer?"

"Now that you mention it, no."

"So you'd better look at Hal Gillis pretty closely."

"You have something against him?"

"No, but he was there and nobody else was. I'd think that would make him a prime suspect."

"I thought I was the professional lawman in this family."

"You are. It just seems logical to suspect Hal."

"I'll put him on my list," Rhodes said, and then he sneezed.

"I dusted in here a couple of days ago," Ivy said.

"It's not dust." Rhodes looked at Sam, who was looking back, his rest disturbed by the sneeze. "It's the cat."

"You aren't allergic to Sam, and I wish you'd quit pretending that you are."

Rhodes sneezed again. "Right." He pulled the paper to his side of the table. "I need to read Jennifer Loam's article about the chicken farm."

"I read it," Ivy said. "Lester Hamilton would be rolling over in his grave if he had one."

Rhodes thought about Hamilton's current autopsied state and said, "I don't think he'll be moving much."

"You know what I meant."

Rhodes grinned. Then he sneezed.

"Go ahead and read the article," Ivy said. "I'm going to shower and go to bed."

When he'd finished reading Jennifer Loam's story, Rhodes laid the paper on the table. Hack and Ivy hadn't been kidding. The article was a powerful indictment of factory farming. Loam said that Hamilton had managed to make such great profits because he'd shifted a lot of his costs to the taxpayers, and that he'd done great harm to the environment. She said that while the chicken farm generated as much pollution as many regulated industries, it was exempt from antipollution laws because it was considered "agriculture."

All in all, it was an article that William Qualls must have loved, and it gave Rhodes at least one bit of new information. Somehow, Loam had found material that proved the incinerators used to burn the carcasses of dead chickens were inadequate. The incinerators were too small, and often the second stage of burning was skipped. Qualls had suspected something along the same lines.

Because the article reinforced everything Rhodes had heard, it gave him all the more reason to suspect everybody who lived in Mount Industry, including, he supposed, Hal Gillis.

Loam concluded with a note saying that there would be more articles to come. Rhodes was sure everybody would look forward to reading them, except Jared Crockett.

The next morning, Rhodes drove to the jail.

"So?" Hack asked as soon as Rhodes stepped through the door.

"So what?" Rhodes asked, though he knew very well what Hack meant.

"So what about Lester Hamilton?" Lawton asked from his usual place by the door to the cell block.

"He's still dead," Rhodes said.

"Yeah," Hack said. "We kinda figured that. You gonna tell us if you found out anything else?"

Rhodes relented. "He was murdered."

"Kinda figured that, too," Lawton said.

"Yeah," Hack said. "When you got as many people hatin' you as Lester did, it's pretty suspicious when you drown."

"That's not what you said yesterday," Rhodes pointed out.

"We were just tryin' to make you feel better. What're you gonna do now?"

"Find out who killed him," Rhodes said.

The first thing Rhodes did was go out to Murdock's rock pit to see if he could find anything he'd missed. He continued to have the nagging feeling that he'd overlooked something, but he still couldn't figure out what it could have been.

It was a bright day, not a cloud in sight, the sky as blue as a baby's eyes. No one was fishing in the rock pit. The only sign of life was a rabbit that hopped away through the weeds when it heard Rhodes's county car bouncing along the rutted road.

Hamilton's car was gone, towed away to the county lot, where it would sit for a while. If necessary, Rhodes would have Ruth go over it again.

Rhodes got out of the Charger. It was too late to look for tracks again. Too many vehicles had come and gone since the previous morning, but it didn't matter. Rhodes was convinced that the only cars that had visited the rock pit before he'd arrived yesterday were the ones driven by Gillis and Hamilton.

Did that make Gillis the guilty party? Ivy seemed to think it might, and she had a point, but Rhodes didn't believe Gillis was strong enough to drown a man like Hamilton.

Rhodes walked to the edge of the pit and worked his way to the spot where Hamilton's body had been. The sun sparkled off the water, and the willows whispered at Rhodes's back. They didn't tell him anything useful, however.

Rhodes looked down at the rock that had half hidden Hamilton's body. If there was a hole under that rock, the giant catfish that Gillis had mentioned might be hiding inside it, all right.

Hamilton would have reached into the hole, which is when the fish would have latched onto him with its bucket-sized mouth had it been there. Could someone have been hidden in the hole? Or could someone have hidden himself some other way? Rhodes didn't know, but he was sure of one thing: He didn't want to find out himself. The county would have to hire a diver, probably a man named Casey Jones. He lived in Milsby, and he'd done that kind of work for several of the surrounding counties.

While Rhodes looked at the rock and the water, the moss-backed turtle floated soundlessly up toward the surface. Rhodes couldn't see it well at first, but then it became a distinct circular shape. When it was a foot or so from the surface, Rhodes could see it plainly. It came up even farther and stuck its head a little out of the water. It looked to Rhodes kind of like a submarine survey-ing the surface through a periscope.

Two much smaller turtles floated beside the larger one. They weren't much bigger than teacups, and they bobbed like fishing corks.

"I wish you could talk," Rhodes said. "I expect you know what happened here."

The turtles didn't answer. The larger one retracted its thick neck and began to sink as quietly as it had surfaced. The two smaller ones sank beside him. It was a neat trick, and Rhodes won-dered how the turtles did it. Maybe he should have paid more at-tention in biology class when he was in school, but he couldn't even recall if the teacher had discussed snapping turtles.

Rhodes leaned out a little to look at the turtles as they sank back down, and that was a mistake. He stepped on a round pebble that turned under his left foot, causing him to lose his balance. He grabbed for the willows but got only the tip of a branch. A couple of leaves tore off in his hand. He felt himself falling and windmilled his arms in an attempt to keep his balance, but it was no use. He tumbled backward, looking up at the blue sky and feeling like a clumsy clown. He shut his eyes and sucked in air, and his worry about what would happen when he hit the water was tempered by his relief that no one was around to see him.

He hoped he wouldn't hit the rock that stuck out from the side of the pit and break his back.

He didn't. He struck the water flat on his back. It stung, and he made a splash that he hoped would scare off any giant catfish and huge turtles.

The water was cold, but not so cold that Rhodes was shocked into insensibility. It chilled him a little, but that was all. The summer had been a warm one, and the fall hadn't been much different, so Rhodes wasn't worried about being incapacitated by the cold. That was a good thing because he had plenty of other things to be worried about.

He sank rapidly, but he didn't reach the bottom. It occurred to him that he didn't know how deep the water was. He knew he didn't want to find out.

He opened his eyes and saw wavery light above him. Righting himself, he kicked his feet, moved his arms downward, and started up. His head popped into the air, and he shook it hard, sending water drops all around. He bobbed like a cork and looked for a place where he could climb out of the water.

Maybe he could save the county some money, however. All he had to do was duck under and make his own inspection of the space underneath the jutting rock.

He didn't have a light or any diving equipment, but he didn't think he'd need a light. He wouldn't go far enough under the water for that.

He didn't have anyone to watch him, either, and that wasn't

good. Still, while he didn't want to make a fatal blunder, he was already wet. It seemed like a shame not to get some benefit from his accident. How long could it take? A minute or two at the most. Then he'd climb out and get dry.

Before he could talk himself out of it, he slipped off his shoes and threw them one at a time to the top of the bank.

He left his pistol in its ankle holster. He didn't want to throw it. No telling what might happen if he did. Considering his luck so far, it might go off and puncture the county car's radiator.

Rhodes slid back under the water and pushed himself over to the rock. It was darker underneath the water than he'd thought it would be, but he could see that there was an even darker area under the outcropping, darker than it should have been. He kicked his feet and went closer.

Sure enough, a big hole gaped in the side of the rock pit, but Rhodes wasn't sure it was big enough to conceal a man, and he wasn't going to try to find out.

He eased back to the surface for a breath or two. He didn't think anyone could have hidden inside the hole and waited there for Hamilton. Even if someone had gotten inside, how could he have held his breath long enough to kill a man? For that matter, he'd have had to conceal himself for quite a while before Hamilton got there. It was impossible.

One more look, Rhodes told himself. He submerged again and paddled over to the hole. Definitely not big enough for anyone to hide in, not that he could really see much. A big catfish could hide inside, even a gigantic one, but not a person.

Rhodes was about to go back up when he saw something else. Just to his right, several small rocks stuck out of the side of the pit. He thought he saw something on the ragged edge of one of them, and he surfaced for a breath before taking a look.

When he dived again, he saw that a piece of cloth, not a big one, had snagged on the rock. Rhodes reached to get it with his right hand, holding on to one of the other rocks with his left hand.

When he pulled the cloth off the rock, he kicked his feet to go up, but when he moved his left hand from the rock, something clamped onto it. Hard.

Rhodes pulled.

Whatever had hold of him pulled back, scraping the top of Rhodes's arm against the rock.

Rhodes was trapped. He wondered if Hal Gillis would come fishing and find his body.

10

▼

RHODES STUCK THE CLOTH IN HIS BACK POCKET AND REACHED into the cleft of the rocks with his right hand. He felt a whisker and a slick muscular skin. A catfish had hold of him, all right.

Luckily it wasn't the giant that Gillis had told him about, but it wasn't tiny, either. Rhodes grasped his left wrist and pulled.

The catfish was lodged securely in the rocks and didn't budge. Rhodes tried to pry its mouth open. He didn't have any luck.

Rhodes didn't know how long he'd been under the water, but he knew it had been too long. He started to worry. He pulled again.

This time the catfish budged, but not much. Maybe it was too big to pull through the opening. That would be too bad for Rhodes. He'd had a lot of embarrassing things happen to him over the course of his life, but it would be hard to top getting drowned by a catfish.

It hadn't seemed so bad when he'd thought Les Hamilton might have gone out the same way, but Hamilton had known the risk he was taking. Rhodes hadn't even thought about the risk.

That was the story of his life. He never thought about the risk until it was too late.

His chest burned, and he had to struggle not to breathe. He fluttered his feet and churned his legs in an attempt to force himself to the surface while dragging the reluctant catfish from its lair.

It didn't work. Rhodes settled back down and felt his thinning hair float above his head. He hoped there'd be enough to cover the little bald spot that was showing up in back when they laid him out.

Giving another hard jerk, he thought he felt the fish give a little ground, but not enough to slip through the crevice in the rocks.

Rhodes drew up his legs, doubled his body, and braced his feet against the rocks. Then he pushed backward as hard as he could. The fish was wedged too firmly to move, and it wasn't about to let go of Rhodes's hand.

It was all Rhodes could do not to take a deep breath and suck in water. Instead, he let the last bit of air bubble out of his lungs and sank farther toward the bottom of the rock pit. He wondered why his life hadn't flashed before his eyes. Wasn't that supposed to happen? He'd be disappointed if that turned out to be a myth.

His left foot touched a stone. It was firmly stuck in the side of the pit, and it gave Rhodes some leverage.

He hadn't tried pulling downward, and he had no real reason to expect it would work any better than what he'd been doing, but he didn't want to drown without giving it a try. He hooked his feet under the rock and gave as hard a downward jerk as he could.

The fish popped out of the cranny, driving Rhodes down even farther into the water. He kicked for the top, but he didn't think he'd make it.

His mouth opened. Water choked him. Then he burst through the surface, gagging, gasping, and coughing.

Rhodes shook his head and sent water droplets flying. They dimpled the water when they struck it. Rhodes floated where he was and drew in deep breaths. It felt good to fill his lungs. He was happy to be breathing, and even happier that he wasn't in Mount Industry, where he'd have to inhale the polluted air of the chicken farm.

After a short time, Rhodes raised his arm to have a closer look at the catfish that was still attached to his hand. The fish was scratched, bloody, and big. Rhodes figured it must have weighed a good twenty pounds, but sometimes things looked bigger under the water.

The catfish looked up at Rhodes with harsh accusation in its black eyes. Then it opened its mouth, released his hand, and disappeared into the deep water with a twitch of its powerful tail.

Rhodes wasn't sorry to see it go. He didn't have any use for it. He was thinking about never eating fish again. If he quit chicken and beef, that left him with vegetables, which didn't seem like an alternative he could live with.

He paddled to the side of the rock pit and moved along until he located a spot where he thought he could climb out. The rocks hurt his shoeless feet, and his clammy clothing clung to him like a heavy winter fog.

When he reached the top of the stony bank, he sat on a rock so the sun could dry his clothes a bit. He removed his ankle holster and set it and the little Kel-Tec .32 automatic beside him.

The .32 was new. Rhodes had carried a .38 revolver for years, but it was heavy and a bother. He'd carried it in different places, but he'd never found one that was comfortable, which explained the .32.

It was tiny, not much bigger than the palm of his hand, and it weighed just an ounce over half a pound with seven hollow points in its magazine. It didn't have the stopping power of a .38, but Rhodes didn't often have to stop anyone with a bullet.

The little pistol also wasn't accurate at any great distance, but that didn't bother Rhodes, either. For his purposes, a .32 was an adequate deterrent, and he didn't plan to get into a firefight with any gangsters armed with tommy guns. If he did, maybe he could use the county's M-16, assuming the county ever purchased one.

The .32 had gray polymer grips. Rhodes wasn't worried about the effect of the water on those. The receiver was aluminum and steel. The steel was what worried Rhodes. He'd have to give the gun a good cleaning when he got home.

Rhodes reached into his back pocket and pulled out the cloth that had been hung on the rock and had almost gotten him drowned. It looked like the belt loop of a pair of jeans. Not much of a clue. Half the people in the county wore jeans, and unless this was some odd brand, it would be impossible to trace. Rhodes replaced it in his pocket. It might yet prove useful. You never knew.

Rhodes took off his socks and wrung some of the water out of them. He stood up and stretched. His clothes hadn't dried much, but it was time to go. He limped over to his shoes and after a little struggle got his feet into them.

It seemed he was always messing up the interior of the county cars he drove, and this was a new one. He hadn't gotten muddy, however, just wet. A little dampness wouldn't hurt the seats and wouldn't even require cleaning. He got in the car and put the cloth from the rock pit into an evidence bag.

Then he started the engine. A blast from the air conditioner momentarily stunned him. He turned it off.

When he got to the gate, another car was about to pull in. It waited for him to come out, and as he passed, the driver called out, "Catch anything, Sheriff?"

80

Rhodes didn't recognize the man, but he gave a friendly wave.

"Almost caught a catfish," he said. "Big one. But it got away from me."

"Too bad," the man said. "Maybe I'll snag him."

"Good luck," Rhodes said.

The man drove on into the field and deposited his money in the mailbox. Rhodes wondered if he'd have done that if the sheriff hadn't been watching him.

Thinking he was too suspicious, Rhodes drove on back to Clearview. He got Hack on the radio and told him he was going home.

"What's the matter?" Hack asked. "Wore yourself out already?"

"I'm hungry," Rhodes said.

That didn't satisfy Hack, but it was all he was going to get. Rhodes didn't feel like having to explain his wet clothing to Hack and Lawton. Bad enough that he'd have to explain it to Ivy when she got home that evening.

Or maybe he wouldn't have to. He went in through the back door of his house after spending a minute or two tussling with Speedo and his chew toy. He undressed on the enclosed back porch and laid his pistol on top of the washer. He tossed his clothes and ankle holster into the dryer and turned it on. Yancey bounced around his feet with joyous yips throughout the whole process, as if it were the most fascinating thing he'd ever seen.

Feeling far too exposed without his clothes, Rhodes went through the kitchen and into the bathroom. Sam hardly bothered to look at him, and Yancey was so happy to see him home at an odd hour that he pranced through the kitchen, completely forgetting to be afraid of Sam.

Rhodes took a hot shower. The water and soap made him feel a lot better. He dried off with a thick towel and put on a robe that he found in the bedroom closet. The robe had been a Christmas gift years ago, and Rhodes couldn't remember the last time he'd worn it.

While the clothes dried, Rhodes spread some newspaper on the kitchen table and retrieved the pistol. He got the gun lube, bore cleaner, alcohol, cloths, patches, and swabs. After field-stripping the pistol, he cleaned and lubed every part thoroughly.

Yancey hopped around for a while but finally gave up and lay down by Rhodes's chair, his head on his paws, his eyes wide open and focused on Sam, who still showed no interest at all in what was going on. Rhodes figured that if Sam so much as moved, Yancey would be off and running.

Rhodes reassembled the pistol, got a fresh magazine, and made sure the slide worked smoothly.

"If only the criminal element could see me now," he said to Yancey, who raised his head and looked at him. "A guy in a robe with a pistol the size of a deck of cards. They'd have a good laugh."

Yancey yipped in agreement.

"Hack and Lawton would get a kick out of it, too," Rhodes said, and Yancey yipped again.

"You don't have to keep agreeing with me," Rhodes said.

Yancey yipped and jumped up. The sudden movement bothered Sam, who opened his eyes and yawned, showing off his fangs.

Yancey gave a short bark and scampered out of the room.

"I wish you'd leave Yancey alone," Rhodes said to the cat.

Sam closed his mouth, closed his eyes, settled his head on his paws, and went instantly to sleep.

Rhodes wished he could be so unconcerned about things going

on around him. He thought about his morning's adventure. He didn't have much to show for it other than a few scrapes on his hand and wrist, not unlike those on Hamilton's wrist, except that Rhodes's had really been made by a catfish and not a rope. He also had a belt loop from a pair of jeans. That was it, if you counted only the physical items.

He had, however, one other thing, a theory about how Hamilton might have been killed.

The theory, of course, involved another person, which was a problem Rhodes hadn't quite worked out. That didn't matter. He was certain someone else had been at the rock pit, and that someone—whoever it was, however he'd gotten there, however he'd gotten away—had killed Hamilton.

The killer had been in the water with Hamilton, probably serving as his backup in case of emergency. Rhodes understood the necessity for a backup better now than ever, and Hamilton wasn't stupid. He'd have had someone with him, especially if he'd been hoping to catch a legendary giant catfish. He wouldn't have taken any chances by going it alone.

Whoever had killed Hamilton had been a friend, which was odd since Hamilton didn't have any friends. That was something to think about.

The friend might have gone to the rock pit early or even days ahead. He would have hidden his rope in a convenient spot, maybe in the big hole that Rhodes had seen under the rock. Under the guise of helping Hamilton, he'd have slipped the rope over his wrist, pulled it tight, and kicked away, pulling Hamilton down and looping the rope over one of the jutting rocks, of which there were plenty.

Maybe the killer had used the same rock that Rhodes had hooked his feet under to save himself. He wouldn't have had to keep Hamilton under the water long. Rhodes wondered if Hamilton had panicked or if he'd kept trying to save himself. Rhodes hadn't panicked, but he'd been pretty sure he was going to drown. Maybe Hamilton had been the same, but not giving up until the last second.

After Hamilton was dead, all the killer had to do was remove the rope and leave. Somehow. Rhodes would keep working on that.

He'd have to keep working on how the killer got there and got away, too. There had to be a way.

The dryer on the porch dinged. Rhodes went out there and got his clothes. The warm cloth felt good, and he gathered it to him as he went back to the bedroom to change.

When he bent down to strap on the ankle holster, Yancey stuck his head out from under the bed.

"I thought you were a dust bunny," Rhodes said, looking him in the eye.

Yancey looked back at him with a pained expression.

"You shouldn't let that cat bully you," Rhodes said. He straightened. "You're bigger than he is."

That wasn't strictly true, but Rhodes was sure Yancey didn't have any idea about relative sizes. He certainly wasn't afraid of Speedo, who was much bigger. His fear of Sam had to do with the old cats versus dogs problem. Some kind of instinct kicked in, and Yancey couldn't overcome it.

Rhodes returned to the kitchen and made himself a peanut butter sandwich. He wasn't going to have time for a fancy lunch, and peanut butter would have to do. He would have preferred bologna, but Ivy didn't like having it around. She thought it wasn't healthy.

Rhodes washed the sandwich down with some Dr Pepper.

When he'd finished, he picked up his pistol from the table. It smelled of gun oil and lube. After he put it in the holster, he gathered up the newspapers and took them outside to the recycle bin in the garage.

He was careful not to get rid of the one with Jennifer Loam's article. He might want to read that one again.

11

▼

HARVEY STONEMAN, THE PASTOR AT THE FIRST BAPTIST CHURCH, had the right voice for a preacher, the kind of voice that could reach the back of the balcony without the aid of a microphone, if there'd been anybody in the back of the balcony to reach.

He was short and stout, with a head of thick black hair that he combed straight back. Rhodes had once had thick hair like that, but it had been a while. Longer than he liked to think about.

A dark maroon carpet covered the floor of the pastor's study, and bookshelves hid the entire wall behind his desk. The shelves were filled with books, not the kind that Clyde Ballinger liked, but serious hardcover tomes whose spines bore titles like *The Life and Letters of Paul* and *In Search of the Historical Jesus*. Rhodes couldn't see the covers, but he suspected they wouldn't be anywhere near as lurid as the ones on Ballinger's preferred reading material.

Stoneman and Rhodes had already gotten through the preliminary discussion of what a shame it was that Lester Hamilton had died, and now they'd arrived at the reason for Rhodes's visit.

"You couldn't say Lester had any real friends in the church," Stoneman told Rhodes in answer to the sheriff's question, his voice filling the entire office. "He did at one time, but they've pretty much deserted him now."

Rhodes thought that was pretty unchristian of them, but he didn't want to get into a theological discussion with the minister.

"Who were his friends before he started the chicken farm?" Rhodes asked.

"Calvin Terrall was one of them. Their land joined, and they'd both lived in Mount Industry most of their lives. They sure had a falling-out about the farm, though."

"Did Terrall ever go noodling with him?"

"That's illegal, Sheriff. They wouldn't tell their pastor about that." Stoneman smiled. "He might overhear them talking about it, though, and I did once or twice. Calvin liked fried catfish a mighty lot."

Rhodes tried to get Stoneman to say more, but Stoneman insisted that was all the information he had to offer. He wouldn't meet Rhodes's gaze. Rhodes thought the preacher was holding out on him.

"Lester was friendly with that professor out there, Qualls, too, before he moved to town." Stoneman said. He frowned. "Qualls isn't a godly man. I'm not judging him. It's just the truth. Lester said Qualls cursed him out more than once after Lester started his farm."

Rhodes hadn't known that Qualls and Hamilton had been friends at one time. It was something to think about.

"Why are you asking about Lester's friends, Sheriff?" Stoneman asked. "I'm sure it's not because you're wondering if there will be enough of them to serve as his pallbearers."

Rhodes wasn't ready to answer Stoneman's question. He asked, "When's the funeral?"

"I haven't heard anything about arrangements," Stoneman said. "Lester didn't have any close kin around here, and he might have wanted just a simple memorial service. I expect he did. He didn't like a lot of fuss being made over him. Maybe he won't need any pallbearers. I should hear from Randy Lawless soon enough, and then I'll know."

Rhodes wasn't surprised to hear Lawless's name. "Lawless was his attorney?"

"That's right. He's a member here, too, and I'm sure he made Lester's will. Lester was always one to plan ahead, so there's no doubt he left instructions for what to do after his demise."

Rhodes didn't think he'd ever heard anybody use the word "demise" in conversation before.

"I'll check with Lawless," Rhodes said, thinking that the will was his business now.

Before he want to Lawless to talk about the will, Rhodes would have Ruth Grady see if it was on file at the courthouse. It should have been. The will might not have anything helpful, but it would at least name Hamilton's heir or heirs. Sometimes that was a clue.

"You still haven't said why you're so curious about this sad affair," Stoneman said. "I don't think the sheriff comes around asking questions if there's not something fishy going on."

"It might be that Hamilton had some help drowning," Rhodes said. "If he did, I want to find out who did the helping."

Stoneman didn't appear too surprised. "You didn't ask me if Lester had any enemies."

"I can think of plenty of those on my own," Rhodes said.

Stoneman shook his head. "I don't doubt that you can. Lester didn't endear himself to anyone over the last several years. He always supported the church, though. He was a good man, no matter what people think of him."

People didn't always equate supporting a church with being a good person, Rhodes thought. Sometimes they expected a little more. Being a good neighbor would have helped.

"What about you?" Rhodes asked. "Were you his friend?"

"I was his pastor. I like to think I was his friend, too."

"The way a pastor's a friend to everybody in the church, or more like a real friend?"

"A pastor always strives to be a real friend," Stoneman said in a hurt tone.

"I didn't mean that the way it sounded," Rhodes said. "I mean, were you the kind of friend who went fishing with him."

Stoneman got that evasive look again. "What do you mean by that, Sheriff?"

"I mean did you ever back him up when he was noodling?"

"No," Stoneman said. "I never did."

He sounded like he was telling the truth, but Rhodes wasn't satisfied.

"You know who did, though. You might as well tell me now, save us both some trouble."

Stoneman was quiet for a while. The silence stretched out, but Rhodes didn't mind. He could wait.

"Calvin Terrall," Stoneman said.

"What about him?"

"I hate to say. It's just something I heard once, not anything that was told directly to me."

"Better go ahead. It might be something I need to know."

Stoneman sighed. "I don't like repeating gossip, but this is something I overheard."

He seemed to overhear a lot of things, Rhodes thought.

"Calvin and Lester talked about noodling one day after church.

Calvin used to go with Lester, but that was before they fell out with each other. I don't think Calvin would go now."

He might, though, Rhodes thought, if he wanted to see to it that Lester didn't get back home.

"Do you really think someone killed Lester, Sheriff?" Stoneman asked.

"Looks that way," Rhodes said.

He still thought Stoneman was holding something back. If that was the case, Rhodes would find out sooner or later.

He always did.

Rhodes drove to Mount Industry. When he got to Garrett's store, he stopped. Might as well have a cold Zero. After all, he hadn't had much lunch, just a sandwich, and that hardly counted.

Garrett was in his usual spot behind the counter with his feet propped on it. Rhodes wondered if he sat that way all the time or if he changed positions now and then.

"Hey, Sheriff," Garrett said.

"Still busy, I see," Rhodes said.

"Busy as usual, anyway. You after another Zero?"

"Don't mind if I do."

"Help yourself," Garrett said, as he always did, and Rhodes went to the refrigerator.

"No Dr Pepper this time?" Garrett said as Rhodes unwrapped the candy bar.

"Already had one today."

"Could have another."

"Better not." Rhodes took a satisfying bite of the Zero. "You ever hear about Calvin Terrall going noodling with Lester Hamilton?"

"You trying to get the game warden's job, Sheriff?"

"I'm satisfied with the job I already have. I was just wondering."

Garrett laughed. "You're the sheriff. You're never 'just wondering.'"

"Sometimes I am. In this case, maybe not. I'd like to know, either way."

"You'll just have to ask Terrall about it, then. I don't have any idea. You ever tried it? Noodling, I mean?"

"Once," Rhodes said.

"You know it's against the law."

"I know. Let's just say there were extenuating circumstances. And I didn't much like it, if that makes any difference."

"Don't blame you for not liking it. Too damn dangerous. I guess Lester found that out."

"I guess he did."

Rhodes finished the Zero and disposed of the wrapper. He paid Garrett and started to leave.

"You didn't ever go noodling with him, did you?" he asked as he reached the door.

"Not me," Garrett said. "It's illegal, remember? I'm a law-abiding citizen myself."

"Just like everybody else in the county."

"Most of 'em," Garrett said. "Not all."

"Don't I know it," Rhodes said.

12

▼

CALVIN TERRALL'S PLACE WAS ON DOWN THE ROAD FROM THE store, and Rhodes didn't have to take the turn that led by the cemetery. As he neared Terrall's, he began to see hand-painted signs nailed to fence posts. All of them advertised Terrall's wares: peaches, tomatoes, potatoes, onions, corn, persimmons, and other produce. Each sign had a picture of the particular item being touted. To Rhodes the pictures looked as if they'd been drawn by six-year-olds. Maybe they had. Terrall's whole family was involved in his business, from his children to his grandchildren.

Terrall's house was set back from the road, and with good reason. His big front yard served as a parking lot for visitors to his produce stand, an open-front building with long tables in front.

At different times of the year, different items sat on the tables in bushel baskets and cardboard boxes. It was long past time for peaches, but Rhodes saw reddish orange persimmons, bright red tomatoes, brown potatoes, onions, and green beans. He figured that the tomatoes, for sure, were trucked in from elsewhere and not grown on the farm.

Rhodes parked his car and got out. There was plenty of room, as Terrall had no customers. The smell from the chicken farm wasn't quite as bad as it had been the previous day, but it was still a palpable presence in the air.

Calvin Terrall and his wife, Margie, sat in metal lawn chairs behind one of the tables. Calvin stood up when Rhodes approached.

"Need you some tomatoes today, Sheriff?" he asked.

Terrall was a rawboned six-footer a little past sixty, with a tanned face and faded blue eyes. He wore a Western-style white straw hat, a blue work shirt, and jeans that were tucked into the tops of a worn pair of boots.

"I don't think so," Rhodes said.

He wasn't fond of tomatoes, at least not raw ones. Cooked or made into sauce, they were all right, but Rhodes couldn't just sit down at the table, slice a tomato, and eat it.

"How about some persimmons, then?" Terrall asked.

Rhodes shook his head. He'd eaten persimmons once or twice, but they were a little too tart for his tastes. The thought made his mouth pucker.

Margie Terrall stood up and joined her husband. "You could get your wife to bake you a nice persimmon cake. Or make you some chutney, maybe."

Rhodes didn't know the Terralls well, but he liked Margie. She always seemed cheerful, or she had in the past. There wasn't much trace of cheer in her face today.

"I didn't come to buy anything," Rhodes said.

Margie waved a hand at the empty parking lot. "Neither did anybody else. I guess you know why."

Calvin didn't wait for Rhodes to answer. "It's the smell from those chickens. People don't like to think about eating fruits and vegetables when the place where they buy 'em smells so much like an open sewer. Can't you do anything about it, Sheriff?"

"Not a thing," Rhodes said. "That farm's a hundred percent legal."

"Legal, maybe, but it's a crime against everybody who lives around here."

"Things might change now that Lester's dead," Rhodes said.

Terrall snorted. "No, they won't. Somebody else will just take over, and it'll be exactly the same. That is, if it doesn't get any worse. Seems to me like you could shut the place down for smelling like that."

"You'll have to take that up with the Commission on Environmental Quality," Rhodes said. "It's a legal operation, so I can't do a thing."

"We've tried the commission. We've about reached the end of our rope. It's our living we're talking about here."

Rhodes looked past the house at the orchards. Most of the persimmon trees were still hung with fruit. Terrall saw where Rhodes was looking.

"We used to have people coming in here by the busload, picking their own fruit, having a good time. Some of 'em would bring their lunches and have picnics here. Now we're lucky if we get more than a carload a week stopping by, and they don't stay long, believe me."

Rhodes believed him.

"Me and Margie can't hardly stand it ourselves," Terrall continued. He was getting worked up, his eyes turning mean. "It's not right, Sheriff."

"You and Lester used to be friends," Rhodes said.

"Used to be, maybe. Not now. Anyway, he's dead, and I'll dance a jig on his grave."

Margie hit her husband on the arm with a small fist. "You hush that kind of talk, Calvin. Next thing you know, the sheriff will think you drowned Lester."

"A catfish drowned him, is what I heard. I'd like to shake that fish's hand."

"Fish don't have hands as a rule," Rhodes said.

"I've shook hands with a couple."

"So have I," Rhodes said. "Well, one." He held out his wrist so Terrall could see it. "Today, in fact."

Terrall and Margie looked at the scratched wrist. Terrall nodded.

"Catfish can do that, sure enough. Lester and me went noodlin' a time or two. I've seen how they hold on."

"It's against the law," Rhodes said.

"Yeah, but that doesn't stop anybody if they want to do it. I never heard of anybody being arrested for it."

"They could be arrested if they drowned somebody."

"What's that supposed to mean?" Terrall said. He looked genuinely puzzled. "You talking about a catfish being arrested, or what?"

"Not a catfish. I think somebody drowned Lester Hamilton, somebody he knew."

"Well, I'll be damned." Terrall grinned and looked at his wife. "'Scuse my language, Margie. Anyway, Sheriff, you really think somebody drowned that skunk? I'll shake that fella's hand, for sure. Better'n shaking hands with a fish anytime."

"You don't get it, do you, Calvin," Margie said. "The sheriff thinks you did it. He thinks you killed Lester."

Terrall's grin disappeared. "That right, Sheriff? You think I'd do something like that?"

"I don't know who did it," Rhodes said. "I'm just checking around. I heard you and Lester fished together, and I wondered if someone was with him yesterday."

"I don't know anything about that. If there was anybody with Lester when he drowned, it wasn't me. I was here trying to sell persimmons. Right, Margie?"

"Right," Margie said. "Here all the time. If you don't want to take our word for it, you can ask anybody."

"Who would anybody be?"

"Customers. You could ask them."

Rhodes looked around. "I don't see any. Were there a lot more here yesterday?"

"Margie's word's good enough," Terrall said. He'd turned belligerent. "Mine, too. You got anything else you want to ask me, Sheriff?"

"Not today," Rhodes said. "I might think of something later."

"Fine. You come back when you do. Right now, though, if you're not planning to buy something from me, I'd appreciate it if you'd just go."

Rhodes went, but he had a feeling he'd be back.

The sheriff's next stop was the jail. The first thing he did was record the evidence he'd found in the rock pit and put it in the locker. The piece of cloth didn't amount to much, but if he could find the owner of a pair of jeans that was missing a loop, it could become significant.

Hack and Lawton tried not to show their curiosity about what Rhodes was doing, and he didn't give them any hints. He wasn't going to tell them anything about his dip in the rock pit's waters, so he couldn't very well tell them about the belt loop and where he'd found it.

After he'd taken care of the evidence, he asked Hack if anything had been going on around town.

Hack grinned, which Rhodes knew was a bad sign. He knew that Hack and Lawton would have their revenge on him now.

"Had an emergency at Lilly Bynum's place," Hack said.

"What kind of emergency?" Rhodes asked, thinking he'd have made a great straight man if he'd gone into show business.

"You might call it a headgear problem," Lawton said.

"The fit wasn't right," Hack said.

"We're fitting headgear now? What kind? Dental headgear? Crash helmets? Help me out, fellas."

"It was already fitted," Hack said. "That was the trouble."

"Yeah," Lawton said. "It went on, but it wouldn't come off."

Rhodes thought he had the picture now. "Lilly Bynum tried on a hat that didn't fit?"

"Wasn't a hat exactly," Hack said. "More like a chair."

"Lilly was wearing a chair?"

"Not a reg'lar chair," Lawton said.

"And she wasn't the one wearin' it," Hack said.

"Was her granddaughter," Lawton said, earning a look from Hack, who hadn't been ready to let the game end so soon.

"Lilly was toilet-trainin' her," Hack said, picking up the story before Lawton could give everything away. "Or she was tryin' to. The kid wound up wearing the potty chair on her head like a hat. Lilly wanted you to come get it off."

"Me?" Rhodes asked.

"She figgered it was your job, you bein' the high sheriff and all."

"I hope you didn't tell her I'd come."

"Nope," Hack said. "I told her that was the fire department's job."

Rhodes was certain the fire department appreciated Hack's efforts on their behalf.

"He was nice enough to call 'em for her," Lawton said.

Hack laughed. "I wanted to hear what they had to say, and they said plenty. They sent somebody out there, though. I haven't heard back, but I guess the kid's okay."

Rhodes hoped so. He wished all their emergencies were that easy to deal with.

He told Hack to have Ruth check on Hamilton's will at the courthouse.

"I think she's on patrol out around Obert," Hack said. "Buddy's closer."

"Have Buddy do it, then. I'll be out at the college, and then I'm going back to Mount Industry."

"The college? What's out there?"

"You mean who's out there. Dr. Benton is who."

"You think he's mixed up in this?"

"Maybe," Rhodes said, "and if he's not, he soon will be."

"I'll bet he's lookin' forward to that."

"Knowing him," Rhodes said, "he probably is."

The college was on the outskirts of town near the highway to Obert. It was a branch of a community college from another county, one with a bigger tax base and one that was looking to expand. The operation in Clearview had started out in one of the downtown buildings, one that hadn't been structurally sound, so as soon as the college built up its enrollment, the new building went up out on the highway.

Dr. C. P. Benton had moved to Clearview from down around Houston to teach math at the college. Rhodes had heard some story about love gone wrong being Benton's reason for the move, but he hadn't delved into it. Benton seemed happy enough in Clearview, and he was a good fit for the community even though most people considered him something of an oddball. Or, to be more accurate, they considered him a major oddball, which he was, but he was also smart and always glad to lend a hand if Rhodes needed one.

Rhodes parked in front of the redbrick building and went inside. Benton's office was on the second floor, and Rhodes found it easily. The door was open, and Rhodes looked in. The place looked as if a small tornado had blown through only moments before. The only chair other than the one occupied by Benton was stacked high with books and papers. Papers littered the top of the desk, and the bookshelves were in no kind of order at all. Books were stacked on end, both right side up and upside down, on their sides, and occasionally on a slant. Books and papers lay on the floor.

The math teacher himself sat at a computer desk looking at some oddly colorful shapes on the monitor.

Without his surgical mask, Benton looked a bit like a puckish rabbi. He had a neatly trimmed beard, and he wore a disreputable black fedora. Rhodes didn't wear hats himself, but if he were ever to wear one, he was sure he wouldn't wear it indoors.

"Fractals," Benton said when he noticed Rhodes standing in the doorway. He pointed at the monitor. "Beautiful things. Would you like to know the math behind them?"

Rhodes shook his head. "I don't think so. Math was never my strong suit."

"English major, huh?"

"Not that, either."

"It figures. You were probably good in PE, though. Could climb the rope and all that."

"I always made an A in PE," Rhodes said.

"I don't doubt it, but I doubt that you came here to tell me that."

"No, I came here to ask if you wanted to take a ride out to Mount Industry with me."

Benton straightened in his chair, instantly alert. "Is something going on out there?"

His body language and the tone of his voice made Rhodes suspicious.

"Do you know something I don't?"

"No, no. Just wondering. I thought you might need my help to solve a crime or something. I'm good at that. I helped out the police in the town where I used to live."

Benton had made that claim before, and Rhodes had checked it out. While it was stretching things a good bit to say that Benton had been helpful, he at least hadn't gotten in anyone's way. Maybe he could use him later.

"I'm going out to talk to your friend Qualls," Rhodes said. "I thought having you along might make things go more smoothly."

This wasn't entirely true. Rhodes believed that Benton and Qualls might be working together. Not that Benton would ever kill anyone, but he and Qualls had been together yesterday. If Qualls was involved in Hamilton's death, Benton might know something. Rhodes wanted to question them both at the same time, so he was taking Benton along under false pretenses.

Benton looked disappointed. "I was hoping it was a criminal matter. I've cracked a couple of cases for you, too."

That was such an exaggeration that Rhodes didn't bother to comment on it.

"I just want to talk to Qualls about Lester Hamilton."

"I heard Mr. Hamilton was dead. Drowned. Murder, right? I knew as soon as I heard about it."

"You knew a lot sooner than I did, then."

"I have skills beyond those of ordinary men." Benton stood up.

"Besides, I was a member of the Citizens' Sheriff's Acacemy. Remember? You could say I'm a trained crime fighter, just like you."

The academy had seemed like a good idea at the time, but Rhodes had come to regret it.

"I wouldn't say you were *well* trained."

"Well enough," Benton said. "My office hours are about over, and I don't think anybody will miss me if I leave now."

Benton shut down his computer and moved a few books and papers around while not improving the state of his office any at all that Rhodes could tell. Opening the bottom drawer of his desk, he reached inside and brought out a surgical mask.

"I'm ready," he said.

"You're not going to wear that, are you?" Rhodes asked.

"Not here in the building, if that's what's worrying you. I won't put it on until the smell gets bad."

"Fine," Rhodes said. "Let's go."

13

▼

ON THE WAY TO MOUNT INDUSTRY, BENTON TOLD RHODES THAT Qualls taught a world literature class on Monday and Wednesday evenings at the college, that he was regarded as a good teacher, if a little eccentric, and that he was interested in the quality of life in his little community.

Rhodes wondered what Benton would consider eccentric. Maybe Qualls wore a respirator mask to class. It wasn't a topic Rhodes wanted to discuss, so he asked how Benton had become involved with Qualls's crusade against Lester Hamilton.

"I'm as interested in the environment as anybody," Benton said. "More than most people, I guess, and Hamilton's farm has really ruined the air quailty around here. Or hadn't you noticed that?"

Rhodes admitted that he'd noticed.

"I have a class on Monday night," Benton said. "Qualls and I talked some in the faculty lounge one evening while we were on break, and he told me about his problems. He has asthma, and there are times he can hardly breathe out at his place. He's been writing letters to everybody he can think of, but so far nothing's been done."

Rhodes didn't think there was much chance of anything being done. He didn't consider himself a cynic, but he knew that the big poultry companies in East Texas made heavy contributions to as many legislators as they could. The legislature would be very slow to pass any laws that would harm those companies, no matter how many people had asthma.

"How far do you think Qualls would go to stop Hamilton?" Rhodes asked.

"He'd march on the capitol building naked," Benton said.

"He would?"

"That's what he said. Not that there's anything wrong with that." Benton looked thoughtful. "Naked marchers can accomplish things sometimes."

Once again Rhodes was suspicious. "Are you sure you don't have something you want to tell me?"

Benton's expression was bland. Rhodes didn't trust him.

"Not a thing. Why are you asking about Qualls? Why do you want to talk to him?"

"He and Hamilton used to be friends."

"Not anymore. Nobody in this county liked Hamilton."

"Qualls did at one time, though."

Benton thought it over. "Now that you mention it, Qualls told me that. When he first moved to Mount Industry, Hamilton was a good neighbor to him. He helped him get moved in, introduced him to people, things like that. Then Hamilton built the chicken farm. Qualls didn't like that. When you move somewhere to get away from pollution, you don't expect to find yourself breathing foul air. No pun intended."

Benton said the last with a straight face, but Rhodes didn't believe him for a minute.

"What do you get when you cross a rooster with a razor?" Rhodes asked.

"You can't cross a rooster with a razor. It's a biological impossibility. Why?"

"Never mind," Rhodes said.

"What about Deputy Grady?" Benton said, as if Rhodes hadn't asked his razor riddle. "Is she working this case? I think she and I would make a good team."

"Mostly she works alone," Rhodes said.

"We've been going out. Did you know that?"

"I don't want to hear about it. Are you still playing at Max's Place?"

Max Schwartz owned a barbecue restaurant near the college campus. Benton occasionally played guitar and sang his own compositions there, supposedly for the entertainment of the guests, but Rhodes thought it was more for Benton's own amusement than anything else.

"I'm the most popular attraction he has, after the food," Benton said.

As far as Rhodes knew, Benton was the *only* attraction other than the food, if you could call Benton's singing an attraction.

"The barbershop chorus sang there last week," Benton said, letting Rhodes know that there was other entertainment at Max's Place. "You should join the group and sing with us."

Rhodes had been asked to join before, but not because of his nonexistent singing ability. The group was having problems they hoped he could solve, and he'd declined the invitation. When he thought about what happened later, he sometimes wished he'd joined.

"I'm not a singer," Rhodes said. "I have other talents. I'm sure you do, too. Archery, maybe."

"I know about Zen archery," Benton said.

Rhodes wasn't surprised. Benton seemed to know a little about a lot of odd things.

"The secret is not to aim," Benton said, "but to *aim*."

Rhodes waited for the rest. Benton didn't say anything further.

"That's it?" Rhodes asked.

Benton nodded. "That's it."

"Do you ever put it into practice?" Rhodes asked. "The secret, I mean."

"I'm not Robin Hood. I just know things."

"Do you know who Robin Hood is?"

"I don't know those kinds of things, but I might be able to find out. I learned a lot of investigative techniques in the academy. If you want me to help out, just let me know. I'm always glad to lend a hand."

Rhodes was afraid Benton might be more of a hindrance than a help if he tried to do any more than accompany Rhodes to visit Qualls. Rhodes was trying to think of a nice way to say that when the radio squawked.

It was Hack. "What's your twenty?"

Rhodes keyed the mike. "About a quarter mile from Mount Industry."

"You better get on out there in a hurry."

"What's the problem?"

"Robin Hood's on the loose, shootin' up the chicken farm."

"I'm on it," Rhodes said.

He hit the switch for the light bar and floored the accelerator. The Charger surged forward, slamming Rhodes and Benton back against the seat.

"Yow!" Benton said. "Little did I realize how much fun it was to be the sheriff."

Rhodes wheeled around the curve at Garrett's store, past the cemetery, around two more curves, and up the hill that led to the chicken farm. Benton bounced around beside him. The seat belt wasn't tight enough to restrain him, and he wasn't holding on to anything to steady himself because he was too occupied with putting on his surgical mask.

Rhodes stopped the car near the red metal headquarters of the chicken farm. No one was in sight, but Rhodes saw a couple of arrows sticking out of the side of the building and another two sticking straight up out of the ground.

"You stay in the car," Rhodes told Benton, who was reaching for the door handle.

"Are you sure you don't need my help?"

Benton's muffled voice sounded relieved, but it was hard to tell, what with the mask he wore.

"What I don't need is you turning into a pincushion," Rhodes said. "You stay put."

Rhodes looked around, but he didn't see any movement anywhere. About the only place the arrows could have come from was the old farmhouse where Crockett lived, but Rhodes didn't think Crockett would be shooting at his own building.

Rhodes and Benton sat in the car for a while, looking and listening.

Nothing happened, and Rhodes said, "I'm getting out."

"I'm staying put," Benton said.

Rhodes opened the door. He heard a buzzing *zing* and then a solid *dong* as an arrow bounced off the metal building.

"Be careful," Benton said. "You don't want the county to have to go to the expense of burying you."

"Your tax dollars at work," Rhodes said.

"He's hiding next to that big tree by the house," Benton said. "That's about as close as we come to Sherwood Forest around here."

Rhodes didn't bother to point out that several trees stood on the hill behind the house and that a mesquite thicket fanned out in the fields beyond that. The thicket might not qualify as a forest, but it would do very well for the hiding and concealment for a whole band of Merry Men if any such thing existed in Blacklin County.

An arrow thudded into the ground in front of the Charger, kicking up a little dust.

"He's not aiming," Benton said.

"You mean he's not *aiming*," Rhodes said.

"That's what I said."

Rhodes felt for a second as if he were back with Hack and Lawton.

"Never mind. I don't think he's very accurate if he can't even hit a car. He's missed the building a couple of times, too."

"He might be trying to lull you into a false sense of security," Benton said.

Rhodes didn't think that was the case. He thought the bowman just wasn't very accurate. He'd been able to hit the tire on Mikey Burns's Solstice, but he might have been standing only inches away when he did it.

First utility poles, then the tire, and now human targets. Well, not human targets, but buildings and cars with humans in them. One thing Rhodes was sure about: Robin Hood was escalating his attacks. Either he was getting more confident that Rhodes and his deputies were too incompetent to catch him, or he was sliding deeper into his delusions, whatever they were.

Rhodes unlocked the shotgun that rode between him and Benton.

"Wow," Benton said. "You're serious about this stuff."

"He's shooting at us," Rhodes said. He pointed through the windshield. "You see what one of those arrows can do to metal. I can't go after him with a peashooter."

Or for that matter with a .32 caliber pistol that wasn't accurate at much more than ten yards. For a second Rhodes wished that he hadn't given up his .38.

Too late for that, though. Rhodes got on the radio and called Hack.

"Send some backup out here," he said. "Robin Hood thinks he has us pinned down, but I'm going after him."

"I'll send Buddy," Hack said. "You better wait till he gets there."

"Robin Hood might be gone by then. I don't want him to get away."

"Ivy won't like it if you get your hide punctured."

"She'll think it serves me right," Rhodes said.

He hung up the mike, took hold of the shotgun, and opened the car door. As soon as his feet touched the ground, he started to run.

Benton gave a muffled yell just as the door closed. "Serpentine! Serpentine!"

Rhodes thought zigzagging might work just as well, or was that the same thing? It didn't matter, as long as he didn't zig when he should be zagging. He held the shotgun in front of him with both hands as he jogged toward the farmhouse.

The first arrow flew past him to the right, missing him by at least ten feet. It didn't miss the Charger, however. Rhodes heard it gong into the side of the car. He thought he heard a muffled scream, but that was probably just his imagination.

The second arrow didn't come any closer, and it was too high. If it came near the car, it sailed over it.

Rhodes didn't look back to see. He'd reached the shelter of the wide front porch that ran along the entire front of the old house. The tree was on the left side, so Rhodes figured he'd go around the house in the opposite direction as soon as he caught his breath. The problem with catching his breath was that he caught plenty of the chicken stink along with it. He breathed through his mouth to minimize the effect.

He looked toward the Charger. Benton still sat in the front seat, and Rhodes thought he could see a couple of cars coming along the road. He hoped Buddy was driving one of them.

Rhodes didn't pause long, but it was long enough to let the bowman make his getaway. When Rhodes got to the back of the house, he could see the mesquite branches moving and hear someone thrashing through them.

There was nothing for Rhodes to do except follow along. He'd told Hack he didn't want Robin Hood to get away, and he'd meant it.

Mesquite thorns clawed at Rhodes as he crashed along in pursuit of the bowman. The trees were a plague all over the county, not as bad as the feral hogs that plowed up the land everywhere they roamed, but not really much better. Any cleared land never stayed cleared for long, not if it wasn't cared for constantly. If the hogs didn't root it up with their snouts as they dug for food, the mesquite trees would grow up and cover it. Sometimes Rhodes thought the hogs spread the mesquites in some kind of parasitical relationship.

Rhodes had no idea where Robin Hood was going, but he was bearing to his right. If he kept going that way, he'd come to the back of Calvin Terrall's land.

If Hamilton had run cattle on his property, there might have been a path to follow, but there were no cattle and there was no path. Rhodes figured that even if Robin Hood knew where he was going, he was running blind.

So was Rhodes, and he didn't think he was gaining any ground on his quarry. The bushes were so thick that he couldn't see much around him or in front of him, but he kept on going.

Then he halted, not because of anything he saw but because of something he didn't hear. The noise of the bowman's running had stopped. It was quiet in the mesquites. A late-season mosquito hummed in Rhodes's left ear.

A much louder hum on his right was followed by the sound of an arrow slicing through mesquite leaves. Rhodes didn't know exactly where it had come from, but he fired the shotgun in what he hoped was the right general direction.

The shotgun wasn't designed for long-distance shooting, but it was deadly against most mesquite limbs within the area. Rhodes looked through thin wisps of gunsmoke at the clearing he'd created.

He didn't see anyone, but through the ringing in his ears he heard somebody running. Rhodes went after him. Before he'd gone fifty yards, he heard a car start.

Rhodes ran as fast as he could, but the bushes in the mesquite thicket slowed him down. He came to a barbed-wire fence that separated Hamilton's property from the dirt road that ran between Hamilton's land and that owned by Calvin Terrall. The fence had been cut, probably when the bowman had made his way onto Hamilton's place.

Rhodes looked to his right and saw a cloud of dust that obscured a car headed in the general direction of Clearview. Because of the dust and distance, Rhodes couldn't tell what kind of car it was, much less read the license plate. He let out a long breath and started back to the farmhouse.

Now that he wasn't pursuing the bowman, he noticed the stink more than ever. It was so strong it could have been tracked on radar.

Rhodes wouldn't have been surprised if birds flying overhead had been overcome by it, dropped out of the sky, and plopped dead at his feet. He breathed through his mouth and walked on.

He was about halfway back to the farmhouse when he saw the arrow that had buzzed by him. It lay near a mesquite that it must have hit. Rhodes picked up the arrow and noticed that it didn't have an arrowhead attached. The rounded wooden tip was blunt and bare.

While he puzzled about that, he heard noises. He started to walk again. The closer he got to the farmhouse, the more the noises sounded like a commotion.

Rhodes picked up his pace. As he got nearer, he could tell that there was an all-out ruckus going on. He wondered what the trouble was this time.

When he rounded the corner of the farmhouse, he got his answer. In front of the red building and surrounding the county car were about a dozen naked women.

14

▼

THE SIGHT MOMENTARILY MADE RHODES FORGET ALL ABOUT THE smell of the chicken farm.

The women weren't entirely naked, Rhodes saw, when he recovered from his initial surprise and took a second look. Or possibly it was a fourth or fifth look. He hadn't counted. At any rate, the women all wore something that might have been bikinis covered with what appeared to be feathers. Maybe chicken feathers, but probably fake ones.

They also carried signs. When Rhodes got closer he could read some of them.

CHICKENS HAVE FEELINGS, TOO!

SAVE OUR FEATHERED FRIENDS!

IF YOU CUT THEM, DO THEY NOT BLEED?

Rhodes thought about his grandfather and that chicken they'd had for Sunday dinner. It was a good thing his grandfather wasn't here to see this. For several reasons.

A number of cars were parked all around. Buddy's county car

was parked beside Rhodes's, and Buddy was making quite a bit of the noise Rhodes heard. The deputy had a bullhorn, and he was yelling into it.

"Put down your signs and get in your vehicles! Vacate these premises at once!"

The women ignored him and chanted the slogans that were on their signs.

Seepy Benton sat on the hood of Rhodes's car, looking like a happy Jewish Buddha in a fedora. Rhodes imagined a wide grin beneath the surgical mask.

Jared Crockett and several of the workers from the chicken farm were standing in front of the red headquarters building. They didn't look happy at the disturbance, but at the same time they were eyeing the women. When they saw Rhodes, they moved away from Crockett and went behind the building. Rhodes figured Crockett had told them to get back to work.

While Rhodes watched the scene, another car arrived. Jennifer Loam got out.

"No press!" Buddy yelled into the bullhorn. "No press!"

Jennifer walked over to him and said something. Rhodes couldn't hear what it was, but he could imagine it. It would have to do with freedom of the press and the Constitution. Buddy didn't stand a chance.

When she was through with Buddy, Jennifer went over to the women. One of them, a redhead, stopped chanting and spoke to the reporter. Jennifer must have identified herself, because the woman smiled, and Loam pulled out her little recorder.

Rhodes walked past a couple of the women, who looked warily at his shotgun. It didn't disturb them enough to quiet them. In fact, they seemed to get louder. Rhodes put the gun in the Charger and closed the door. Benton watched him from the hood of the car. The arrow poked up beside him.

"You knew this was going to happen," Rhodes said.

Benton's voice was muffled but cheerful. "I didn't know for sure. I thought it might. Dr. Qualls got in touch with a couple of animal rights organizations and asked for their help. I guess one of them decided to do something."

Before Rhodes could respond, Buddy ran up to him, the bullhorn at his side.

"I'm glad you're here, Sheriff. Just look!" Buddy was scandalized. "These women are indecent! They're outside agitators, and they're out of control! Hack said something about you needing help with Robin Hood, but he never mentioned anything about this!"

Buddy had a puritanical bent, and Rhodes knew he'd like nothing better than to arrest the women and toss them in the clink for eighty years, if not a hundred.

"They have a right to assemble peaceably," Rhodes said.

"Peaceably! They're not even dressed. They could cause a riot."

"I don't see anybody who's likely to riot." Rhodes turned to Benton. "Are you thinking of rioting?"

"Not me," Benton said. "I'm just enjoying the scenery."

Jennifer Loam, having finished her interview, got a camera from her car and started to take pictures.

Buddy saw what she was doing. "Stop that! You can't put pictures like that in the paper!"

"Sure she can," Rhodes said. "If the publisher will let her."

Jennifer snapped a shot of Rhodes and Buddy. She didn't give them any warning, so Rhodes didn't get a chance to frown appropriately. He didn't care. He didn't think the picture would ever appear in the newspaper.

Jennifer put the camera back in her car. She shut the door and walked over to the lawmen.

"Hey, Sheriff. What do you think of the demonstration?"

"We think it's unlawful assembly and a disgrace besides," Buddy said. "We're gonna arrest all of them."

"No, we're not," Rhodes told him. "We'll let them have their fun, and then they can go back home."

"We can't let them get away with this, Sheriff." Buddy put the bullhorn to his mouth. "Return to your vehicles! Clear the area at once!"

The women ignored him. They weren't bothering to chant anymore, but they walked around, raising and lowering their signs.

"Nobody's paying any attention to us, Buddy," Rhodes said. "You can go on back to town. Robin Hood's escaped, and I think I can handle this on my own."

"I'm not so sure about that, Sheriff," Buddy said. "I've seen TV commercials for those *Girls Gone Wild* tapes. I don't think you know what we're dealing with here."

"I'll take my chances."

"Indecent exposure," Buddy said. "We could arrest them for that. You gotta admit that they're indecently exposed."

"I'll make a closer examination before I'm sure," Rhodes said.

Buddy looked at him. "You wouldn't be making fun of me, would you, Sheriff?"

"No way. You know me better than that. You already have the demonstration under control. There's nobody here to see it, so the appearance of the demonstrators isn't threatening the county's morality. I can take it from now on. You get back on patrol, and I'll get these people moved out."

"Well," Buddy said. "If you're sure."

"I'm sure."

Buddy nodded and went to his car. He tossed the bullhorn into the backseat, then turned to look at Rhodes.

Rhodes gave him a two-fingered salute. Buddy shook his head, got in his car, and drove away.

The women began to chant again. This time Benton chanted with them. Rhodes ignored all of them and went to talk to Jared Crockett. Jennifer Loam followed him.

"This place smells terrible," she said.

"Tell me about it."

Jennifer looked at the ground. "What are all these arrows doing here?" she asked.

Rhodes hadn't noticed before, but several arrows lay at their feet. They weren't sticking out of the ground. Like the one he'd picked up, they had only blunt tips. It could be that Robin Hood wasn't trying to hurt anyone. He used the arrowheads only when shooting at buildings. Or cars.

"What was the deal with the shotgun?" Jennifer asked. "What did Buddy mean about Robin Hood?"

"It's a long story," Rhodes said.

"This is a real mess, Sheriff," Crockett said as they reached him. "What's this woman doing with you?"

"I'm not with him," Loam said. "I represent the *Clearview Herald*, and I'm here to get a story."

"I don't have anything to say to you. I read what you wrote in yesterday's paper. Not a word of truth in it. I don't know where you got your information."

"My sources are confidential."

"They're confidential liars, then."

"I don't think so."

"Well, I'm telling you they are." He waved a hand at the demonstrators. "I guess you're gonna write this up, too."

"It's news, so it should be in the paper."

"Publicity's exactly what those people want," Crockett said. His face had started to get red. "Lester's dead, so what good is this going to do anybody?"

"What difference would it make if Lester was alive?" Rhodes asked. "They're calling attention to a situation they think is wrong. It doesn't matter to them if Lester's dead or not. They didn't know him. It's the situation they don't like."

Jennifer Loam looked at him. "You're pretty good, Sheriff. That's almost exactly what Maddie Spencer told me."

"Who's Maddie Spencer?" Rhodes asked.

"The woman I interviewed. She says she and her friends object to the inhumane treatment of the chickens here, and it doesn't matter if the owner's around or not. The harm is still going on."

"There you have it," Rhodes said to Crockett. "Aren't you going to invite us in?"

Crockett clearly didn't want to, but he said, "All right, come on."

He turned and went into the building. Rhodes and Loam were right behind him.

Once inside, Crockett sat behind his desk. Rhodes and Loam took the two folding chairs without waiting to be asked.

"Tell me about Robin Hood's attack," Rhodes said.

Loam got out her little recorder and turned it on.

"This is all off the record," Crockett said.

"Nothing's off the record," Rhodes said. "It'll all be in my report, and that's a public document."

Jennifer smiled and got out a notebook to use for backup in case the recorder failed, which Rhodes figured wasn't impossible.

"All right, then," Crockett said. He turned to glare at Jennifer. "Print this. Some maniac tried to kill me and some of the employees. Then a bunch of crazy people came out here and danced around naked."

"Tell me more about the maniac," Jennifer said.

"I was outside, giving some instructions to the fellas who work here. The next thing I knew, something banged into the roof of this building." Crockett looked up as if he expected to see the tip of an arrow protruding into the office. He looked back down. "Before we could run, I got hit."

"You don't look wounded," Rhodes said.

"The arrow bounced off. A couple of the guys were hit, too."

"The arrows bounce off them, too?"

"Yeah, and then we got our butts inside. We could hear the arrows hitting the building. Sounded like a hailstorm."

Rhodes doubted that. There were quite a few arrows lying around, but not enough to have made that much noise. Rhodes would have to remember to gather up the arrows. He wondered if there was a note attached to any of them.

"Nobody was hurt, though?" Jennifer asked.

"No. Make a better story for you if they were, wouldn't it."

Jennifer didn't bother to answer.

"You said you'd have another story about the farm in the paper today," Crockett said. "What's it about?"

"You'll have to buy a copy and see."

"I wouldn't buy that rag. Mr. Hamilton subscribed. I'll read his copy."

"Who do you think might have been shooting the arrows?" Rhodes said, to get things back on track.

"I can give you plenty of names. Nobody who lives here likes me."

"You?" Rhodes asked.

"I meant Mr. Hamilton. They complain about the smell. I don't know why."

"I know," Jennifer said. "They complain about other things, too."

"That stuff about the incinerator was a lie."

Jennifer smiled.

"Back to the arrows," Rhodes said. "Any ideas?"

"I told you. Anybody around here. They're all whiners and complainers."

Crockett was a charming guy. Rhodes wondered if he had any more friends than Hamilton did.

"Can you be a little more specific?" Rhodes asked. "Is there anybody in particular who has a grudge?"

"You want specific?" Crockett asked. "Okay, I can be specific. I'd check out that Garrett fella, and that other old geezer, too."

"Which other old geezer would that be, exactly?"

"Gillis," Crockett said. "Hal Gillis. You know who that is?"

"I know him," Rhodes said.

15

▼

RHODES DIDN'T GET MUCH MORE FROM CROCKETT, AND NONE OF what he got was helpful. Crockett might have had more to say if Jennifer Loam hadn't been there, or if she'd turned off the recorder, but Rhodes doubted it.

Benton was still sitting on the hood of the county car when Rhodes and Jennifer went back outside. All the protestors had left except for one, the redhead who had talked to Jennifer eariler. Now she stood by the car, where Benton had engaged her in conversation.

"This is Maddie Spencer," Benton said when he noticed Rhodes.

A good bit of Spencer's bare skin was exposed, and after noting that she had an innie, Rhodes tried to focus on her eyes, which were green. She had a band of freckles across her face, and of course she wore mostly fake feathers. She put our her hand, and Rhodes shook it.

"Pleased to meet you," she said.

"My pleasure," Rhodes said and hoped as soon as he said it that she didn't take it the wrong way. "You've already met Jennifer Loam."

Maddie smiled, showing white, even teeth, the result of either good heredity or expensive orthodontia.

"Jennifer's going to do a story about us," she said.

"I'll include it as part of the series I'm doing on this farm," Jennifer said.

Maddie's smile disappeared. "This is a terrible place, and Seepy tells me there's nothing that can be done about it, legally."

Seepy? Rhodes thought.

"That's right," Jennifer said. "The only way to get anything done is to bring public pressure to bear on some of the state agencies. Even then, they can't close it down."

"They can investigate," Benton said. "They can find out if everything's being done in accordance with whatever laws there are."

"They've investigated before," Rhodes said. "The farm's come out all right."

"That might be because they haven't looked closely enough." Benton slid off the hood of the car and stood between Maddie and Jennifer. "If they come out again and if they know what they're looking for, they might find something. What with Hamilton dying, Jennifer's articles, and this demonstration, they might feel the urge to take another look."

"Not to mention the attack by Robin Hood," Jennifer said.

"I hope your bunch didn't trample any of the evidence," Rhodes told Maddie.

"Seepy told us to be careful," Maddie said. "So we were. I don't think we touched a single one of the arrows."

Rhodes looked around. The arrows he could see didn't appear to have been disturbed.

"I think I'll pick them up now," he said.

"I'll help you," Benton said. He looked first at Maddie, then at Jennifer. "I've been trained in crime-scene investigative techniques."

"The Citizens' Academy doesn't count," Rhodes told him, "so quit bragging. I'll pick up the arrows."

Benton gave in and continued to talk to the women while Rhodes picked up the arrows on the ground. He put those into the Charger and then looked at the ones sticking out from the side of the metal building. No way was he going to climb up on top to remove the one there, and he found that taking the ones from the side would be no easy job. The only way to do it was to cut a hole around them, and he wasn't willing to do that. They had no message attached, and they appeared to be no different from any of the others, though Rhodes knew they had arrowheads attached. He decided to leave them where they were.

"What about this one?" Benton asked. He pointed to an arrow on the ground near the Charger. "It nearly hit me. I'm lucky I'm still alive."

Rhodes rolled his eyes, but the women didn't see him. They were too busy admiring Benton for his bravery under fire.

"That one doesn't appear to have an arrowhead on it," Rhodes said. "I don't think it could have hurt you much even if it had hit you."

"That was lucky," Maddie said. "This has been fun, but I'd better be going. It's a long drive back to my town."

"Where would that be?" Rhodes asked.

"Fort Worth," Benton answered for her. "She's a math instructor at Tarrant County Community College."

Rhodes figured that explained Benton's connection to the group of protestors. He'd probably arranged for them to be there, even though he'd tried to make it sound as if Qualls had been involved.

"Actually I live in Arlington," Maddie said, "but Fort Worth is close enough." She grinned. "This was fun. I hope we helped."

"If you did, you'll see it in the paper," Benton said.

"I doubt if she subscribes," Jennifer said.

Benton waved that away. "You don't have to worry about that. I'll send her a copy."

Jennifer walked Maddie to her car, a Prius, which figured. They talked a minute or so, and Maddie left. Jennifer waved to Rhodes and got into her own car.

"Seepy, huh?" Rhodes said to Benton as Jennifer drove away.

"I met her at a math convention," Benton said.

"So she knows what you look like without your mask."

"Yeah."

"I'll bet those math conventions are pretty wild."

"You have no idea," Benton said.

"That's the truth. Get in the car and let's go see your buddy Qualls."

Benton got in the car. Rhodes thought he was smiling beneath the mask.

Qualls lived in the only new house in Mount Industry. It was just past the second curve of the road on the way to the chicken farm, but set well back on a little hill. To get to it, Rhodes had to drive through an open gate and up a road paved with white gravel.

About fifty yards behind the house, dark green cedar trees stood in a clump. A couple of oak trees were nearer the house, but most of the land was clear. Rhodes wondered what it had cost Qualls to get rid of all the mesquites. A lot, he was sure.

Qualls probably thought he'd have a nice view when he'd built the house, and it wasn't too bad even now if you didn't consider all the chicken barns an eyesore.

The house had two stories, like most houses seemed to these days. Rhodes thought that houses for people Qualls's age should be on one level, but maybe Qualls didn't mind the stairs. He'd seemed to be in good enough shape when Rhodes met him. The stair-climbing would help with that, Rhodes supposed.

Qualls must have seen them coming, or heard them. By the time Rhodes had stopped the car, he was out of the front door and standing in the entranceway. He had on his breathing mask and still looked like some kind of alien creature. It occurred to Rhodes that he'd never seen the man without the mask.

"What are you doing here?" Qualls asked through the tinny speaker when Rhodes got out of the Charger.

"We're here to ask you a few questions," Benton said as he got out on the other side.

Qualls might have been surprised to see Benton, but Rhodes couldn't tell. He hadn't thought about it, but questioning a man whose expression you couldn't see wouldn't be easy. Rhodes didn't think Qualls would remove the mask voluntarily.

"Are you part of the sheriff's posse?" Qualls asked Benton.

"Just helping out. The sheriff asked me to come along, and since I'm a graduate of the Citizens' Sheriff's Academy, I'm qualified to do interrogations."

"I wish you'd quit telling people things like that," Rhodes said. "You know better."

"I thought we got the best of training," Benton said. He sounded hurt. "Are you telling me we didn't?"

"Never mind that." Rhodes turned to Qualls. "Can we go inside?"

"We can talk out here," Qualls said.

"What about the mask?"

"It stays on."

Rhodes didn't insist on its removal. He didn't want to get into a tussle. He was afraid Benton might try to help out and get hurt.

"What did you want to ask me about?" Qualls asked.

"Let's start with the demonstration that just happened."

"What demonstration?"

Rhodes couldn't tell if Qualls was puzzled by the question or not. The combination of the mask and the little speaker was too much for him.

"The women from Tarrant County," Benton said. "They showed up."

"Great," Qualls said. "I wasn't sure they'd do it. Was anyone from the paper there?"

"Yes. Someone must have let one of the reporters know they were coming."

Rhodes thought he had a pretty good idea who that someone might have been.

"Excellent," Qualls said. "Sooner or later the state's going to have to take notice of the situation over there."

"Speaking of the situation," Rhodes said, "do you own a bow?"

"Who, me?" Qualls asked. "What would I do with a bow?"

"Shoot arrows," Rhodes said. "You know. At utility poles, car tires, people, things like that."

"I'd never hurt anyone," Qualls said. "I'm a college professor."

As if that made a difference. Besides, Qualls's statement was ambiguous. The blunt arrows hadn't been intended to hurt anyone.

"Did you ever practice archery?" Rhodes asked.

"Look at me," Qualls said. "Do I look like an Errol Flynn?"

It was hard to tell because of the mask, but Rhodes suspected that Qualls looked nothing like Errol Flynn. Or like Kevin Costner, for that matter.

"You don't have to look like a movie star to shoot arrows from a bow," Rhodes said. "You just need a little practice."

"Are you making an accusation, Sheriff?"

"No, just asking a question that I'd like to get a straight answer to."

"What he wants to know is were you the one shooting arrows over at the chicken farm this afternoon," Benton said.

So much for subtlety. Again, Rhodes couldn't tell anything about Qualls's expression.

"Me?" Qualls's voice gave nothing away because it came from the speaker. "I was here all afternoon. I listened to music and corrected some papers for my class at the college."

"What music did you listen to?" Benton asked.

Rhodes didn't mind the irrelevancy. The interview had gone so far downhill already that it didn't matter what questions got asked, and Rhodes already knew that Qualls and Benton were working together, if not on the Robin Hood imposture, then on the protest.

"I prefer Peruvian flute music when I'm correcting papers. It relaxes me."

"The pan flute," Benton said. "Very nice. Did you know I play the Native American flute?"

"I didn't know, but I'd like to hear you."

"It's hard to play a flute with a face mask on," Rhodes said. He knew about Benton's alleged guitar playing, but not about the flute. "I'm going back to town. If you want to ride along with me, come on. Or would you rather stay here and discuss flutes?"

"I'll come," Benton said. "I need to correct a few papers myself."

*   *   *

The sun had dropped down nearly to the horizon and outlined the low clouds in orange and red by the time Rhodes dropped Benton off at the community college campus. Benton removed his face mask after they left Qualls's house, but he didn't have much to say as they drove back to town. Rhodes didn't push him.

"You think I had something to do with those women protestors," Benton said when Rhodes parked in front of the building.

"I think it's a good possibility," Rhodes said. "Even a likelihood."

"Okay, I confess. I did have something to do with it." Benton paused. "Let me amend that. I had a lot to do with it. Qualls knew about it, but I'm the one who set it up."

"I had a feeling you were."

"I could tell. I don't want you to think Qualls was guilty of it."

"Is he guilty of anything else? Like being Robin Hood?"

"I don't know about that. If he's been running around with a bow and arrow, he hasn't told me about it."

Rhodes believed him. While Benton wasn't much good at keeping secrets, Rhodes was sure Qualls was.

Benton got out of the car. Rhodes thought it was too late to grade papers, but Benton assured him that it wasn't.

"College teachers don't keep regular hours," Benton said. "We work all the time, day and night."

"I'll be sure to vote for your next pay raise."

"Thanks. I'll do the same for you. We both have tough jobs."

"Not exactly the same," Rhodes said.

"If you think yours is tougher, try standing in front of a classroom of college kids and see. Come to think of it, that might be a good idea. You could talk to my classes and see what it's like."

"What would I talk about?"

"Something simple. How to factor second-degree polynomial equations, maybe."

Rhodes was never sure when Benton was kidding. "We'd better start with something a little easier. Like converting one-half into a decimal figure."

"That could be arranged."

"Never mind," Rhodes said. "I think I'll stick to arresting people for breaking the law."

"You have to catch them first."

"Thanks for the reminder," Rhodes said.

16

▼

AFTER DROPPING BENTON OFF AT THE COLLEGE, RHODES WENT to the jail. He was glad to see that Buddy was there, working on his report about the incident at the chicken farm. That meant Rhodes could ask him about Lester Hamilton's will instead of trying to get the information from Hack.

It turned out that Buddy didn't have the information. He hadn't found out who Hamilton's heirs were.

"You mean there's no will on file?" Rhodes said.

"That's right. There was one, but now there's not."

Thinking about that answer, Rhodes wondered if Hack had somehow inhabited Buddy's body. He told himself that wasn't possible, but it *was* possible Hack had been coaching Buddy as part of an insidious plan to drive Rhodes crazy. Rhodes couldn't rule it out.

"You mean they can't find the will?" he asked.

"No," Buddy said. "I mean it was there, and now it's not. It's been pulled. The way I understand it, Hamilton's lawyer's making a new one."

"Means you'll have to talk to Randy Lawless," Hack said. He'd been listening in. "I know you'll love that."

Rhodes wondered how much he'd be able to get from Lawless. Sometimes he cooperated. Sometimes he didn't.

"Did they tell you when the old will was removed?" Rhodes asked.

"Last week," Buddy said.

Rhodes appreciated getting direct answers. Hack hadn't been coaching Buddy after all. Rhodes had misjudged them.

"That means you might have you a suspect," Hack said. "Could be the old heir killed Hamilton before the new will could be put into effect."

"Or the new one killed him because he wanted to run the chicken farm," Buddy said.

"Why would anybody want to run the chicken farm?" Hack asked.

"Naked women," Buddy said. His mouth twisted with disdain. "Some people like that kind of thing."

"What naked women?" Hack asked.

"The ones at the chicken farm," Rhodes said.

"Just awful," Buddy said, shaking his head in disapproval. "Stiff-starch naked."

"They weren't stiff-starch naked," Rhodes said, enjoying the look on Hack's face. "They wore feathers."

"Might as well have been naked," Buddy said. "It's not decent to talk about it. I still can't believe you didn't put every one of them in a cell."

"Nobody told me anything about naked women," Hack said.

"The jail doesn't have room for them," Rhodes said. "We'd be cited for overcrowding."

"What are you two talking about?" Hack asked.

"You don't want to know," Buddy said.

"He's right," Rhodes said. "You're way too old to be interested in something like that. What would Miz McGee say?"

Mrs. McGee was the woman whom Hack was dating, if that was the right word. Rhodes had never quite figured out their relationship.

"Don't you bring her into this," Hack said.

"Into what?" Lawton asked, coming into the room from the cellblock. "What's Miz McGee been up to now?"

"Nothing," Buddy said. "We weren't talking about her. I think we ought to get off this subject. It's not fit to talk about naked women on the loose."

"Whoa!" Lawton said. "Don't be in such a rush. What naked women?"

"The ones wearing feathers," Rhodes said.

"I still say we should've arrested 'em," Buddy said.

"Hold on, hold on," Lawton said. "What're you talkin' about?"

"Buddy can tell you," Rhodes said. "I have work to do."

With that, he left the jail.

Rhodes grinned all the way to the Lawj Mahal, thinking about Buddy's consternation at the protestors and their lack of attire, and about the problems Hack and Lawton would have in getting him to talk about it.

As Rhodes had suspected they might be, the lights were on in the Lawj Mahal. It was the only place in the old downtown area where a light burned. The other buildings, what was left of them, were dark and deserted. Nothing new in that. They were dark and deserted even during the day for the most part. Even the town's two traffic lights had been removed.

The only car in the parking lot was a big black Infiniti, which had probably cost as much as or more than Lester Hamilton's Lexus. Lawyering was about the only thing in Blacklin County that paid as much as chicken farming.

Rhodes parked beside the gleaming Infiniti and went into the building. The secretary had gone home long ago. Rhodes walked down a lighted hallway to the end where Randy Lawless had his office.

The attorney sat at a desk that could have doubled for an aircraft carrier had the need arisen. Its beautifully polished top was covered by a sheet of glass so spotless and slick that a speck of dust would have slid right off had it dared to settle there in the first place.

Lawless wore his usual expensive dark suit, white shirt, and designer tie. Rhodes figured the shirt alone cost more than his monthly salary. Being an attorney with a reputation for winning sure had its benefits, though Lawless hadn't always come out so well when he represented clients Rhodes had arrested.

"Good evening, Sheriff," Lawless said. "I had a feeling you might be stopping by. I didn't expect you this evening, though."

"A sheriff's work is never done," Rhodes said, taking a seat in one of the big wingback chairs without being asked. "We're like teachers that way."

"And attorneys," Lawless said. "As you can see, I'm burning the midnight oil."

"More like the early evening oil," Rhodes said.

"All the same, it's late, and I'm here, working for my clients."

"And being well paid for it."

"Just like teachers and sheriffs. The workman is worthy of his hire. Are we through beating around the bush yet?"

"I guess so," Rhodes said. "I want to know about Lester Hamilton's will."

"I figured that was why you were here. I heard that your deputy was asking about it over at the courthouse this afternoon."

Rhodes wasn't surprised that Lawless had spies in the courthouse. Unpaid spies, no doubt, but spies nevertheless.

"It's interesting that Lester was making a new will," Rhodes said. "I'd like to know about that."

"What do you want to know?"

Rhodes wondered if everyone in Clearview was taking lessons from Hack.

"Let's start with why Lester changed his will."

"All right." Lawless leaned forward and rested his arms on the spotless desktop. "He changed his will because he wanted to change his heirs."

"Aha."

"Is that what you professional lawmen say when you think you've uncovered a clue?"

"Sometimes we say *oho*."

"Right. Well, congratulations. You might very well have uncovered a clue."

"It's about time," Rhodes said. "Tell me about it."

"Lester's original heir was a cousin named Lafferty. He was the only living relative Lester had, and they knew each other pretty well when they were kids. Lafferty was a little younger than Lester, and Lester thought it would be nice to leave his property to him. Not his money, mind you. That was going to charity."

Rhodes was a little surprised to hear that. "Lester wasn't as bad as people made him out to be."

"True. Most people aren't. Lester was leaving his money to cancer research, but of course he didn't think he'd be leaving it so soon."

"That doesn't get us to why he changed the will."

"The short version is that his cousin died. No need to start thinking up conspiracy theories. His death doesn't have any connection to Lester's."

"Are you sure of that?"

"As sure as I can be," Lawless said. "The cousin died of a heart attack while he was on vacation in Colorado last week. He was backpacking and had a heart attack. Nothing suspicious about it. He had some kind of heart problem that he didn't know about. They found it in the autopsy. If he'd known, he wouldn't have been backpacking in Colorado."

"Shows the value of regular medical checkups, I guess," Rhodes said.

"Could be. Sometimes they miss things, of course, so you can never be sure."

"You can be sure about who the new heir is, though," Rhodes said.

"I can indeed." Lawless smiled. "That's the good part."

"What's so good about it?"

"You'll know when I tell you."

"Tell me who it is, then."

"It's William Qualls," Lawless said.

17

▼

"I STILL THINK YOU NEED TO TALK TO HAL GILLIS," IVY SAID AS she served Rhodes another helping of vegetarian chili. "Did I get this too hot?"

"With pepper or fire?" Rhodes asked.

He sat at the kitchen table with Yancey cowering under his chair because Sam was looking at him.

"Pepper. I'm never sure how hot to make things, and the peppers kind of vary. Sometimes they're a lot hotter than others."

Rhodes took a bite of the chili. His eyes almost teared up, but not quite.

"It's just right," he said, reaching for his water glass.

"You're not just saying that?"

"Nope. I like it hot."

Ivy had eaten earlier. She'd learned that Rhodes turned up at odd times and that dinner wasn't something that could be scheduled, so Rhodes often got warmed-up meals. The chili wasn't bad, even if it didn't have any meat in it. Maybe he'd become a vegetarian after all.

"Are you going to talk to him?" Ivy said. "Hal Gillis?"

"I just haven't gotten around to it," Rhodes said. "I'm having checks run on Jared Crockett and William Qualls. I know Hal's background, and I know Garrett's and Terrall's. They've never been in any trouble."

That wasn't strictly true. All of them had been in trouble of one kind or another, though nothing had been serious. Gillis had been arrested for assault once, but that had been thirty years or more ago, and he'd never been in trouble since.

Terrall had been sued by a man who accused him of assault, but the suit had been dropped before it reached court. Rhodes didn't know if Terrall had paid the man off or if he'd just thought better of having filed the charges.

In his younger days, Garrett had gotten quite a few tickets for traffic violations, mostly for speeding. He'd always paid his fines and never complained. As he got older, he wised up and stopped being so lead-footed. Or he got too smart for anyone to catch him at speeding.

"You never know what somebody might do," Ivy said. "Past performance is no guarantee of future results."

"You heard that on TV."

"Doesn't matter. It's the truth."

Ivy sat across from Rhodes at the table and watched him eat. And drink. Rhodes needed a lot of water with the chili, but he hadn't lied to Ivy. He liked it hot.

"What about Qualls?" he asked. "He has the best motive."

"You think he'd want to be the owner of the chicken farm?"

"Sure. He'd like nothing better. Not for the money. Looking at his house, I'd say he doesn't need money. If he owned the place, though, he could close it down."

"But you don't even know if Lester had told him about the will."

"That's the catch. Qualls has kept quiet about it if he knew, and Lawless says he didn't tell him. Lester might have told him, just for meanness, but I don't know if he did."

"Qualls might have told his friends if he knew about it."

"Seepy Benton is as close a friend as he has here, and he didn't mention it. I'm sure he would have told me if he'd known. He can't keep a secret for very long. I think Qualls can, though."

Yancey stirred under Rhodes's chair. Rhodes looked down at him, and Yancey yipped. Not loudly. Rhodes glanced over at Sam, who'd closed his eyes and gone to sleep, which explained Yancey's bravery.

"So can you," Ivy said.

"What does that mean?"

"It just means you haven't told me what you did this afternoon." *Uh-oh.*

"Robin Hood showed up at the chicken farm," Rhodes said. "I thought I might catch him, but he got away."

"Did you catch anybody else?"

Rhodes put his spoon down on the plate that held the chili bowl. The spoon clinked against the china.

"I helped Buddy break up a demonstration. Some animal rights people showed up to protest the inhumane treatment of chickens."

Ivy smiled at him. "Sometimes people who protest inhumane treatment of animals show up without any clothes on. There's even a Web site for that kind of thing."

"You're kidding me," Rhodes said.

"No. You could check it out."

"I'm not too good with a computer."

"Some of the county employees are. Good with the computer, I mean."

"Hack," Rhodes said. "You've been talking to Hack."

"What would give you that idea?"

"Knowing Hack, is what. I've been beating him at his own game lately, so he found a way to get back at me."

"I'm not admitting anything, copper. I'm no stoolie."

Rhodes laughed. "You're not much of a James Cagney imitator, either. That's all right. You don't have to squeal. I know who told you."

"Told me what?"

"About the protestors and how they were dressed."

"Or not dressed," Ivy said.

"You could put it that way, but they were dressed, all right. They were wearing feathers. Not real ones. They'd never do that. Fake feathers."

"How did they look?"

"I think I'll take the Fifth on that one. You could ask Buddy for his opinion. I'm sure he'd be happy to share it with you."

"I can just imagine. I'd rather hear your version."

"Later, maybe. I still haven't read Jennifer Loam's article today."

Ivy got up and went into another room. When she came back, she was holding a newspaper.

"You're going to like this one. Lester Hamilton wouldn't have, though."

"He doesn't have to worry about it anymore," Rhodes said

Ivy handed him the newspaper. The article was on the front

page, and it took up several columns. Rhodes didn't have to read far before he came to the part Ivy must have been referring to. Not only were the incinerators inadequate, but the litter hadn't been changed between batches of chickens. No law required it, but the litter also hadn't been rototilled. According to Loam, nothing had been done with the litter for at least a year, which had led to a higher mortality rate, which had led to more improper incinerations. A vicious, smelly circle if Rhodes had ever heard of one. No wonder people had been complaining. Their health was in danger, all right.

"So," Ivy said when Rhodes laid the paper aside. "What do you think of that?"

"I think Hamilton was guilty of slipshod management and that he should have been watched more closely. I think some of the state agencies should step in and do something about what's going on out there."

"Do you think they will?"

"Supposedly tomorrow's article will be even more startling," Rhodes said, referring to the teaser at the close of the story. "Taking that and today's demonstration into account, you have to think something will be done."

"Maybe. But what? They won't close down the farm. You know that."

"They can at least make them follow the proper procedures. Or maybe they won't have to. Maybe Qualls will just close the place down."

"It'll take a while for the will to be probated," Ivy said. "Sometimes those things take forever."

Rhodes felt something move against his feet. He looked and saw that Yancey had crept out from under the chair and was crawling on his belly toward Sam.

"This ought to be good," Rhodes said.

"Shame on you, Dan Rhodes," Ivy said. She got up and swept Yancey into her arms. "Sam would kill Yancey."

"I don't think Yancey would get within six feet of him even if you let him go," Rhodes said. "As soon as Sam opened his eyes, Yancey would be long gone."

Ivy sat down with Yancey in her lap. She patted his head, and he looked up at her adoringly.

"You spoil that dog," Rhodes said.

"And you don't."

"Not all the time." Rhodes stood up.

"Let's clean up the kitchen, and then we can go see if there are any old movies on TV."

He didn't really expect to find anything he wanted to watch. The kind of movies he preferred had long since been relegated to the dustbin of history. Not even TCM would touch them, and hardly anybody other than Rhodes even remembered things like *Hercules in the Haunted World,* or so he thought. While there was probably a good reason for that, Rhodes didn't want to think about it.

"What are the odds you'll get to sit through a whole show before you get a call?" Ivy asked.

Rhodes didn't want to think about that, either.

"I recorded something for you," Ivy said. "I think you'll like it."

Rhodes was apprehensive, but he asked what it was.

"Abbott and Costello Meet Captain Kidd."

"A classic," Rhodes said, suddenly enthusiastic. "Thanks."

After they'd cleaned up the dishes, they went into the living room and turned on the TV and DVR. Rhodes got to watch almost twenty minutes of the movie before the phone rang.

The caller was one of his deputies, Duke Pearson, who'd run the background check on Jared Crockett.

"I don't think he's going to be much of a suspect," Pearson said. "His record's pretty clean."

"Not entirely?" Rhodes asked.

"No, he's had a few run-ins with the law. When he was a kid, he got picked up a time or two for shoplifting, and he lost his last job because he got into a fight with his foreman at a furniture factory."

"That sounds serious to me," Rhodes said.

"It wasn't a physical fight. They just had words."

"What about?" Rhodes said.

"That's not in the records. He seems to have had a good bit of trouble holding jobs, but lots of people have that problem."

"You might as well check it out. Not that it'll do us any good. Anything else?"

"Not a thing," Pearson said. "Aside from those things, the guy's a saint."

"So is everybody else," Rhodes said. "I'm beginning to think a catfish did drown Hamilton after all."

"What are the odds?" Pearson asked.

"Not good," Rhodes admitted, "but they're better than the odds on anybody else."

"Want me to do a background check on the catfish?"

"We're not that desperate," Rhodes said. "Yet."

After he hung up, he and Ivy started to watch the movie again.

"Those two remind me of somebody," she said as Abbott and Costello engaged in one of their routines.

"Me, too," Rhodes said, "but it's not nearly as much fun to deal with people in real life as it is to watch them in a movie."

It was one of the few color films that Abbott and Costello had done, and Rhodes was enjoying it, especially Charles Laughton as Captain Kidd. Laughton must have felt like he was slumming to appear in a movie with a former burlesque team, but he was a good sport and got right into the slapstick spirit of things as he tried to get his treasure map back from the two comedians.

"Charles Laughton reminds me of somebody, too," Ivy said.

"His size or his attitude?"

Ivy poked Rhodes with her finger. "Maybe around the stomach a little bit."

Rhodes was saved from responding by the ringing of the phone. This time Rhodes had gotten to watch only ten minutes of the movie. The caller was Mikey Burns.

"I hear Robin Hood shot up the chicken farm," Burns said.

"News travels fast around here," Rhodes said.

"Never mind that. You didn't catch him, did you."

Rhodes admitted that he hadn't. "I got close, though."

"Close doesn't count except in hand grenades and horseshoes," Burns said.

Rhodes thought about asking if he should write that down, but he restrained himself. Instead he said, "I'll catch him sooner or later."

"You'd better make it sooner. Some of the other commissioners are just as unhappy as I am."

Rhodes thought it was odd that they didn't seem to worry as much about the chicken farm as they did about Robin Hood, but then Lester Hamilton had been a major taxpayer. The commissioners liked taxpayers.

"I'll do what I can," Rhodes said.

"And next time, arrest the naked women," Burns said. "We can't allow that kind of thing in Blacklin County."

"I sent them on their way," Rhodes said.

"Domestic terrorism," Burns said. "That's what it is. Robin Hood and those women, too. That's why we need an M-16."

Rhodes was a little taken aback. "To shoot naked women?"

"Terrorists," Burns said.

"You're making light of terrorism," Rhodes said. "Robin Hood might be guilty of malicious mischief, if that, and the women were peaceful protestors. There's a big difference between killing people and destroying property and protesting."

"You know what I mean."

Rhodes wasn't sure that he did.

"Take care of it. I don't want any more incidents like that happening in the county."

Rhodes was an elected official, just like Burns. Burns hadn't hired him, and Burns couldn't fire him. Commissioners had control over the sheriff's department's budget, but they could be swayed by public opinion just like anyone. They couldn't cut too much law enforcement without giving their opponents some good arguments for the next election. So Rhodes wasn't too worried about what Burns wanted. Sometimes men in Burns's position forgot that they couldn't order other county officials around.

"I'll do my best to see that you aren't disturbed again by naked women," Rhodes said.

Burns was quiet for a little too long, and Rhodes wondered if he knew he'd been kidded.

"I know you'll see to it," Burns said finally. "You keep me posted."

"Roger," Rhodes said and hung up before Burns could comment further.

"Do naked women disturb you?" Ivy asked before Rhodes started the movie again.

"In certain ways."

"Would you rather be disturbed or watch Abbott and Costello?"

Rhodes was quiet. The silence stretched.

"Well?" Ivy said.

"I'm thinking it over."

Ivy hit him with a throw pillow and left the room.

Rhodes wasn't far behind. Abbott and Costello would have to wait, and Rhodes didn't really care if Captain Kidd ever got his treasure map back.

18

▼

THE NEXT MORNING WAS WARM AND DAMP, A SURE SIGN THAT A cold front would be moving through later in the day. The backyard was wrapped in fog, and while Rhodes didn't like it, Speedo didn't seem to mind. Neither did Yancey, who lolloped through the damp grass yipping with delight.

Rhodes sat on the damp back step and watched them. He'd dreamed something about the rock pit, but he couldn't remember what it had been. When he woke, the remnants of the dream fragmented and drifted away like pieces of a ragged cloud. He didn't think the dream would have been any help to him even if he'd been able to recall it, but it did remind him that he still hadn't figured out how whoever killed Lester Hamilton had gotten away from the rock pit.

If he'd thought of it, Mikey Burns might have blamed the killing on terrorists who'd come up from Mexico and were now roaming the back roads of Texas on their way to assassinate as many government leaders as they could. Burns would say they'd just been practicing on Hamilton before making good their escape into the countryside.

Rhodes wasn't being fair, he knew. Burns was normally a level-headed man, and he'd just let that flat tire get the better of his good judgment.

So that left the problem of the killer's exit from the area around the rock pit. The only person who'd been there when Rhodes arrived on the scene was Hal Gillis. It would be like something from an old TV show if Gillis had killed Hamilton, called the law, waited around for the sheriff to arrive, and then claimed innocence.

Rhodes wondered if anyone had ever tried a trick like that before. It had been his experience that there were no new tricks, just variations on old ones, so it had most likely been done, and more than once.

Ivy was still convinced that Gillis had been involved, and while Rhodes had eaten his cereal (with skim milk) earlier that morning, she'd told him again that he should pay Gillis a visit and have a long talk with him.

Ivy thought more of Rhodes's abilities than he did. She was sure that Gillis would confess if Rhodes would just ask him the right questions.

Maybe that was true, but Rhodes didn't know what the right questions were. Gillis had already claimed his innocence in the face of Rhodes's questions after the body was found, and it didn't seem to Rhodes that the old man was likely to change his story.

However, he might have seen someone or something that he hadn't remembered at the time. A good talk might be able to jar loose the memory.

Could someone have just walked away from the scene? It was possible, but where had he been parked? Rhodes hadn't found any tire tracks.

Did that mean the killer had been in the car with Hamilton? That was possible, but how could anyone walk back to town without being seen? By sticking to the fields? They were too open. No one could have walked through them without being conspicuous.

Hide a car along the road? Wouldn't Hamilton have wondered about someone who came walking up? A flat tire would make a good excuse, though.

Rhodes knew he'd have to go back out to the rock pit and examine the road to see if a car had been pulled off nearby. He should have done it sooner.

Someone would have to talk to Hal Gillis, too, and Rhodes wanted to confront William Qualls about his inheritance. He could visit both of them since they lived at Mount Industry, or he could call them in for interviews at the jail. That would be more formal, get the men out of their comfortable and familiar surroundings, and maybe be more likely to produce results, so he decided to take that approach. He'd call Hack before he left the house and have him make appointments for Gillis and Qualls to come in for interviews.

Sitting on the step while watching the dogs play wasn't the way to get anything done, however. Rhodes stood up without putting his hands on his knees to push. He'd read somewhere that having to push up from a sitting position was a sure sign of old age, and he didn't want to think he was getting old.

He whistled for Yancey, who of course ignored him. When he was playing with Speedo, Yancey was as good at ignoring Rhodes as Sam.

"Yancey," Rhodes called. "Either you come in with me now, or you'll have to stay out here all day."

Yancey stopped in his tracks. Speedo, who'd been chasing him, had to swerve aside and narrowly missed trampling him.

Yancey looked at Rhodes. Speedo, who had managed to come to a less than graceful stop, did the same, his tongue lolled out.

"Well?" Rhodes said.

Yancey trotted over, and Rhodes let him in through the screen door.

"I don't think I'll come with you," Rhodes said. "I have work to do. You leave the cat alone, you hear?"

Yancey turned and sat down, looking at Rhodes with a hurt expression.

"I know the cat's more likely to bother you than the other way around," Rhodes said. "I was just joking. Go on and look for Ivy. Tell her I'll see her this evening."

Yancey turned and trotted off as if he'd understood every word. For all Rhodes knew, he had.

"Maybe I should put you on the case," Rhodes said. "How about it?"

Yancey didn't turn around to accept the challenge.

"Smart dog," Rhodes said.

The fog hung over the smooth surface of the water in the rock pit and drifted through the weeds and grass of the field like smoke. Rhodes felt it on his skin almost as if it were rain. The warm dampness made his shirt stick to his back.

No one was around, and no one was likely to be. Even the most avid fisherman would think twice before coming to wet a hook on a day like this one.

Rhodes wasn't sure what he was doing. He still thought he'd overlooked something at the crime scene, but returning hadn't jogged loose any answers. Maybe he hoped an arm would rise up out of the dark water, holding a clue in its hand instead of a sword.

He'd seen an illustration of the hand and the sword in a book about King Arthur many years ago, when he was a boy.

Rhodes shook his head. When he started thinking about half-forgotten stories from his childhood, it was time to get moving. He didn't think the rock pit was anything like the Arthurian lake, and there was certainly no island of Avalon in the middle of it. There was nothing out there except a giant turtle, and even the turtle was staying under cover this morning. Rhodes didn't blame it.

Getting back in the county car, Rhodes drove along the road that led to the bridge across the river. He saw several places along the way where a car could have pulled off the road and been left safely. Unfortunately all of them were entrances to other pieces of property, and all had gravel topping that wouldn't show any tracks even if there'd been any. A car stopped at any of them would have drawn attention from someone passing by, and because Blacklin County was like any other small place, someone would have reported it to the sheriff's department after hearing about Hamilton's death. Rhodes didn't think the car was a possibility.

He drove on over the steel bridge, his tires humming. Down below, the river flowed sluggishly along. Rhodes had fished in the river long ago, but now it was low most of the time because of all the lakes that had been built above it. There was still a slope beside the road that a car could drive down, but nothing had driven along it lately, as the weeds attested. Trees grew along the bank, and their branches extended out over the brown water.

Past the bridge, the road got a bit narrower. The trees grew closer to the sides, almost making a canopy over the road. When Rhodes was young, he'd ridden down many roads like that on his bike, taking his fishing pole to some stock tank or other, never even considering the possibility of drowning. He wondered if kids did that sort of thing anymore. He doubted it. Their parents wouldn't dare let them because of the dangers involved, and certainly the kids were safer for it. For all the safety, though, something was lost along the way. Rhodes wasn't just sure what, and he didn't want to think about it. The next time he came to a good place, Rhodes turned around and went back to town.

Hack and Lawton were glad to see him when he stopped by the jail. Hack had just gotten a call about an emergency.

"Woman wanted to know if we could get her out of a moving car," he said.

"A moving car?" Rhodes asked. "Wouldn't it be easier if she just stopped the car and got out? That's a whole lot safer."

"Would you believe that's exactly what Hack told her?" Lawton said.

Hack turned to the jailer. "I'm telling this story." He turned back to Rhodes. "That's exactly what I told her."

"Good decision," Rhodes said.

He went to his desk, hoping that was the end of the matter, though he knew in his heart that it wasn't.

He was right.

"There was a problem with that solution," Hack said.

Rhodes had been afraid of that, but he didn't ask what the problem was.

"She couldn't stop the car," Hack said when he saw that Rhodes wasn't going to take the bait.

"Accelerator stuck?" Rhodes asked.

"That's exactly what Hack asked her," Lawton said.

Rhodes thought Hack might get up and throttle Lawton, but Hack didn't like to get up unless he had to, and throttling Lawton wasn't worth the trouble.

"That's exactly what I asked her," Hack said. "See, I was think-ing that we could do something like in the movies. We have Duke drive alongside her car, and she gets the window down. You're on the hood of Duke's car, and when you get to just the right spot, you jump in through the window and save her."

Rhodes didn't think he could jump in through the window, much less save anybody.

"How was I supposed to do that?"

"I'm not the sheriff," Hack said. "You'd have to figure it out for yourself."

"Wouldn't have worked, though," Lawton said.

"Why not?"

"The accelerator wasn't the problem," Hack said. "The driver was."

Rhodes was getting confused, a not unusual thing when Hack and Lawton were telling him something.

"The driver?" he asked.

"Yeah," Lawton said. "The woman who called wasn't doing the driving."

"That's not good," Rhodes said.

"It's sure not," Hack said. "When she told me that, I figured she was trapped in the car with a serial killer, or maybe somebody trying to sell her insurance."

"Then she hung up," Lawton said.

That wasn't good, either, but Rhodes was determined not to ask what had happened next. Hack watched him. Lawton watched him. The silence in the room stretched out until Rhodes gave in.

"All right. What happened? Did you send somebody out to find her?"

"Nope," Hack said. "She called right back."

"And?"

"And she said she'd just been mad at her boyfriend, who was doing the driving. She thought she could get back at him by threatening to phone the law, and he called her bluff. They'd made up, though, so everything was all right."

"Good thing, too," Lawton said. "I'm not sure the sheriff would've fit through the car window."

"I'm not sure he could even have made the jump," Hack said.

"Sure I could have," Rhodes said. "I'm a regular Jackie Chan. Did you set up those appointments I called about?"

"Sure did," Hack said. "You think I'm not on the ball or something?"

"Just checking. What time are they coming in?"

"When you said. Qualls at ten, Gillis at eleven."

"I'd better check out the room, then," Rhodes said.

"You think it's not clean," Lawton said, hurt.

"Just want our visitors to be comfortable."

"Yeah," Hack said. "Right. Like anybody's comfortable in a jail."

"You are," Lawton said.

Hack took in a breath as if readying a retort. Then he let the air out slowly.

"You know what?" he said. "You're right."

19

▼

THE ROOM IN WHICH RHODES INTERVIEWED PEOPLE AT THE JAIL wasn't exactly the way people expected it to be, and its appearance often threw them off stride. That was the way Rhodes wanted it.

People expected the room to look like something they'd seen on TV, with two-way mirrors, a microphone hidden in a light fixture, a scarred wooden table with nothing on it but an ashtray, and a couple of metal folding chairs.

The room held a table, all right, but it was a dining table with a Formica top that was hardly scarred. There was no ashtray because no smoking was allowed in the jail, not even in the cells, a policy that put a severe strain on some of the prisoners.

The table matched the chairs, which were also part of the old dinette set Rhodes had picked up at a yard sale at a price so cheap that he hadn't even charged the county for it. He wanted the interview room to look more like a kitchen where you'd find Julia Child, not a place where Torquemada would have been at home.

The idea was to make people comfortable so they'd confide in

Rhodes or whoever was doing the interview. Rhodes thought the casual approach worked better than intimidation.

The room also didn't smell the way anybody expected. No fear-sweat odor permeated the walls. Rhodes had read that the smell of vanilla made people comfortable and improved their mood, and Ivy had found some vanilla-scented trash bags for him. Rhodes always made sure to have a fresh one in the room's trash can.

There was a microphone in the light fixture, however, though nobody could see it. All the interviews were recorded, just in case.

As for the two-way mirrors, the county had never seen any reason to go to the expense of installing them, and Rhodes didn't miss them. He'd never needed any witnesses to his interrogations other than the people he had in the room with him, usually one of the deputies.

Today, the witness would be Ruth Grady. She showed up at fifteen minutes before the hour. She and Rhodes went to the interrogation room and sat at the table while Rhodes told her what was going on.

"That's a strange way for things to work out," she said when he got to the part about Qualls being Hamilton's heir. "I wonder if he knew."

"So do I," Rhodes said. "That's the main reason I want him here. The lawyer says he didn't tell him, but Hamilton could have. We need to find out."

"Who gets to be the good cop, and who gets to whack him with the rubber hose?"

In the distant past, the rubber hose was a distinct possibility in the Blacklin County jail. Or some said a battery cable was more likely. Rhodes didn't use either. He didn't think pain worked very well when it came to getting information. Just about anybody would confess to just about anything to stop a painful beating.

Rhodes didn't want a false confession. He wanted the truth. So no pain, no intimidation. Ruth knew that, of course. She was only joking.

"You can use the rubber hose," Rhodes said. "When I step out of the room for coffee, let him have it."

"You don't drink coffee," Ruth said.

"Right, but Qualls doesn't know that."

"Good. Where do we keep the rubber hoses?"

"You'll have to pick one up at the hardware store."

"We don't have one of those anymore."

Rhodes thought about the old hardware store. It had been gone for a while. Everyone bought hardware at Walmart now. Rhodes was about to tell her that when Hack came in.

"Qualls is here," he said.

"Good," Rhodes said. "Bring him on back."

The one intimidating thing about the room was that it was located right next to the cellblock. Might as well give the person being questioned a glimpse of the hard life, not to intimidate him, but to let him know that what was about to happen was serious business.

When Hack let Qualls into the room, both Rhodes and Ruth were standing. Hack ushered Qualls over to the table and told him to have a seat. Qualls sat, and Hack left the room.

Rhodes took a good look at the former professor. It was the first time Rhodes had gotten a good look at the man without his respirator mask. His eyes were sunken, with black circles beneath them as if Qualls hadn't been sleeping too well. He had a prominent nose and a wide mouth. He clasped his hands and put them on the table. Rhodes glanced at them, and Qualls unclasped them and dropped them to his lap.

"I assume you've called me here for a good and sufficient reason," Qualls said. Without the mask and speaker, his voice was low and pleasant. "If I'm a suspect in some crime or another, I'd like to have an attorney present."

"You don't need an attorney," Rhodes said. "I just wanted to talk to you. Funny you should mention a lawyer, though."

"I don't see anything funny about that."

"Coincidence," Ruth said. "That's what it is. Some people think coincidences are funny."

Qualls wasn't laughing. "Then why don't you let me in on the joke."

Rhodes had planned to ease into the question of Hamilton's will, but Qualls was impatient. Rhodes didn't blame him. Being called in for an interview with the sheriff would bother anybody, even if an informal discussion was the intention.

"I talked to Randy Lawless yesterday," Rhodes said. He hooked one of the chairs with his foot and pulled it away from the table. The metal runners scraped on the concrete floor. Rhodes sat down across from Qualls. "Lawless mentioned your name."

Qualls looked genuinely surprised, but Rhodes supposed a teacher would be a pretty good actor when the occasion called for it.

"Why would he do that?"

"You tell us," Ruth said. She stood just behind Rhodes's chair. "Don't you know?"

Qualls shook his head. "I have no idea. I've never met the man."

"He knows you, though," Rhodes said.

"That's not surprising," Qualls said. "I've become a fairly well-known citizen since I moved to Blacklin County. I didn't want it that way. It's just something that happened, thanks to Lester Hamilton and his chickens."

"That's how your name came into the conversation," Rhodes

said. "Lawless and I were talking about Hamilton and those chickens."

"Did someone hire Lawless to file suit against Hamilton? I'd be more than happy to be a party to something along those lines."

"Nothing like that. We were discussing Hamilton's will."

"His will?" Qualls squirmed a bit in his chair. "What does that have to do with me?"

"You're saying you don't know?" Ruth said.

Qualls looked up at her. "I'm saying I have no idea what you're talking about. This whole conversation is like something out of Samuel Beckett."

"Who's he?" Rhodes said.

"A writer. Never mind. You wouldn't know him."

Rhodes was pretty sure he'd just been insulted, but he didn't care. He might not know much about literature, but he figured Qualls didn't know much about law enforcement, either.

"You haven't talked to Randy Lawless lately?" Ruth said.

"No. As I said, I don't even know the man."

"How about Lester Hamilton? Have you heard anything from him?"

Qualls made a noise that was a cross between a snort and a laugh. "When he was alive, Lester Hamilton wouldn't give me the time of day, and the only times I spoke to him are well in the past. He stopped taking my calls long ago, and we didn't meet each other in the course of the day." Qualls paused and looked at Rhodes. "Is this conversation going somewhere, or are you just trying to drive me crazy?"

Rhodes wondered if he'd been hanging around Hack and Lawton too long. He'd let the interview get well off track.

"I asked you here for a reason," Rhodes said. "I wanted to talk to you about Lester Hamilton's will."

"What does that have to do with me?"

"You're his heir," Rhodes said. "Once the will is probated, you're going to be a chicken baron."

It was as if someone had struck Qualls in the back of the head with a rubber hose. His eyes widened, and his mouth opened, but no sound came out. He gulped a couple of times, jittered around in the chair, then started coughing.

Rhodes thought Qualls might be strangling, but Qualls held up a hand to let them know that he was all right. When he stopped coughing, he gasped for breath. His face and nose were an unhealthy red.

"Are you okay?" Ruth asked. "Maybe you need a Heimlich."

"I'm fine," Qualls gasped, pushing back from the table. "Or I will be in a minute. You shouldn't surprise me like that. Of course, I know you're only trying to get a reaction from me."

"We got one," Rhodes said, "but we weren't trying. What I told you is the truth."

Qualls took in a deep breath, and Rhodes was afraid he'd start coughing again. Instead, Qualls held his breath and pounded on the table a couple of times with his fist.

Rhodes turned and looked at Ruth, who shrugged. Rhodes looked back at Qualls and waited.

"Could I have some water?" Qualls asked. His voice was a rasp. "Or a soft drink?"

"I'll get some water," Ruth said and left the room.

Qualls leaned back in his chair, not looking at Rhodes or anything in particular as far as Rhodes could tell. Rhodes didn't say anything. He just sat and waited.

Ruth was back in less than a minute with a plastic bottle of water that she handed to Qualls. Rhodes knew she kept water in her desk and in her county car.

"The county will pay you back for that," he said.

Ruth waved him off, and they watched Qualls drink. He took several swallows and lowered the level of the bottle by about half. He set the bottle on the table and leaned forward.

"As you might have gathered," he said, "your news took me by surprise."

Either that, or he was an even better actor than Rhodes had first thought.

"I had no idea that I was named in Lester Hamilton's will," Qualls went on. "I can't quite get used to the idea."

"It might take some time," Ruth said, "but you'll get used to it."

"I don't think so. It's more than I can take in. Why would he do a thing like that?"

"He must have had a good sense of humor," Rhodes said.

"Not that I ever noticed," Qualls said. His face grew thoughtful. "I can see now what you've been thinking. Because I'm now the owner of the farm, or will be eventually, you consider me a suspect in Lester's murder."

"You have to admit it's a powerful motive, any way you look at it," Rhodes said. "If you keep running the farm the way Lester did, you'll make a lot of money. If you want to close it down, you can. You won't have to wear your mask anymore."

Qualls gave Rhodes an accusatory look. "You said I wasn't a suspect when I came in. You lied to me."

"Now just a minute," Ruth said. "I didn't hear the sheriff say anything like that."

"I see. So that's how it works. It's my word against his. And yours."

"And the tape recorder's," Rhodes said.

Qualls stiffened. "I wasn't aware this conversation was being recorded. It's not legal to record someone without permission, is it?"

"It is," Rhodes said. "Trust me."

"You tricked me."

"First it's lies, then it's trickery," Ruth said. "That's how we operate."

"We didn't trick anybody," Rhodes said. "We might have sprung a surprise on you, but we didn't trick you."

"Very well. You have your opinion, and I have mine. Have I been charged with anything?"

"No," Rhodes said. "Not yet."

"Then I'm leaving." Qualls stood up. "I hope you realize I won't be voting for you in the election."

"I'm sorry to hear it," Rhodes said. "I need all the help I can get."

"Not from me," Qualls said as he left the room.

"That went well," Ruth said when Qualls was gone.

"About as well as could be expected," Rhodes said. "We might have learned something, though."

"What?"

Rhodes was about to answer when Hack came in and said, "Gillis hasn't showed up."

"Did you give him a call?" Rhodes asked.

"I gave him two. No answer either time."

"He could be on the way to town," Ruth said.

"Could be. All I know is, he ain't here."

"I'll go check on him," Rhodes said. "Ruth can stay here in case he shows up. You let me know if he does."

"Like I don't know my job," Hack said.

"He's kind of old," Ruth said.

Hack looked at her.

"No offense. I just meant that something might have happened to him. He could have taken a fall, or—"

"You're not helpin' yourself any," Hack said.

"Sorry."

"I'll check on him," Rhodes said. "He could have decided not to come in because he has something to hide."

"Be careful, then," Hack said. He was still looking at Ruth. "Some of us old guys can still give plenty of trouble when we want to."

"Then again, some of you are just softhearted pushovers," Ruth said.

"Don't you believe it," Hack told her.

20

▼

RHODES DIDN'T STOP AT GARRETT'S FOR A DR PEPPER AND A candy bar. He considered it, but he had a bad feeling about Hal Gillis. Rhodes didn't know the man well, but he believed he'd have come to the jail if he'd been able. Or if he'd had nothing to hide. Rhodes wondered if Ivy had been right all along.

Gillis lived next door to Calvin Terrall, if you could consider living a quarter mile away as being next door. Rhodes thought of it that way because no other houses stood between where Gillis lived and the Terrall property.

Calvin and Margie Terrall sat in their chairs at the roadside stand. Rhodes waved to them as he passed by. They watched him drive by, but they didn't wave back. Rhodes figured that was another couple of votes he couldn't count on.

Hal Gillis had lived in Mount Industry all his life. The house where he lived was the one his parents had owned, which was more common in Blacklin County than outsiders might think. Gillis had gone to school in Clearview. After graduation, he'd worked various jobs, clerking in grocery stores, pumping gas, doing a little carpentry work, whatever came to hand, but he hadn't really had to do anything if he didn't want to. His father had owned mineral rights on some land in another county, and the land had a couple of producing oil wells on it. The family had always had enough money to get by on without anyone having to worry about a job.

Gillis had stopped working and started fishing when he was around fifty, and that's what he'd done ever since, when he wasn't working on his old two-story house. He was handy with tools, and he'd kept the place in good shape. He painted every ten years or so whether it was necessary or not, and he made sure the roof was tight, the trees were trimmed, and the grass around the house was mowed. It was a pleasant place if you could disregard the pungent smell of the chicken farm, though right now the smell wasn't as bad as it often was. The morning breeze had been from the south, but the wind had switched around to the north. It was cool, bordering on cold, and it carried the smell away.

Tall pecan trees stood around the house, and its wide veranda ran around three sides of it. A porch swing hung from the ceiling, and a couple of old lawn chairs stood beside it. They hadn't been used much lately, Rhodes figured. Nobody in Mount Industry sat outside much since the chicken farm had moved in. Not counting the Terralls, of course. They had to watch over their business.

Gillis's beat-up old Chrysler sat in the side yard in front of a big detached garage that wasn't in such good shape as the house. Gillis didn't put much time into maintaining it. The garage doors were closed.

Rhodes parked the county car in the dirt driveway behind the

Chrysler and got out. The fog was gone with the wind, but heavy clouds covered the sky and darkened the day. The wind rattled the dead pecan leaves and sent a couple of pecans hurtling down. They thumped off the roof of the veranda and fell to the grass near where Rhodes stood. The house was quiet.

Rhodes walked up the wide front steps to the veranda and crossed it. A brass knocker shaped like a chili pepper hung on the frame by the screen door. It had been cleaned recently, and Rhodes used it to give three hard taps. He didn't hear anything from inside, so he tapped again, even harder.

No answer.

Rhodes walked around the veranda, first to the left and then to the right, looking in the windows. The lacy curtains, which must have been musty relics left behind by Gillis's parents, were pulled back and tied. Rhodes saw nothing unusual, just the old-fashioned furniture that looked as if it had been there since Gillis was born, if not before.

The veranda didn't extend all around the house, so Rhodes had to go back down the steps and walk around to the back. The backyard had an old well-house in it, but Rhodes didn't think Gillis used the water for anything, even if there was still any water in the well. With all the dry weather they'd had in the last few years, the water table had dropped dramatically.

The back steps were concrete and went up to a screen door that opened onto a long screened porch. The screen door wasn't latched, but Rhodes didn't open it. At the moment he didn't think he had probable cause to go in the house. Gillis might be there, sick or hurt, or he might not. Rhodes wanted to look around a bit more before he went inside.

The first place Rhodes checked was Gillis's old car. Nothing unusual there, just a couple of fishing rods and a tackle box in the backseat. Gillis always kept them there so he wouldn't have to load the car when he left to go fishing and so he'd have them if he happened to pass a place that looked as if it might be good for a few casts.

Rhodes walked on past the garage. Gillis had a big stock tank on the property, and he often fished there when he wasn't fishing somewhere else. The tank dam was lined with willow trees. He might have gone down there this morning before the interview and forgotten about the time.

Rhodes didn't see anyone on the dam, but Gillis could have been hidden by the willows. Rhodes called out, but he got no answer. He decided he'd walk to the dam and see if Gillis was there.

It wasn't much of a walk, about a quarter of a mile, and it didn't take Rhodes long to find Gillis when he got there. The old man lay at the lower end of the tank. There were no trees there. Gillis lay facedown, his head in the water and his legs on the land. There wasn't much doubt that he was dead. The wind blew across the water and moved the body gently.

Rhodes went around the dam to where the body lay. Gillis hadn't died of natural causes. He hadn't fallen into the green water and been unable to save himself. Someone had hit him in the back of the head and let him drop into the water. Rhodes could see blood on Gillis's thin hair.

A fishing rod lay on the ground beside the body. The monofilament line extended into the water. Gillis must have known whoever had hit him. He hadn't been distracted from his fishing, and it wouldn't have been possible for anyone to sneak up on him, not unless Gillis was totally deaf. Rhodes didn't think that was the case.

Rhodes crouched down beside the body. He tried to stay detached, but he felt a rush of sadness for the old man who'd never done anything to anyone as far as Rhodes knew. Now he was dead, and for no good reason. Rhodes was sure of that.

He stood up and looked out over the water. The breeze riffled the top, and something splashed over in the shallows. After a few seconds, he walked back to the county car and called Hack.

"Send Ruth out here to Gillis's place," he said.

"The old man givin' you trouble?" Hack asked.

"He's not going to give any trouble again," Rhodes told him. "Not to anybody."

Ruth and Rhodes didn't find any clues. The ground was hard, and there were no tracks. Gillis's killer hadn't stood near the edge of the water where the earth was soft.

"Nobody came to the house in a car," Rhodes said. "Not unless he managed to do it without leaving tracks."

He'd examined the area as soon as he'd called Hack. He'd found no sign that any car other than the Charger had been there. Though it was possible that Rhodes had obscured any tracks in the dirt driveway when he arrived, he didn't think so.

"Sort of like the situation at the rock pit," Ruth said. "You think somebody's flying in, killing people, and flying away?"

"Not too likely," Rhodes said. "I don't think anybody has a jet backpack yet."

"Have you looked inside the house?" Ruth asked.

"No, but I will. Call for the ambulance and the JP. You wait here for them, and I'll give the place the once-over."

"What do you think you'll find?"

"Nothing," Rhodes said, but he was wrong.

* * *

Rhodes entered the back porch through the screen door on the back. Like the rest of the house, it was clean and neat. Because the screen was no protection from the weather, Gillis didn't store anything there other than some of his fishing equipment that water couldn't damage: long cane poles lying on the floor, fishing rods leaning against the wall, a couple of black plastic tackle boxes beside them.

The door from the porch opened into the kitchen. Nothing of interest there, either.

Rhodes had a choice of two doors from the kitchen. One went into a dining room, and the other went into a hallway. Rhodes took the one into the hall, where he found something he hadn't expected: a bow and a quiver of arrows.

Rhodes didn't know much about bows, but he was surprised to find one here. He'd thought for sure that Qualls was Robin Hood. He looked at the bow, but he didn't know a thing about archery. He didn't know what kind of bow it was or what kind of arrows were in the quiver. He knew what kind Robin Hood used, and if these were the same, Ruth would be able to tell.

Rhodes went through the rest of the house but found nothing else that would tie Gillis to Robin Hood, and there was nothing of a suspicious nature. Gillis had been a lifelong bachelor, and he hadn't accumulated many worldly goods. He had a fine fifty-two-inch television set, a bookshelf with a lot of old hardback books, most of them about fishing, and a nice collection of antique fishing lures. A pair of good binoculars. That was about it. Gillis didn't even own a computer.

The second story of the house was almost bare. It was clean, and Gillis had a couple of chairs up there, but nothing else. He'd apparently confined his activities to the bottom floor.

Thunder rattled the windowpanes, loose in their frames after so many years. Gillis would have taken care of that if he'd lived, Rhodes thought.

Lightning brightened the interior of the house for a second. Rhodes stood in the middle of the living room, hoping he might see something that would help him figure out why someone would kill Hal Gillis. He didn't.

By the time Rhodes was finished going through the house, the JP had declared Gillis officially dead. The ambulance had come and picked up the body. Ruth met Rhodes in the kitchen.

"Just in time," she said as rain began to patter down on the roof.

Rhodes told her about the bow and arrows. "You want to have a look?"

She nodded and followed him into the hallway. Taking one arrow from the quiver, she gave it a look and said, "Wrong brand." She looked at the others and held up one of them. "But this one's right."

She went through the entire quiver, nodding now and then.

"Some of these are the brand Robin Hood used, but there are a couple other brands mixed in. That's funny. Not ha-ha funny. You know what I mean."

Rhodes knew. "I do. We'd better take these in as evidence. I'll let you handle it."

"What's on your agenda?"

"I'm going to talk to the Terralls."

"What about?"

"About Gillis. They were neighbors, and the Terralls are outside a lot of the time. Maybe they saw something or heard something."

"Like a man with a jet backpack."

"I'd settle for just a man on foot. Or a woman."

"Don't get your hopes up."

"You don't have to worry about that," Rhodes said.

The rain had never been heavy, and it had stopped by the time Rhodes arrived at the Terralls' vegetable stand.

The Terralls still sat where they'd been sitting when Rhodes had visited them earlier, but this time they wore matching sweaters, both gray. They didn't get up when Rhodes stopped his county car, and they didn't get up when he got out and approached them.

"Afternoon," Rhodes said.

"What do you want?" Calvin Terrall asked. His tone was anything but friendly. "I know you didn't come to buy any persimmons. You can see we aren't exactly covered up with customers, either. I don't blame 'em for staying away, not with the stink around here."

"It's not so bad today," Rhodes said.

"Yeah, it's not making my eyes water, but that's thanks to the wind. Wind's not good for business, though, and neither is rain."

"Some days you just can't win," Rhodes said.

"Most days," Terrall said. "Lately, anyway. You didn't say what you wanted."

"You told me to come back when I had another question for you."

"So? You got one?"

"It's not a question. Hal Gillis is dead. Somebody killed him."

Margie Terrall sucked in a sharp breath. Calvin looked stunned. Rhodes didn't think it was an act, but he'd learned that you could never be sure about something like that.

"Who'd want to kill Hal?" Calvin asked. "What did he ever do to anybody?"

"That's what I'm going to find out," Rhodes said. "I hoped you might be able to help me."

Terrall's face darkened. "You accusing me of killing Hal? Seems to me like you're always coming here to accuse me of something."

Terrall was awfully touchy, just as he'd been on Rhodes's previous visit.

"I don't remember that I accused you of anything," Rhodes said. "You just keep assuming that I have. Maybe there's a reason for that."

Terrall took a step toward Rhodes. Rhodes didn't move.

"Maybe there's not a reason for it, either," Terrall said. "Hal and I have been friends for a long time. He came by here every now and then to buy something. Just to help out. Not like some people I know."

Rhodes knew who Terrall was talking about. He started to say that he'd helped out Garrett by buying candy bars, but he didn't think Terrall would appreciate it.

"Speaking of helping out," Rhodes said, "what I wondered was if you'd seen anybody walking along the road or maybe crossing Gillis's property."

"Not me." Terrall turned to his wife. "Not anybody that's not usually on the road here, anyhow. What about you, Margie? You were out in the orchard before it rained. You see anybody walking around?"

"It was foggy," she said. "I couldn't see more than a few yards on either side of me, and I sure couldn't see over onto Hal's property. I liked Hal. I can't believe he's dead."

"He's dead, all right," Rhodes told her. "Somebody was there with him this morning. I don't know how he got there, though."

"There's a county road that runs back of both our places," Terrall said. "Anybody could park on the road and walk to Hal's house through the pasture."

"I'll check that out," Rhodes said, but he didn't think there was much chance he'd find anything. "About those people who usually drive on the road that goes by here. Who were they?"

"Well, Snuffy Garrett was one of them," Terrall said. "I don't remember who else. Margie?"

"I can't think of anybody. We don't have a lot of traffic, not since—"

"Since the smell," Rhodes said. "I know. Thanks for the help. I'll stop by and talk to Garrett. If you remember later that you saw somebody else, give me a call."

"I'll do that," Terrall said, his tone not as surly as it had been. "I want you to catch whoever killed Hal. He might get after me and Margie next."

Rhodes didn't think so. He had a feeling that Gillis's death was connected somehow to Hamilton's and that the Terralls weren't in any danger unless they'd seen something that they hadn't told Rhodes about. Or heard something.

The bow and arrows worried Rhodes. He asked, "Did you ever know Hal to go bow hunting?"

"He didn't hunt with a bow or a gun or anything," Terrall said. "He was a fisherman, not a hunter."

"What about target shooting?"

"With a bow? Nope. Not with a gun, either. Like I said, Hal was a fisherman. He didn't go in for that other stuff."

That's what Rhodes had thought, too, so the bow and arrows didn't figure, not unless Gillis was indeed Robin Hood. That would make Mikey Burns a prime suspect in the murder.

"I'll make sure the deputies make a regular check out this way," Rhodes told Terrall. "If you see anything suspicious, call the jail, and Hack'll alert them."

"Thanks," Terrall said, "but we'll worry anyway."

Rhodes didn't blame him.

21

▼

"HOW ABOUT A DR PEPPER, SHERIFF?" GARRETT ASKED WHEN Rhodes walked into the store.

This time Garrett wasn't sitting behind the counter. He was standing on a chair, replacing a lightbulb, one of three that hung from twisted cords from the ceiling of the store.

Garrett screwed in the bulb and stepped down from the chair, resting his hand on the back to do so.

"Gettin' too old for that kind of thing," he said. "Nobody else here to do it but me, though. How about that Dr Pepper? I could use one myself."

Rhodes didn't argue. Having missed lunch for what seemed like the tenth day in a row, he needed a little pick-me-up.

"I'll take a Zero, too," he said and went to the refrigerator to get one.

He unwrapped it, and Garrett brought him a Dr Pepper. Rhodes had to admit that when it came to lunch, a Zero and a Dr Pepper were hard to beat. Two of each would have been better, though.

"You sure been out this way a lot lately," Garrett said, taking a swig from the Dr Pepper bottle. "That chicken farm must be causing a real ruckus with folks out here."

"That's not all," Rhodes said. He bit the end off the Zero and chewed it. He swallowed and said, "Somebody killed Hal Gillis this morning."

"Damnation." Garrett set his Dr Pepper on the counter and wiped his mouth with the back of his hand. "Who?"

"I don't know, but I'm looking to find out. Could've been anybody. Have you seen him lately?"

"Funny you should ask that."

"Why?"

"I guess you talked to the Terralls. They must've seen me drive by this morning."

"They did." Rhodes ate some more of the candy bar and washed it down. "They didn't know you'd been to Gillis's place, though."

"Well, that's where I went. Hal and I go back so far it's hard for me to believe. Grew up together right here in Mount Industry. I go to see him now and then."

"You just close the store and take off?"

"Sure. No reason not to. Nobody ever comes by."

"So you haven't had any customers today, say somebody who might have gone on to Gillis's place."

Garrett looked at Rhodes. "Nobody. Except you, that is."

"Maybe if you stuck around somebody would come in."

"I don't think so. Anyway, I'm never gone long. Me and Hal just talk over old times, and then I come back. We can remember when this was a hoppin' little community. Been a long time, though." Garrett picked up his drink and took a sip. "You sure he's dead?"

"I'm sure."

"Damnation." Garrett's voice cracked. "I'm gonna miss that old boy. He was about the only friend I had left here."

"What about the Terralls?"

"You never mind about them. They're not bad folks, but they're not friendly. What happened to Hal?"

"Somebody hit him," Rhodes said.

He thought about that, wondering what the murder weapon might have been and where it was. Maybe in the middle of the stock tank, sunk in the mud under several feet of water.

"Must've been somebody he knew," Garrett said. His eyes were red. "Damnation."

"Who were his other friends around here?"

"He didn't have many. Not many people around, if you've noticed. Most of the ones we grew up with left long ago, and nobody much has moved in."

"What about Dr. Qualls?"

"He's moved in, all right. Hal knew him. I don't know how well. He'd mention him now and then, mainly when we got to talking about the chicken farm."

Rhodes thought about that. Qualls didn't live too far from Gillis. He could have cut across the back of his own property and walked to the back of Gillis's place that morning before driving into town for his appointment at the jail.

"Hal didn't like the chicken farm, I guess," Rhodes said.

"No more than anybody else here did, which is to say not one damn bit."

Garrett looked as if he had more to say on the subject, but instead he stuck out his hand and asked Rhodes for the Zero wrapper. Rhodes had finished the candy bar, and he gave Garrett the wrapper. Garrett tossed it in the trash while Rhodes drank the last of his Dr Pepper.

"You ever think back, Sheriff? About the way things used to be around here?"

"All too often," Rhodes said.

"Yeah, I know what you mean. I hate it when things change. They don't ever seem to change for the better, but then I guess all old men feel like that."

"I'm not that old," Rhodes said.

Garrett laughed. "Compared to me, maybe. Compared to the young whippersnappers I see when I go into Clearview, well, I don't know."

Rhodes said he got the point.

"Seems like most of the people I used to know are gone off or in the cemetery," Garrett continued. "The new folks don't act like they care much about the town or the way it used to be. Can't blame 'em, I guess. They weren't here then."

"It's not a bad town," Rhodes said. "Just different."

"The people are different, all right. You take that Qualls fella. He's a strange bird if there ever was one. You might oughta talk to him."

"I will," Rhodes said.

He didn't mention that he'd already talked to Qualls without producing much of a result, other than becoming convinced that Qualls was Robin Hood. If that was true, then Qualls had a motive for killing Gillis. He could plant a bow and arrows in the house and throw suspicion on Gillis. If Gillis was dead, he couldn't very well deny anything. Of course, if Gillis was dead, there would be quite a search on for his killer, and murder was a more serious crime than anything Robin Hood had done.

"You watch out for him," Garrett said. "He's always got that mask on. Bound to be something funny about a man like that."

"He doesn't like the smell," Rhodes said, "and he's afraid he's going to catch some kind of disease from the chickens. Bird flu or something."

"That bird flu's bad stuff," Garrett said. "Or so they say. So far nobody's caught it that I know of, not around here anyway."

"You know," Rhodes said, "you still haven't told me why you went to see Hal this morning."

"Just to talk. He was about to go fishing. He was headed for his tank when I left. Said it was likely to get cold, and he wanted to wet a hook before it did."

"What time was that?"

" 'Round eight o'clock. I was back here a little after that."

Rhodes didn't know what time Gillis had died, and he doubted that Dr. White would be able to pin it down closely enough to clear Garrett, if that's what Garrett hoped, even if he was telling the truth.

"Did he say anything about having an appointment to see me at the jail?"

"Nope. Didn't mention it. His memory was good, too. He was sharp as he ever was. Damnation."

"Did you see anyone else around?" Rhodes asked. "Anybody on the road or the property?"

"Not a soul. Only people I saw were the Terralls, sitting out in their stand. They didn't even wave to me when I went past."

"They didn't wave to me, either," Rhodes told him.

"Sure are unfriendly," Garrett said, shaking his head, and Rhodes had to agree.

Rhodes drove from Garrett's store to Qualls's house. The weather had gotten progressively colder, and Rhodes was glad it wasn't raining.

Qualls came to the door, still without his mask.

"I thought we'd said all we had to say to each other," he said when he saw Rhodes standing at the door.

"That was then," Rhodes said. "This is now. We need to have a talk, and it might take a while. You can ask me to come in."

"Why should I?"

The cold wind blew against the back of Rhodes's shirt, a thin one that he had put on that morning in hopes that the cold weather wouldn't arrive until much later in the day.

"Because it's cold and damp out here and because if you don't invite me, I'm coming in anyway."

Qualls didn't look happy with that response, but he stepped back, and Rhodes went past him into the house. It smelled new, the combination of new lumber and carpeting and fresh paint. Qualls was such a neat housekeeper that the place looked as if he'd moved in only days before.

"This way," Qualls said.

He led Rhodes to a room just off the hall. It looked a little like Benton's office at the college except that it was much more orderly. It held bookshelves, a computer desk, another desk, a couple of chairs, and a small TV set.

"This is my office," Qualls said. "I got used to having one when I taught, and I find I can't do without one now."

He sat in the chair at the desk. Rhodes took the other one. He noticed that Qualls was keeping his hands pretty much out of sight.

"Now, then, Sheriff," Qualls said. "What brings you out here? I don't have anything more to say than I've already told you."

"That's what you think," Rhodes said.

He looked at the bookshelves, which, like the others he'd seen lately, held none of the kind of books that Clyde Ballinger liked to read. Not unless Ballinger had recently switched to Shakespeare or Faulkner or Hemingway.

"You read?" Qualls said.

"Newspapers," Rhodes said. "Sometimes. When I'm not chasing criminals."

"Of course. I'm sure you watch television, though."

"Not much. I watch a DVD now and then. Just last night I was watching an old Abbott and Costello movie."

Qualls couldn't quite keep the sneer off his face. "I don't believe there's any such thing as a *new* Abbott and Costello movie."

"I guess not," Rhodes said. "The old ones will have to do."

"No doubt you found the one you saw hilarious."

"Oh, yeah," Rhodes said. "Those two guys crack me up. You ever watch them?"

"No," Qualls said. "I prefer foreign films."

"This one had Charles Laughton in it," Rhodes said. "He's not from around here, so I guess you could call it foreign. It was about Captain Kidd. He's not from around here, either."

Qualls opened his mouth, closed it, and peered at Rhodes. "Sheriff, I think you're putting me on."

"Now why would I do that?"

"I can think of several reasons. One might be that you're posing as an ignorant hayseed to lull me into a false sense of security."

"Hayseed," Rhodes said. "Now there's a word you don't hear very often. Ignorant, though, that one I hear all the time."

"You can drop the act, Sheriff," Qualls said. "It's not going to work."

"Well," Rhodes said, "you never know until you try."

"That act might work on some of the people you deal with around here," Qualls said, "but it won't work with me. Let's just get on with it. Say what you came to say."

"Good enough. I came by to ask you if you killed Hal Gillis."

"What? Gillis? Isn't he the man who lives not far from here in that old house he inherited from his parents?"

"That's the one. 'Lived' would be the right word, though, if you want to get technical about it."

"You think I killed him? Why in God's name would I do that?"

"Maybe to keep people from thinking you were Robin Hood," Rhodes said. "It wouldn't do your reputation any good if people thought you were going around shooting arrows into the air and letting them fall to earth in the tire of a county commissioner's nice red car. I know the earth and a tire are different, by the way."

"All right, all right, I underestimated you. I have a feeling I'm not the first one."

"It happens now and then," Rhodes said.

"I apologize," Qualls said. "You don't have to keep rubbing it in. You're probably some mute, inglorious Milton who'd have been chief of police if you'd lived in some big city like Houston."

"I seem to remember from high school that that's what you'd call a mixed metaphor, unless you're talking about Neal Milton. He's the sheriff about two counties over and a whole lot smarter than I am."

"You never let go of a thing, do you."

"Not usually," Rhodes said. "Not until I get the answers I'm looking for."

"If you think I killed Gillis, you're looking in the wrong place. I hardly knew the man."

"I found a bow and some arrows in his house."

"What does that have to do with me, or with anything?"

"I wondered if you might be missing something like that."

It was an idea that had occurred to Rhodes on the short drive from Garrett's store. Gillis might have seen the bow and arrows on a visit to Qualls's house and found a way to get them as evidence. He could have been planning to take them with him to his interview with Rhodes and let him know who Robin Hood was. Qualls had discovered they were missing and killed Gillis. He hadn't gotten them, though, possibly because he had to leave for his own interview and had thought he could go back for them. Rhodes had showed up, however, and spoiled his opportunity.

"I'm not missing anything," Qualls said. "I'm certainly not missing your implication that I'm somehow involved in the murder of Hal Gillis, with which I had nothing to do. I didn't even know he was dead until you told me. I still don't know that he's dead, for that matter. You might be trying to trick me."

"I'm not trying to trick you," Rhodes said. "I'm just an ignorant hayseed looking for answers to some simple questions."

Qualls sighed. "I've already apologized. I'm not going to do it again, and I'm not going to confess to murder. You can give up on that idea."

"If you went over to Gillis's pasture today, someone will have seen you. I'll find out about it sooner or later."

"You'll find out about it only if I've been there, which I haven't. Look, Sheriff, this kind of talk is getting you nowhere. I'm sorry to hear Hal Gillis is dead, but I hardly knew the man."

" 'No man is an island.' "

"You must read more than you let on," Qualls said.

"I stayed awake in English class when I was in school."

"Fine. But you didn't let me finish. I was going to say that I hardly knew the man, but that I'd be glad to do whatever I could to help you find the killer. Unfortunately, there's no way I can help you. I was in the house this morning until I drove to the jail to talk to you. I drove straight there, and I came straight back here when I left. I've been here ever since. That's the truth."

"You don't have any witnesses to confirm that, though," Rhodes said. "That's the truth, too."

"Yes," Qualls said, "I suppose it is. Are you going to arrest me?"

"Are you guilty of anything?"

"Many things, I suppose, but not of killing Hal Gillis."

"How about Robin Hood?"

"I didn't kill him, either."

"That's not what I meant."

"I know what you meant. I'm not confessing to anything, and if I'm not under arrest, isn't it time for you to go?"

Rhodes stood up. He looked around the office again. Qualls certainly had a lot of books. Rhodes wondered if Qualls had read all of them. He hoped he'd see an archery book, but there wasn't one. Or if there was, it was kept somewhere out of sight. He turned to Qualls, whose hands were folded carefully and half hidden in his lap.

"You never let me see your hands," Rhodes said. "Anything to hide?"

"Nothing at all," Qualls said. "I'm sure you can find your way out."

"And back again."

"Just do what you have to do. I'll leave that to you."

" 'Just leave the world to darkness and to me,' " Rhodes said, turning to leave.

He heard Qualls sigh behind his back.

22

RUTH HAD ALREADY FILLED HACK AND LAWTON IN ON THE Gillis murder by the time Rhodes got back to the jail, saving Rhodes the trouble of sparring with them.

Hack wanted to know who Rhodes thought had done it.

"If I knew that, I'd be a better lawman than Sage Barton," Rhodes said.

"I thought you already were," Hack said.

"If I am, it's not helping me much. Or Hal Gillis, for that matter."

"Hal's been around this county for more years than I can remember," Lawton said. "People sure are going to miss him."

"You don't even have an idea who did it?" Hack asked.

"I have too many ideas," Rhodes said. "I need to talk to Seepy Benton. Give him a call at the college and see if he's still there."

"It's not even five o'clock," Hack said. "He's bound to be there."

"College teachers don't keep regular hours," Ruth said, repeating Benton's earlier words to Rhodes. "He might be at home."

"Since when do you know so much about college teachers?"

Ruth smiled and said nothing.

"Okay," Hack said. "I'll call him. I don't much like talking to him, though. I never can figure out half of what he's telling me."

"I know the feeling," Rhodes said, but Hack wasn't listening. He was already making the call.

"No answer," Hack said after a while. "You want me to try his home phone?"

"He probably doesn't have one, but he has a cell number," Rhodes said. "Like everybody else. Call the switchboard at the college. They'll give it to you."

Hack got the number and called it. Benton answered, and Hack said, "The sheriff needs to talk to you. You at home?" He listened. "Good. He'll be there in a little while."

Hack hung up the phone and swiveled his chair so that he faced Rhodes. "He says he'll be out in his yard."

"You need backup?" Ruth asked.

"You just want an excuse to go see him," Hack said. "I think you're soft on him."

"What if I am? He's smart and sweet, and he knows how to treat a woman."

Lawton fanned his face with his hand. "Wooooeee. Too much information."

Rhodes escaped and left them to it.

Seepy Benton lived not far from the college in a little house that he'd freshened up considerably since he'd gotten interested in Deputy Grady. At least on the outside. Rhodes had never seen the interior.

Rhodes parked in front and walked around to the backyard,

where he found Benton hard at work laying paving blocks. Bruce, Benton's canine companion, thanks to Rhodes, sat near the fence, watching.

"Hey, Sheriff," Benton said, looking up from his work. "Say hey to the sheriff, Bruce."

Bruce barked. He was some kind of leopard dog, and he looked as if he might also be part wolf. Rhodes had run across him during the course of an investigation, but instead of adopting him as he'd done with his other dogs, he'd managed to talk Benton into taking him. Benton and Bruce were made for each other.

Benton knelt on both knees in the wet grass. Rhodes saw that he was wearing some kind of knee pads.

"Hack says you wanted to talk to me," Benton said.

"I do," Rhodes said. "What on earth are you doing out here? It's a little cold to be working outside."

"Does that mean you think college teachers are softies?"

"Not you. I know how tough you are. What're you doing?"

"I'm building a golden rectangle."

Rhodes looked at the paving stones. They looked grayish white, not golden.

"A golden rectangle is one where the ratio of length to width is exactly one hundred sixty-one plus," Benton said. "The ratio can be approximated by using successive numbers from the Fibonacci sequence."

Rhodes held up his hand and repeated Hack's words to Ruth. "That's way too much information."

"But there's more."

"I don't need to hear it. I came to talk about archery."

Benton smiled. "The secret is not to aim . . ."

". . . but to aim. I know."

"Then I have no more to teach you, Grasshopper."

"You might. I need some information."

Benton stood up. The knee pads he wore were muddy, and the mud had dead grass stuck in it.

"I'm all about information," he said. "I'm a teacher, and that's my job. Imparting information, I mean. We can go inside if you're too cold out here."

Rhodes had put on an old denim jacket that he kept in the Charger in case of emergency. "I'm fine out here. I wouldn't want Bruce to think we were deserting him."

Bruce barked when he heard his name. It was a nonthreatening bark, very much unlike the one Rhodes had heard from him on their first encounter. Living with Benton was good for Bruce, and Bruce was also good for Benton, or so Rhodes had convinced himself.

"Fine by me," Benton said. He got a wistful look. "I like it out here, and when I get the golden rectangle finished, it's going to be great to come and sit outside late in the afternoon and watch the sunset. It'll be even nicer if I have someone to watch it with me."

Rhodes thought that over. "I don't think you're inviting me."

"You'd be welcome to come, but I was thinking more of someone else in your department."

"Never mind," Rhodes said. A blast of wind from the north ruffled his hair. "Maybe we'd better go inside after all. I don't want to catch a cold."

"Good idea," Benton said. "Walk this way."

He turned and did a passable imitation of a Groucho Marx amble as he started toward the house.

" 'If I could walk that way,' " Rhodes said, " 'I wouldn't need the talcum powder.' "

"Not bad," Benton said, "but you need a cigar and a painted-on mustache if you want to do it right."

"No, thanks," Rhodes said.

Benton laughed and stopped at the screen door. "I'm not a very good housekeeper. You might think it's a little messy."

"I don't mind," Rhodes said, wondering how bad it could be and a little afraid to find out.

Benton opened the screen and then the wooden door behind it. He went in first and was removing his knee pads when Rhodes entered.

The back porch was covered with boxes, some of them open with papers spilling out. Rhodes also saw a lawn mower, an edger, several trash bags whose contents Rhodes couldn't distinguish (which was probably just as well), cartons of bottled water stacked four high, an open toolbox, and a jumbled pile of dull green quilts, the kind used to pad furniture in shipping. Benton tossed the knee pads onto the quilts.

"We can talk in the kitchen," he said.

The door from the back porch opened into the kitchen, and Benton led Rhodes in. After seeing the porch, Rhodes had been afraid the kitchen sink would be heaped with dishes, but it wasn't. It was empty, and the stove and table were clean.

"I could use something to drink," Benton said. "What about you?"

"No, thanks," Rhodes said, thinking that he'd had a Dr Pepper already that day.

"I have Dr Pepper, Diet Pepsi, and absinthe."

Rhodes looked at him.

"I'm joking about the absinthe. Not about the Dr Pepper and Diet Pepsi, though."

"I'll take a Dr Pepper, then," Rhodes said. "If it's not diet."

"It's not."

Benton got two cans out of the refrigerator. "You want a glass?"

Rhodes didn't want to push his luck. "No. I'll just drink from the can."

"Me, too, then," Benton said. He looked under a cabinet and found a couple of napkins that he wrapped around the cans. "Let's sit at the table."

They sat, and Benton handed Rhodes the Dr Pepper, keeping a Diet Pepsi for himself. They opened the cans and took a sip.

"So," Benton said. "What kind of information are you looking for?"

"It's about your friend Qualls."

"We're not really friends. Just interested in some of the same things."

"You know what I mean. You're as close to a friend as he has here in Clearview."

Benton drank some Diet Pepsi. "That might be true. I hadn't thought of it. I don't know him very well, though. We don't exchange confidences."

"What I want to know is whether you've talked to him about his past, his interests. His hobbies."

"Hobbies? I'm not sure he has any if you don't count writing letters to the *Herald* and trying to get rid of the chicken farms."

"How about getting rid of Hamilton?"

"I don't think he'd do that, not the way you're thinking."

"Somebody got rid of Hal Gillis today," Rhodes said.

"Hal Gillis? Who's he?"

Rhodes explained who Hal Gillis was, or had been, and told Benton some of his theories about the murder. He and Benton sipped from their cans.

"I can see you're going to need my help on this one," Benton said. "I'm an experienced crime solver, you know."

"So you keep telling me, but I don't need you to solve anything. Just tell me about Qualls."

"What do you want to know?"

"I want to know about his archery skills."

"I'm not sure he has any. Do you think he's the one going around shooting up the town? Not to mention Hamilton's place yesterday afternoon."

"I think so."

"Why would he do that? Shoot up Hamilton's place, that is. If the protest was partially his idea, and I'm not saying it was, why would he shoot the arrows?"

Rhodes had thought about that, and he had a ready answer. "To add to the confusion and get more publicity."

"It might work that way. Speaking of that, I wonder if the paper's come yet." Benton pushed back his chair and stood up. "I'll go see."

Rhodes didn't try to stop him. He was interested in seeing what the paper had to say about the demonstration at the chicken farm, and he wanted to read the new article about the farm that Jennifer Loam had promised in the previous day's edition.

Benton came right back, holding the paper. He unwrapped it and looked at the front page.

"Very nice," he said. "Except that I'm not in any of the pictures. Neither are you."

He handed the paper to Rhodes. There on the front page were two photos of the demonstration. As Rhodes had figured, the one of him and Buddy hadn't been printed, but there was one of Maddie and one of the group. Both pictures were from an angle that used the signs to hide the fact that the women weren't wearing much more than feathers.

Rhodes scanned the article but didn't see anything that he hadn't expected. Jennifer Loam was a good reporter. She got the quotations right, and she didn't twist the facts.

Only one thing was missing. The scheduled article about the chicken farm was nowhere to be seen. Rhodes opened the paper and checked the inside pages. Nothing.

"What are you looking for?" Benton asked.

Rhodes told him.

"Maybe she didn't have time to write it," Benton said, "what with doing the article on the protestors and all. You have to admit they're a lot more interesting. A lot more photogenic, too."

Rhodes was willing to concede that point, and Benton could have been right. Still, it seemed odd that the paper had promised an article that didn't appear. It was even odder that there was no mention of it, no hint that it might appear in a future edition of the *Herald*.

Rhodes laid the paper aside and finished drinking the Dr Pepper. Benton took the can, along with his own. He threw the napkins in the trash and put the cans in a box under the sink.

"For recycling," he said. "I believe in recycling everything I can. No pun intended."

Rhodes doubted that.

"Did you know that aluminum has been recycled since the early twentieth century?" Benton continued. "It's a lot cheaper to recycle than to produce new aluminum, so over thirty percent of the aluminum we use is recycled."

"Too much information again," Rhodes said.

Benton laughed and sat at the table. "I tend to lecture too much. It's a habit that's hard to break after you've taught as long as I have."

"I thought the Socratic method was supposed to be a better approach."

"And I thought you didn't want to teach."

"I know a little about it," Rhodes said. "That's all."

"Well," Benton said, "if you ever tried to teach math, you might find out that the Socratic method doesn't always work with college students who can't do fractions."

"I won't ever try," Rhodes promised. "Let's talk about William Qualls instead."

"I don't know what to tell you. He's never mentioned archery to me, and I think you're on the wrong track if you have the idea he killed Hal Gillis or anybody else. Do you have any kind of evidence?"

"Just one thing," Rhodes said.

"You haven't told me what it is."

Rhodes had debated with himself whether he wanted to tell Benton or not, but he couldn't see that it would hurt anything to reveal one little fact.

"It's his hand," Rhodes said.

"What about it?"

"It's more like his finger, the index finger on his left hand. He has a red welt on it, more like a callus."

"What does that have to do with being a killer?"

"It's not about the killing," Rhodes said. "It's about bow shooting. I know some bow hunters, and they all use shooting gloves. If they didn't, the feathers in the arrow would cause a callus like that."

"Ah," Benton said. "Ha."

"Now that I think of it," Rhodes said, "you might be the one to talk to him about that callus. Since you want to help and since you're a graduate of the academy and all."

"Are you serious?" Benton had a huge grin. "You really want me to help with the case?"

"Yes. I'd get a search warrant for Qualls's house, but the judge won't give me one based on such flimsy evidence."

"I thought you were friendly with the judge."

"That doesn't mean he's going against his conscience and the law for me, and neither should you. I don't want you to compromise your friendship, either. Just talk to Qualls casually, hint around, don't make him suspicious. When we both talked to him, he wouldn't open up. If you did it alone, he might tell you something that would help me."

"I'll be great at this," Benton said. "Sherlock Holmes is nothing compared to me."

"You don't want to get confused. If you feel loyal to Qualls because of your friendship, you might make a misjudgment."

"Being confused can be the first step toward realizing what is and what isn't the true reality."

"Yeah," Rhodes said, wondering if he'd made a terrible mistake in asking for Benton's help. "Right."

23

▼

RHODES WENT HOME AND PLAYED WITH THE DOGS FOR A WHILE. Sometimes when he was in his backyard, he could almost imagine that Clearview, and all of Blacklin County for that matter, was really as quiet and peaceful as it seemed on the surface. But then he'd think about the rock pit. It had a placid surface, too, but right below it had been a dead man, and the dead man had floated to the top soon enough.

Ivy came outside when she got home, and Rhodes told her about Hal Gillis.

"I was wrong, then," Ivy said.

"Probably," Rhodes said. "Unless somebody killed him in revenge for his killing Hamilton."

"How likely is that?"

"Not very."

"If someone thought he killed Hamilton, it could have happened that way."

"Possible," Rhodes said. He didn't like the idea of having two killers on the loose. "But not likely."

Ivy wasn't one to give up easily. "How about this one. Hal lied to you that morning at the rock pit. He knew more than he told. He saw something or someone, but he kept quiet about it. Maybe he wasn't sure, so he asked somebody something, and it backfired on him."

Rhodes had considered that possibility. "Or he tried a little extortion."

"That wouldn't have been like him."

"No, but people are strange. They can do things that seem way out of character when a murder is involved."

The more Rhodes thought about it, the better he liked the idea of Hal's having held back some bit of information. He might even have asked the killer to come by and see him that morning because of the scheduled interview. Hal would have wanted to make sure that he was right, or it was even possible that he had used the upcoming interview as a threat to extort more money. If either of those had been the case, things hadn't worked out at all the way Hal had planned.

"Do you have any clues besides the bow and arrows in Hal's house?" Ivy asked.

Rhodes shook his head. "I think that's a false clue."

"How can a clue be false?" Ivy asked.

"I think that stuff was planted by someone to confuse the investigation, to throw us off the track."

"Is it working?"

"It must be," Rhodes said. "I'm pretty confused."

"Do you have any suspects?"

"More than I need."

Ivy shivered. "It's cold out here. Let's go somewhere and eat."

"Where would you like to go?" Rhodes said.

"Barbecue," she said. "Max's Place."

"That's not very healthy," Rhodes said, secretly happy not to have another vegetarian meal in store.

"Man does not live by pasta and vegetables alone, and neither does this woman. Don't you like barbecue?"

"As long as it's not chicken," Rhodes said.

The phone rang while they were getting ready. Ivy answered it and called Rhodes.

"It's Mr. Burns," she said.

Rhodes took the phone. Burns started talking as soon as he said hello.

"So now Hal Gillis is dead," Burns said. "This is getting out of hand, Sheriff. It's been out of hand ever since somebody shot my tire. Now we have bodies all over the place. What are you going to do about it?"

"Catch whoever's behind it," Rhodes said.

"It's that Robin Hood," Burns said. "You have to stop him."

"Maybe it's terrorists," Rhodes said. "Out to wreck the economy of the county."

"That's not funny, Sheriff."

"No, I guess not."

"You quit making jokes and put a stop to this. It's making all of us look bad."

Burns didn't care how bad Rhodes looked. He was more interested in making sure his own constituents voted for him next time around.

"I'll get it taken care of," Rhodes said.

"You'd better," Burns told him.

*   *   *

Rhodes and Ivy drove to Max's barbecue restaurant, which wasn't far from Seepy Benton's house, and parked in the big parking lot. Rhodes could smell the mesquite smoke before he even got out of the car. Lots of barbecue places used applewood these days, while others used hickory, but in Texas, mesquite was still the thing for a lot of barbecuers.

"Is Seepy Benton performing tonight?" Ivy asked as they walked to the entrance.

"I don't think so," Rhodes told her. "No barbershop singing, either."

Max Schwartz was a member of the local barbershop chorus, and he'd been one of those who'd asked Rhodes to join. The group met at the community center, but now and then they'd come out to Max's Place and sing in the big room that he rented out for parties.

"That's good," Ivy said. "We can use the quiet. I think we need to talk some more."

"What about?"

"The murders," she said.

Max Schwartz greeted them when they got inside the restaurant. Rhodes heard the Kingston Trio singing "John Hardy" over the restaurant's speakers. Schwartz was a fan of the trio, and he featured them at his other local enterprise, a music store.

"You have to pay royalties on that music," Rhodes said.

"Don't I know it," Schwartz said. "Are you working for ASCAP now?"

"Just reminding you of the law."

"As if I needed reminding."

Schwartz had been a lawyer before moving to Texas to try his hand at some new enterprises, at both of which he'd been successful, at least so far. He'd taken to wearing a big Stetson hat at the restaurant because he thought it went with his decor, which changed from time to time, though its theme was always Western. Tonight Rhodes saw a couple of posters advertising Roy Rogers movies complemented by a display of saddles and bridles resting on stacked bales of hay. Rhodes wondered if the Kingston Trio would give way to the Sons of the Pioneers in Schwartz's affections.

"Where's the live entertainment tonight?" Ivy asked as Schwartz led them to a table.

"Benton's too busy with his teaching to come in except on Friday evenings. I haven't signed up anybody else. We're doing all right without anything."

"I think you're on the right track," Rhodes said, not that he had anything against Benton's singing.

"Best table in the house," Schwartz said, pulling out a chair for Ivy. "I recommend the ribs, but the brisket's fine, too. The secret's in the sauce."

It was the same thing he said every time, but maybe he had a point.

When they were seated comfortably, Schwartz left to go to the lobby and wait for the next customer. He believed in the personal touch almost as much as he believed in his sauce.

After the server had brought the menus and taken their orders, Rhodes asked Ivy what she wanted to talk about.

"About Hal Gillis and all the rest of it," she said. "You need to relax and think about the whole situation. Maybe there's some little something you're overlooking that's the key to the whole thing."

If there was, Rhodes didn't know what it could be. The only

thing that had nagged at him was the feeling that he'd missed something from the very beginning. Maybe talking it over with Ivy in a different setting would help. He was willing to give it a try.

"The main problem is that I don't know where either killer went," Rhodes said. "There's just not much way anybody could get from the rock pit back to town without somebody seeing him, and if a getaway car had been parked alongside the road anywhere close by, somebody would have seen it and said something about it after reading about the murder."

"Not everybody reads the paper," Ivy said.

Her mention of the paper reminded Rhodes of the missing article about the chicken farm, but that was just a distraction at the moment.

"Somebody would have reported a car, anyway," Rhodes said. "You don't just see an abandoned car on a county road and not call someone about it."

Ivy said she wasn't so sure. "Besides, there has to be another way to leave that place. Could the car have been hidden somewhere?"

"Somebody could've parked down by the river," Rhodes said, "but there haven't been any cars there in a long time. I checked."

The server brought their plates then: lean brisket, beans, and potato salad, with the sauce on the side, which was the way Rhodes preferred it. They began to eat, and Rhodes thought things over.

After his third or fourth bite of the tender brisket, he said, "I have an idea."

"Let's hear it," Ivy said.

"The river," Rhodes said. "I should've thought of it before. Somebody could have put a boat down by the bridge or anywhere along there and hidden it in the brush on the riverbank. It's not far from the rock pit to the bridge, and it would be easy to get there without being seen by cutting through the fields. Get in the boat, and you'd be home free."

"Where would home be?"

The river flowed south to one of the big lakes, where there were plenty of places to park a pickup. Row downstream, put the boat in the truck, and drive away. Who'd see you? Nobody, most likely. The hard part would be rowing up to the bridge in the first place, but it could be done easily enough since the river wasn't flowing rapidly, if at all.

"Sounds reasonable," Ivy said when Rhodes had explained it. "You have barbecue sauce on your shirt."

Rhodes wiped off the sauce with his napkin and got a fresh one out of the dispenser in the middle of the table.

"I think I'll have dessert," he said. Schwartz had a serve-yourself cobbler and ice cream bar in the restaurant. "Do you want cherry cobbler or peach cobbler?"

"See if there's any apple tonight," Ivy said.

There was, and Rhodes got a heaping bowl for her, with vanilla ice cream on top. For himself he got a bowl of cherry cobbler with plenty of ice cream as well.

They didn't talk while they ate dessert, but when they were finished, Ivy said, "Somebody could have walked away from Hal Gillis's tank even more easily than somebody walked away from the rock pit. Now all you have to do is figure out who it was. I knew talking it over would help."

"Right. Now that the hard part's over, I rush right out and make an arrest."

"Who are you going to arrest?"

"I wish I knew," Rhodes said.

*　*　*

Rhodes wasn't in the mood for a movie when he got home, though the cobbler had cheered him up some. He sat on the couch and looked through the paper again, hoping that he'd get some ideas from the article about the demonstration at the chicken farm. He would have settled for one idea, for that matter, but nothing came to him. He was about to give Abbott and Costello a try when the phone rang.

The caller was Jennifer Loam.

"I think I'm in trouble," she said. She sounded nervous and upset.

"What kind of trouble?" Rhodes asked.

"The bad kind."

"Just because you didn't get your article on the chicken farm done today?"

"That's part of it, but it's more complicated than that. I need to talk to you."

"Come on over," Rhodes said. "Ivy will make some coffee."

He didn't drink coffee himself, but it seemed essential to some people, and he thought it might help Jennifer.

"I don't want to come there. We should meet somewhere that nobody will see us."

"Nobody will see us here except Ivy, and she won't tell anybody."

"You don't understand," Jennifer said. "I might be followed. If I am, I don't want anybody to know I talked to you. Can you meet me somewhere? You'd need to be there when I got there."

"A public place?"

"That would be fine, as long as it's somewhere that it wouldn't be suspicious for us to run into each other. This isn't a pass, Sheriff.

It's business. Not that you aren't attractive, but you're a little too old for me."

Rhodes's feelings weren't hurt. After all, it was only the truth.

"We can meet at Walmart," Rhodes said. "I'll be where the books and magazines are. If anybody's following you, it'll look like a coincidence that we've met."

"Good. I'll be there in half an hour."

Rhodes hung up and told Ivy that he had to go out.

"Where to this time?" she asked.

"Walmart. I'm meeting Jennifer Loam."

"You're much too old for her."

"So she told me. This is business, though, not pleasure. She made that clear."

Ivy grinned. "When will you be home?"

"Good question," Rhodes said. "One of many I don't have an answer for."

"I'll see you when you get here, then. Be careful."

"Nobody would hurt me in Walmart," Rhodes said.

"Don't count on it," Ivy told him.

24

▼

RHODES STOOD IN FRONT OF THE BOOK RACK IN WALMART, thumbing through a paperback copy of *The Doomsday Plan* and marveling anew at the adventures of Sage Barton. The guy was everything that Rhodes wasn't, and the book's cover was a perfect example of that. It showed Barton crouched behind some kind of all-terrain vehicle at the edge of a forest as villains half hidden in the trees blazed away at him with a variety of weapons, maybe even including an M-16. Barton was grinning as if he were having the time of his life.

Rhodes wondered how anyone could think the character was based on him, not that he wasn't flattered that some people did think just that.

A male employee in a blue Walmart vest came up to him and saw what Rhodes was reading.

"That Sage Barton really is something," the man said. "I hear he's a lot like you, Sheriff."

Here we go again, Rhodes thought.

"Not counting all the guns, the fistfights, and the women, sure," Rhodes said. "Other than that, we're practically identical."

The man laughed. "The women go for him in a big way, all right. You sure you never have that trouble?"

"Never," Rhodes said, and about that time Jennifer Loam walked up and put a hand on his arm.

"Never?" the man asked. He wiggled his eyebrows and laughed. "I wouldn't say that, Sheriff."

Rhodes put the book back on the rack, and the employee went away. Rhodes hoped he wouldn't start any rumors.

"This is too public," Jennifer said. "I shouldn't have agreed to meet you here."

"Just say hello and go on your way," Rhodes said. "Head for the stockroom. I'll talk to you in there."

"Can we do that?"

"They know me here. We won't have a problem."

Jennifer left, and Rhodes picked up another book. He had no idea what it was, and though he pretended to look at it, his eyes followed the reporter. It was still early enough for Walmart to have a number of customers, but as far as Rhodes could tell, they were all intent on their shopping. Nobody seemed to have any interest in Jennifer Loam, but there were too many people around for Rhodes to be absolutely sure.

Loam disappeared into the stockroom. Rhodes waited a bit longer, then followed. He went down a long aisle with clothing on one side and groceries on the other. Right past the section of baby clothes and diapers were the big double doors to the stockroom. Rhodes pushed through them. Jennifer was waiting just inside.

"Are you sure this is all right?" she asked.

"I didn't see anybody following you," Rhodes said.

"That's not what I meant. The sign on the doors says this area is restricted to employees only."

"I can go pretty much anywhere," Rhodes said. "Who's going to arrest me?"

"An ambitious deputy, maybe. It would make a good story for the paper."

Whatever was bothering Jennifer, she hadn't lost her sense of humor. Rhodes looked around. There were a couple of men working over on one side of the big storage area, unpacking cardboard boxes. Another man was assembling a bicycle nearby, but no one else was around.

"Let's go over there," Rhodes said, pointing.

He led Jennifer to a spot in the back of the stockroom near the delivery doors, where they stepped behind a row of ten-foot-tall stacks of wooden pallets.

"Nobody's going to bother us here," Rhodes said. "Now tell me about this trouble you're in."

"I don't know if I should," Jennifer said.

Rhodes wasn't surprised. The symptom wasn't new to him. It was a little like buyer's remorse. Jennifer was sorry now that she'd ever said anything about having a problem, and she regretted having called him. Maybe she knew she hadn't been followed and thought that she'd let her imagination run away with her.

"You don't have to tell me if you don't want to," Rhodes said.

Most of the time that statement was all it took to get people to launch into the story they had to tell. It didn't work with Jennifer.

"You don't understand," she said. "This is an ethical issue with me."

"Ethics?"

Rhodes was surprised. That was one word he hadn't expected to hear.

"That's right. Ethics. All reporters have them, some more than others."

Rhodes heard the double doors open and close. He couldn't hear the man working on the bicycle now, so he figured the job was done.

"I know that," Rhodes said, "but I didn't think you'd called me about ethics. I thought you were in trouble."

"I am," Jennifer said. "Or I think I am. I could be. It's hard to explain."

"Give it a try," Rhodes said. "You can stop whenever you think you're about to compromise your ethical code."

"It's about Hal Gillis."

Rhodes held up a hand. He wasn't surprised that Jennifer had heard the news. She always knew when something happened in the county.

"Stop right there," he said. "If you know anything about who killed Hal, you're going to have to tell me, ethics or no ethics."

"I don't know who killed him. I don't have any idea."

"What, then?" Rhodes asked.

"I might know why he was killed."

Rhodes thought he had a pretty good idea, too, and he wondered if Jennifer had the same one.

"That's why you think someone's following you?" Rhodes asked.

He wondered if the reporter was getting paranoid. He didn't think anyone would be following her just because she might have some idea of why Gillis had died. He had two or three ideas, and he didn't think anyone was following him.

"I'm not paranoid," Jennifer said, "if that's what you're thinking."

"I didn't think you were," Rhodes lied.

Jennifer grinned. "I wouldn't blame you if you did. I sound a little paranoid even to myself. I'm probably just overreacting."

"If you're having a reaction, something must have caused it."

Jennifer looked around, but of course she and Rhodes were the only people in sight. The big stockroom was quiet, except for their voices and the sounds of the men opening the boxes on the other side of the area.

"I think someone was skulking around outside my house earlier," she said.

Rhodes hadn't heard anybody use the word "skulking" in a while, if ever, but then Jennifer was a writer.

"You didn't mention that on the phone," he said.

"Nobody was around then. Quite a few of my neighbors have dogs. There was a lot of barking, and whoever was outside went away. If there was anyone outside at all."

Rhodes heard a noise on the other side of the pallets, like the sound a shoe sole might make, scraping on the concrete floor.

Jennifer heard it, too. She gave Rhodes a wide-eyed look.

"Somebody's back there," she said.

Rhodes could have told her that was exactly the wrong thing to say, but it was too late now. He turned and moved toward the end of the row of stacked pallets as quietly as he could.

He managed no more than a couple of steps before the stacks moved with a splintery squeal. Rhodes turned back toward Jennifer as the upper pallets toppled. He grabbed her and pulled her down and toward the base of the pallets, where they hunkered down and tried to cover their heads as the wooden skids thundered down around them and onto them.

Rhodes tried to protect the reporter, but there wasn't much he could do. The heavy pallets landed on his back, his shoulders, and his head.

When the pallets stopped falling, Rhodes was pinned by their weight. Jennifer was beneath him. He tried pushing upward and felt a bit of a give at his shoulders. He pushed again.

"Who's under there?" someone called, and Rhodes heard scraping above him as pallets were shoved aside.

"The sheriff," Rhodes said. "Get these things off me."

He pushed upward, and the pallets moved with him. As the workers moved more of them, he was able to stand up. He reached down and helped Jennifer to her feet.

"Are you all right?" he said.

Jennifer looked dazed. "I'm not sure."

Two men stood nearby. Rhodes recognized them as the two who'd been opening and unpacking boxes.

"Did you see who shoved those things over on us?" he said.

"Nope," one of the men said. "Just heard 'em falling. Somebody ran out of here, though."

"Who was it?"

"Didn't know the fella. Don't know what he was doing back here. Employees only. What're *you* doing back here?"

Rhodes didn't answer or wait around to hear more. He ran to the double doors, pushed through them, and burst into the shopping area. He saw a woman with a basket full of groceries, and another woman with a basket that held diapers and baby clothes. Neither of them looked as if she'd just pushed a stack of heavy wooden skids on him and Jennifer Loam. Other shoppers were farther away but looked just as innocent.

Rhodes went up to one of the women. "Did you see anybody run out of the stockroom?"

"Nobody but you," she said.

"I mean before me."

"No. I was looking for black olives. You don't know where they are, do you?"

Rhodes told her he didn't and went to the front of the store. There were two entrances, each with a greeter. He went to the nearest one first. The greeter there didn't remember anybody who'd left the building in a particular hurry. He'd been occupied with putting a sticker on a returned item and hadn't noticed anybody for the last few minutes.

Rhodes didn't have any better luck at the other entrance, even when he asked if the greeter had noticed anybody who hadn't been pushing a basket or carrying a bag. Whoever had shoved the pallets over had been calm enough to make his escape without drawing any attention to himself.

On his way back to the stockroom, Rhodes walked around the store, looking for familiar faces just in case the pusher had stayed in the store. It was a big store, and it was crowded with people who'd come in to make purchases after work or dinner. Rhodes had a nodding acquaintance with some of them, but he didn't see anyone who was connected with the murders, at least as far as he knew. That didn't mean the pusher wasn't there, skulking around somewhere, but if he was, Rhodes couldn't find him.

Back in the stockroom, Rhodes checked on Jennifer. She seemed to be fine, with only a few bumps on one arm. Now that he had time to think about it, Rhodes realized that he had a bump on his head and that his back was sore. It would be bruised and colorful by morning, he was sure.

"I think somebody did follow you," he told Jennifer after he'd thanked the two men for helping him and sent them back to their work. "I missed seeing him."

"At least you know I'm not paranoid. Somebody must not want me to talk to you."

"Now all I need to do is find out who that is. Maybe what you were going to tell me will help. Once you've told, you shouldn't be in any more danger. It'll be too late for anybody to do anything about it."

"I should have thought of that sooner."

"I should have told you sooner, but now that you know, what's the secret?"

Jennifer hesitated. Rhodes shifted his shoulders to work out a little of the soreness that was already setting in. It was plain that even though Jennifer knew something that might help him in his investigation, she didn't want to violate her ethical code.

"Mr. Gillis was kind of a snoop," Jennifer said after a while. "Did you know that?"

Rhodes shook his head. Nobody had mentioned it.

"Well, he was," Jennifer said. "He kept an eye on things out there around his place. It was kind of a hobby with him."

"Keeping an eye on things isn't snooping."

"No, you're right. I was trying to be nice. He was nosy, and when I say he kept an eye on things, I mean he watched people from his house. He knew what they were up to all the time."

Rhodes remembered the binoculars. Gillis could have pulled one of the chairs on the second story up to a window and had a good view of the Terralls' roadside stand and their house, too. He could have seen Garrett's store, Qualls's house, and the chicken farm equally well.

No wonder nobody had mentioned that Gillis was watching them. They wouldn't have known. Gillis would have been careful to keep that kind of thing to himself. People didn't like it when somebody pried into their lives, and if they found out it was happening, they wouldn't be happy about it. Rhodes figured that gave everyone he suspected a motive to kill Gillis.

"I see what you mean about knowing why Gillis was murdered," Rhodes said. "He might very well have known who Robin Hood is. He might even have known who killed Lester Hamilton."

"He could have known, all right," Jennifer said. "That's not all he knew, either."

"There's more?" Rhodes asked.

"Yes, and it's why I didn't have an article about the chicken farm in today's paper."

Rhodes finally made the connection between Hal Gillis and an ethical problem.

"You see what I mean?" Jennifer asked.

"I think I do," Rhodes said. "Gillis was your source."

"Reporters don't like to reveal their sources," Jennifer said. "Why don't we just say that my source was supposed to come by yesterday and tell me what I needed to know for the article today. He didn't come because he said he couldn't bring the proof he'd promised. I told him I couldn't publish without proof. He said he'd have it today."

"He won't be showing it to you today."

"No. He had it, though. He called and told me he did. He said he had an appointment in town and that he'd bring me the proof after he'd taken care of it. The article would have been in tomorrow's paper, and nobody would have noticed it was a day late, not with today's news."

Gillis's death was the kind of thing that would make anybody forget about the chicken farm.

"Let's get out of here," Rhodes said.

25

▼

RHODES FOLLOWED JENNIFER HOME AND CALLED HACK ON THE way, telling him to make sure that Jennifer's house got a regular drive-by from Duke that night.

"What kinda trouble's she in?" Hack asked.

"Probably no kind at all," Rhodes told him. "The patrol's just to make her feel secure."

"I'll take care of it," Hack said.

Rhodes stopped at Jennifer's house and checked the inside to make sure nobody was waiting for her with an axe, or a bow and arrow. He told her that a patrol car would be coming by regularly all night.

"I appreciate it," she said. "I hope you don't think I was silly for worrying."

"You were right to worry," Rhodes said. "Somebody was after you, all right."

"The question is, who?"

"That's what I'd like to know," Rhodes said.

*   *   *

Ivy was waiting up for Rhodes when he got home. He gave her the short version of what had happened, leaving out the falling pallets, and then took a shower. His head started to throb, so he took a couple of aspirin after he'd dried off. He wrapped the towel around his waist and looked at his back in the mirror. The bruises were already turning dark.

"You seem to have forgotten to mention something about your evening," Ivy said from the bathroom door.

"It's nothing," Rhodes said. "There was a little accident with some pallets in the stockroom. I'm fine."

"I'll take your word for it. Anything else you forgot to tell me?"

"I didn't forget. I was just cutting out the stuff you didn't need to hear."

"I need to hear everything. You know that. If you're hurt, I want to know."

"I'm not hurt. Just a few bruises."

Ivy just looked at him.

"Okay," Rhodes said. "I'll tell you the next time something falls on me."

"Or anything else."

"Right. Or anything else."

"Come to bed now before you collapse."

"I have to brush my teeth. You know how I hate cavities."

"You're a big baby about the dentist, all right. Brush your teeth and then come to bed."

Rhodes got the toothbrush.

*   *   *

When Rhodes got up the next morning, he didn't know any more than he'd known the night before. He'd hoped that somehow his unconscious mind would put all the pieces together while he slept and have the answer ready for him as soon as he got out of bed. It didn't work like that, however.

Nothing came to him while he and Yancey visited Speedo in the backyard, either. The only change for the better was that the weather had gotten a bit warmer.

As far as Rhodes could tell, it now appeared that almost everyone in Mount Industry had a motive for killing Hal Gillis, or everyone would have if any of them knew that he'd been spying on his neighbors.

Rhodes took Yancey back inside. The little dog skittered through the kitchen and ran off to hide from Sam, who instead of lying in his usual spot was walking around the room. It was, Rhodes supposed, the cat's two minutes of exercise for the day.

"You don't look too chipper this morning," Ivy said.

Rhodes rolled his shoulders, hoping to work out some of the soreness.

"It's nothing physical," he said. "I'm just bumfoozled about these killings."

"You'll figure out what's going on," Ivy said. "You always have."

Rhodes wished he felt as confident as she sounded.

"The only thing I know is that I'm glad nobody's running against me this year."

"You'd win even if someone was."

"At least I'd get your vote."

"Always," Ivy said.

* * *

Ruth Grady had some news for Rhodes when he got to the jail.

"That bow and arrows you found in Hal Gillis's house?" she asked. "Never been used."

"How do you know?" Rhodes asked.

"*CSI: Blacklin County* strikes again," Hack said.

"It didn't take any fancy lab work to figure it out," Ruth said. "All you need to do is take a close look and you can tell the bow's never even been strung. You want to know what I think?"

"I can tell you without asking," Rhodes said. "You think it was a plant."

"Right. You know what else?"

"I'll bite," Rhodes said. "What else?"

"I think the reason the quiver had different kinds of arrows is that whoever put them there didn't know what kind Robin Hood used. He must have thought he could throw us off by buying several kinds and hoping that at least a couple of them would be the right brand. That's what happened. He bought the major brands and got lucky."

"Not so lucky," Hack said. "He didn't fool you."

"The important thing," Rhodes said, "would be fingerprints."

"If there were any," Ruth said, "but there aren't."

"That's a clue, too," Rhodes said.

"Wait a minute," Hack said. "How is that a clue?"

"See, that's why you're behind a desk," Ruth said. "We trained lawpersons figure out that kind of thing in the blink of an eye."

"I got it, too," Lawton said.

"No, you don't," Hack said.

"Sure I do. No fingerprints means that somebody wiped it. Why would Hal do that if it was his?"

"Maybe 'cause he didn't want anybody to know it was his," Hack said.

"It was in his house. Bound to be his."

"Unless somebody wiped it and put it there," Ruth said, closing out the argument. "I think that's what happened."

"You sound like you know it for sure," Hack said.

"Not for sure. I'd say about ninety-nine percent."

"More like a hundred," Rhodes said. "Now all we have to do is find out who put it there and why."

"You don't think Robin Hood did it?" Lawton asked.

"Robin Hood would know what kind of arrows he used," Ruth said.

"Sure he would, but he might've run out. He might've had those others around all the time."

Lawton had a point, but Rhodes didn't think that he was right. No need to start an argument about it, though. Rhodes had other things to worry about.

"Any hope you can find out where the bow and arrows came from?" he asked Ruth.

"Very little," she said. "You can order that stuff from dozens of places on the Internet. We won't have any more luck tracing them than we did those first arrows. It's going to be hard to prove any-thing against Gillis with these. I think it was just something to confuse us."

"If that was it," Rhodes said, "it's working."

The phone rang, and Hack grabbed it. Rhodes heard excited jabber on the other end before Hack said, "Slow down. Slow down."

Whoever was on the line must have taken a deep breath, be-cause Rhodes couldn't hear what came next. He did, however, hear Hack say, "I'll send somebody right out there."

"What now?" Rhodes asked.

"Got some kinda hoo-raw goin' on at the college," Hack told

him. He looked at Ruth. "Don't know what it is exactly, but somebody's boyfriend is mixed up in it."

Ruth blushed.

Rhodes knew immediately what the trouble was without being told if it involved Seepy Benton. No doubt it had to do with William Qualls, and it was all Rhodes's fault. He should never have asked Benton to help out.

"I'll take it," he said.

"I'm going as backup," Ruth said.

Rhodes hesitated. He didn't think he'd need any help if Benton was mixed up in it, but backup might be a good idea anyway.

"Whoever's goin', you better get on out there," Hack said. "They're all excited about it."

"We'll be there in five minutes," Rhodes said.

When Rhodes arrived at the campus, Ruth was right behind him. They parked side by side and got out. Students crowded the walk in front of the redbrick building, their faces turned up to look at something on the roof.

"You see anybody?" Rhodes asked.

"No," Ruth said, "but they must be looking at something."

Rhodes didn't necessarily think that was true. Let one person look up, and everybody else would do the same. He craned his neck to see if he could spot anybody from the administration. One of the deans, a woman named Sue Lynn King, stood near the double glass entrance doors, and Rhodes started in her direction. Ruth followed him.

"What's going on?" Rhodes asked when he reached the dean.

Sue Lynn King was a tall, stout woman with dyed black hair and an imposing manner.

"I'm glad you're here, Sheriff," she said, raising her voice to be heard over the hum of the students' incomprehensible running commentary on whatever was happening. "You, too, Deputy. We have something of a situation."

"I can see that," Rhodes said, "but I can't see what the situation is."

"We're not exactly sure. All we know is that Dr. Benton and Dr. Qualls seem to have gotten into some kind of tussle."

"Tussle?" Ruth asked.

"Yes. Not a fight. A tussle. Dr. Qualls ran out of the part-timers' office, and Dr. Benton was with him, or chasing him. It isn't clear."

"Where are they now?" Rhodes asked.

"Well, that's the problem. It seems they're up on the roof."

So that's what the students were looking for. Maybe they hoped someone would jump or fall. Although the building had only two stories, a fall to the concrete would do plenty of damage. It might even be fatal. So far as Rhodes could see, however, no one was near the edge.

"What are they doing up there?" he asked.

"That's another thing we don't know," Sue Lynn said.

There was a lot more they didn't know than they did know. Rhodes decided he'd have to go to the roof himself if he wanted to find out.

"What about your campus security?" he asked.

"That would be Officer Sanders," the dean told him. "He's keeping order inside."

"We'll go have a look," Rhodes said, and he and Ruth entered the building.

Officer Sanders wore a black uniform and looked quite official, but he wasn't doing much to keep order. Students milled around in the hallway, and their chatter echoed off the walls and floor. Rhodes didn't see any of the instructors. He supposed they were in their classrooms and offices, staying out of the way. A wise decision.

"How do I get to the roof?" Rhodes asked Sanders, who was trying to herd the students back into their classrooms.

"There's the stair," Sanders said, jerking his head toward the stairs leading to the second floor. "Goes right on up to the roof."

Rhodes thanked him, and he and Ruth took the stairs.

"It's not like Seepy to get into trouble," Ruth said. "He's very calm, and he doesn't like violence."

"Nobody mentioned violence," Rhodes said.

They reached the second floor and continued up to the door that opened onto the roof. Rhodes stood by the door for a while, listening, but it was made of steel, and he couldn't hear anything from the outside.

"I'll go first," Ruth said. "You're not armed."

Rhodes hoped they wouldn't need weapons, but you didn't go unarmed through a door onto a roof when there was "a situation," not if you didn't know what the situation was.

"Try not to shoot anybody," he said.

Ruth drew her sidearm, a .38 revolver.

"I won't shoot to kill," she said.

She moved past Rhodes and threw open the door.

Rhodes hoped she was telling the truth.

26

▼

RHODES DIDN'T SEE ANYONE ON THE FLAT ASPHALT ROOF OTHER than Ruth as she stepped out the door, her revolver at the ready in a two-handed grip.

The day was clear and cool, and a north wind blew across the roof. A piece of crumpled paper that might have been part of a student's homework skittered across the asphalt.

At the opposite end of the building there was an enormous cooling tower, and Rhodes thought he heard voices coming from behind it.

Ruth started in that direction, and Rhodes was right behind her. When they reached the tower, they turned, putting their backs flat against it. Ruth pointed the .38 at the roof and looked at Rhodes.

He put a finger to his lips, and they stood silently, trying to hear what Qualls and Benton were saying. Rhodes couldn't make out any words because of the wind. He glanced at Ruth. She shrugged, so he figured she couldn't hear, either. He pointed to the right, and Ruth moved out.

They turned the corner. Seeing no one, they continued to inch along the side of the cooling tower. Ruth paused just before the corner and looked back. Rhodes indicated that it was okay for her to go on.

She turned the corner with the .38 extended in front of her.

"Freeze," she said.

Rhodes stood behind her. Benton and Qualls looked as frightened and as guilty as if they'd just burgled the bursar's office.

"Hands in the air," Ruth said.

"But we—" Benton said.

Ruth wiggled the pistol. "I said, hands in the air."

Benton and Qualls raised their hands. It was apparent that neither of them was armed, not that Rhodes had expected them to be.

"It's okay," he said to Ruth. "You don't have to shoot them."

"What if I want to?"

"It wouldn't be legal."

"What's the use of being a cop if you can't shoot whoever you want to?"

Rhodes grinned. "You have the satisfaction of taking the perps off the streets."

"I guess that'll have to do," Ruth said, and she lowered her pistol.

"Let's go back inside," Rhodes said. "This wind bothers me."

"You two go first," Ruth told Benton and Qualls. "I'll be behind you with the pistol."

"You wouldn't really shoot us, would you?" Benton asked.

"Try me," Ruth said, and the two men got in front of her, looking hangdog.

"Go on," she said, and they did.

Before they got to the second floor Rhodes suggested that Ruth holster her pistol.

"We don't want to frighten the students," he said. "Or Officer Sanders, if he's there."

Sanders wasn't there, and the students moved out of the way as the four people made their way to Benton's office. The office didn't look any better than it had the day before, and there was no more room than there had been, either. Rhodes told Ruth to go downstairs and let everyone know that things were under control.

"Tell them nobody's going to jump off the roof," he said. "Nobody's going to get shot or hurt. They can go on with their classes."

"What about these two?" Ruth asked. "Are you sure you don't need my help with them?"

"I think I can handle them. You can go on patrol when you have the campus settled down."

Ruth looked at Benton. "I'm not sure I'd trust them."

Benton looked woebegone. He slumped and sighed, but he didn't say anything.

"I didn't say I trusted them," Rhodes told her. "I said I could take care of them."

Ruth was reluctant to leave. "Well, if you're sure."

"I'm sure." He didn't add that he'd made A's in PE. "You two sit down."

Benton sat in the desk chair. Qualls shoved a couple of books out of the other chair onto the floor, then sat in the chair. Qualls didn't look at all woebegone. He looked angry, and he sat with his hands in his lap, the right covering the left.

"They won't cause any more trouble," Rhodes told Ruth. "You can leave now."

Ruth gave Benton a withering look and left the office, closing the door behind her. Rhodes stood where he was and looked from one man to the other, saying nothing.

Benton cracked first.

"I didn't mean to cause any trouble. Do you think Ruth is upset with me?"

"That would be my guess," Rhodes said, "but at least she didn't shoot you."

"She was only joking," Benton said, but he didn't sound entirely sure of himself.

Qualls had nothing to say about any of this. He sat unmoving in the chair.

"What caused the little tussle between you two?" Rhodes asked.

"Tussle?" Benton said.

"That's what the dean called it."

Benton sighed. "She's going to do worse than shoot us."

Qualls spoke up. "If she dismisses me, I'll see you in court. This was all your doing."

Now they were getting somewhere.

"How was it his doing?" Rhodes asked.

"That's between us," Qualls said. "Or it had better be."

"Is that a threat?" Rhodes asked.

Qualls wasn't going to cooperate. "Take it any way you want to."

"All I did was talk to him," Benton said. "A friendly conversation. That's all it was."

Qualls laughed without humor.

"What was the conversation about?" Rhodes asked.

Benton sat up straighter. "I noticed that he had something wrong with one of his hands. I wondered if he'd hurt himself, and I asked him about it. He didn't like that."

"My hands are my own business," Qualls said.

"They look all right to me," Rhodes said.

Benton pointed. "He has his left hand covered. It's his index finger that's hurt. Ask him to show it to you."

"I don't have to show anything to anyone," Qualls said. "In fact, I don't have to sit here and listen to this unless I've been charged with something. Have I been charged, Sheriff?"

While tussling wasn't against the law, Rhodes thought he might charge Qualls and Benton with disturbing the peace. In the long run, though, that would be more trouble than it was worth for both him and the college. Not to mention for Benton and Qualls.

"No," Rhodes said. "You haven't been charged with anything."

"Are you going to charge me?"

"I don't think I will."

"I'm glad to see you're sensible." Qualls stood up, careful to keep his hand concealed. "Now if you two gentlemen will excuse me, I'll be going. I have a class to teach if the dean doesn't fire me."

"I'll talk to her about that," Rhodes said.

"I thought you might." Qualls opened the door with his right hand. He held his left in front of him where Rhodes couldn't see it. "Good-bye, gentlemen."

When the door closed behind Qualls, Benton said, "I don't much like the way he said 'gentlemen.' I don't think he was sincere."

Rhodes didn't respond.

"Okay," Benton said, "maybe I made a mistake. Maybe I wasn't subtle enough. I didn't think Qualls would overreact the way he did, but you can see he's guilty. Otherwise, why would he run out of the office when I mentioned his hand?"

Rhodes was surprised, too, now that he stopped to think about it. Qualls had seemed to Rhodes to have better control of his emotions than he'd displayed with Benton. Maybe it was the setting, or the surprise. Or maybe Rhodes should have confronted Qualls about his hand during the interview at the jail, though at the time Rhodes hadn't thought Qualls would be so easy to crack.

"You're right," Rhodes said. "He's guilty. The question now is, how much is he guilty of?"

"Do you want me to try to find out?"

"No," Rhodes said. "Somehow I don't think that would be a good idea."

Rhodes left Benton to his own devices, of which Rhodes was certain there were many, and went down to talk with Dean King. The dean wasn't too receptive at first, but when Rhodes explained that Benton had been working for him, unofficially, of course, she relented.

"I hope you aren't going to arrest them," she said. "If you do, then there'll be all kinds of trouble."

Trouble, in the college setting, was likely to involve considerable paperwork, Rhodes assumed. Not to mention meetings. Lots of meetings.

"I don't have any reason to arrest them," he said. "Neither one of them will cause any more trouble."

"*More* trouble? Is one of them in trouble now?"

"No. You don't have to worry about them. They'll be on their best behavior. I can guarantee it."

That was overstating things, particularly in Benton's case. Rhodes could never predict what Benton might do, nor could anyone else, but if the math teacher was interested in keeping Ruth Grady happy, he'd have to watch his step.

Qualls, on the other hand, would have to be careful not to do anything to attract attention to himself. Whatever he did now would be open to scrutiny, and he knew that Rhodes was onto him. Rhodes believed that meant the end of Robin Hood. Qualls wouldn't risk trying anything with his bow and arrows again.

Rhodes could have arrested him and charged him, but not with anything serious. At best, Qualls would have had to pay a fine. At worst, Rhodes wouldn't be able to prove his case. Certainly the callus on Qualls's hand wasn't enough to convict him. It wasn't even enough for Rhodes to bring the charges.

"I'll have to trust you, Sheriff," the dean said. "If you promise there'll be no more trouble, we'll let this go. I'll have a word with Dr. Benton and Dr. Qualls just to make sure they understand."

Rhodes didn't think that would hurt. He thanked Dean King for her time and left the college.

Rhodes's next stop was Mikey Burns's office. The commissioner wouldn't be happy to see him. It seemed as if nobody was happy to see Rhodes these days.

"I think he's still upset about the car," Mrs. Wilkie told Rhodes when he presented himself.

"Or about Hal Gillis," Rhodes said.

"That's so sad." Mrs. Wilkie put on what Rhodes assumed was supposed to be a mournful expression, though it looked more like she'd swallowed a pickle. "Mr. Gillis was a nice man."

Not so nice if what Jennifer Loam had said was true, but Rhodes didn't tell Mrs. Wilkie that. No need to disillusion her.

Mrs. Wilkie let Burns know that Rhodes was there and told Rhodes he could go on into Burns's office.

"Should I carry my hat in my hand?"

"You don't have a hat," Mrs. Wilkie pointed out.

"Maybe I should buy one," Rhodes said.

"I don't think you'd look good in a hat."

"I wouldn't. You can take my word for it. I'm the only sheriff in Texas who doesn't wear one."

"You'd better go on in," Mrs. Wilkie said, puzzled by the direction of the conversation. Once again Rhodes reflected that he spent too much time talking to Hack and Lawton.

"Thanks," he said and entered Burns's office.

27

▼

BURNS'S ALOHA SHIRT WAS MAINLY RED, WITH GRAY LEAVES AND flowers. The red was about the same color as his Solstice, and it matched the color of his face. Rhodes wondered if the commissioner had blood pressure problems.

"This chicken mess has gotten out of hand," Burns said. Then, as if realizing that didn't sound right, he said, "Situation. That's what I mean. This chicken situation. Hal Gillis is dead, Les Hamilton is dead, and there's a maniac running loose and shooting tires out with hunting arrows. It has to stop."

"How many tires have been shot?" Rhodes asked.

Burns gripped the edge of his desk with both hands and pulled himself forward an inch or two in his rolling desk chair. Rhodes was surprised he didn't leave thumbprints in the wood.

"The number of tires isn't what's important," Burns said. "It's the idea that the maniac's out there ready to strike at any time."

"He won't strike again," Rhodes said.

Burns opened his mouth. Closed it. Tried again. "You've made an arrest?"

"Not exactly."

Burns's upper lip curled. "How can you 'not exactly' arrest somebody?"

"It's easy. Let's just say I think I've put a stop to Robin Hood's reign of terror."

"You know who he is?"

"I'm pretty sure I do, and I'm pretty sure he won't be doing anything else to harass you or anybody else."

Rhodes wished he were as confident as he sounded. What worried him most was that he still suspected Qualls might have done worse things than shoot a few arrows. He might have killed a couple of people. Rhodes wasn't going to mention that to Burns.

"You have to arrest him," Burns said. "He has to be punished for what he's done. He has to make restitution."

"There's a problem with that," Rhodes said.

"What's the problem?"

"Evidence. I have enough to be convinced that I'm right, but I don't have enough to convince a judge to issue a warrant. You'll just have to take my word for it that Robin Hood's not going to be around anymore."

"Fine. I'll take your word for it. However, that's not going to pay for my tire."

"Sorry about that," Rhodes said.

"Right. And what about Hal Gillis and Les Hamilton? Are you going to 'not exactly' arrest anybody for killing them?"

"Sooner or later."

"It had better be sooner. We don't need to have any more killings around here."

Rhodes couldn't have agreed more, but he couldn't guarantee anything along those lines.

"Well," he said, "I won't take up any more of your time. I just wanted to let you know that Robin Hood was out of the picture."

Burns didn't look thrilled. Rhodes hadn't expected him to be.

"Speaking of getting things done," Rhodes said, "what about the problems with the chicken farm? Have you managed to get anybody from the state to do anything?"

"Not exactly," Burns said.

Rhodes grinned.

Burns didn't, not for a couple of seconds, and then the corners of his mouth turned up. Not much, but a little.

"All right," he said. "You got me on that one. I've been on the phone most of the day, but I can't get anybody to promise me anything. They're as bad as you are."

"At least they're listening."

"They have to. Qualls has flooded them with letters and petitions, and that demonstration yesterday got their attention. I think they'll send somebody up here eventually."

"That might not be soon enough for the people in Mount Industry."

"I know that," Burns said. "It's the best I can do."

Rhodes had been ready to leave, but he didn't move.

"I know how that sounds after my mouthing off," Burns said. "I was wrong. You want a written apology?"

"I think we can call it a draw," Rhodes said.

For some reason Rhodes found himself drawn back to the rock pit. He didn't know what kind of answer he thought he'd find there. He was pretty sure the turtle didn't have any wisdom to impart, and the giant catfish wouldn't be any smarter, not if Rhodes knew catfish.

Rhodes went by his house and got his fishing tackle. The tackle box was dusty, and Rhodes hoped the monofilament line hadn't deteriorated. It had been a long time since it had been in the water.

After leaving his house, Rhodes drove by the Dairy Queen and bought a burger, fries, and a drink. He told himself that he would've gotten a vegetarian burger if there had been one on the menu. It wasn't his fault that one wasn't offered, and, after all, he'd passed on getting a Blizzard. They were on sale, too. He could at least feel virtuous about that.

When he got to the rock pit, he put his five dollars in the mailbox, this not being an official investigative visit. He drove close to the willow trees to park. No one else was around, maybe because it was a little too cool for fishing or because it was the wrong time of day. Rhodes sat in the car and ate his burger and fries. If he'd been expecting inspiration to hit, he'd been fooled. The fries were good, though.

Rhodes finished his meal and made sure to get all his trash into the paper bag the food had come in. Then he got his rod and tackle box out of the car and walked to just about where Hal Gillis had been when he spotted Lester Hamilton's body. The breeze ruffled the leaves of the willows, making a sound as if invisible sparrows were flitting around in them.

Clicking open the tackle box, Rhodes took out a spinner bait with a yellow and black plastic skirt. He tied the spinner to the monofilament and cast it into the rock pit. He reeled it slowly back toward the bank, never thinking he'd get a strike, which he didn't.

He made another cast, remembering everything that had happened in the last few days, from the discovery of Hamilton's body to the death of Hal Gillis to the tussle between Benton and Qualls.

It was Qualls who occupied most of his thoughts. What would he do, now that he was the owner of the chicken farm? Would he shut it down, or would the lure of the money be too much for him to resist? It might be that he could take steps to make the operation more acceptable to the people in Mount Industry without the state having to intervene, but would it be as profitable if he did? Having fought against the place for so long, what would he do without it? He'd have to find a new hobby. Maybe he'd like to take up fishing.

Or maybe that was too dangerous. Look what had happened to Hamilton. Rhodes wondered if Qualls had been mixed up in Hamilton's death, but he just couldn't see it.

Rhodes reeled in the spinner. As it got nearer the bank, it rose higher and higher, and the silver blade glinted under the water's surface. It should have looked enticing to the fish, and Rhodes couldn't believe they were able to resist it. They were, however. As far as Rhodes could tell, the rock pit was as empty of fish as his bathtub at home.

He made another cast. The sinker hit the water with hardly a splash and began to sink. Rhodes reeled it in.

He thought about what he'd found at the scene after Lester's death. Something about the experience had bothered him at the time, and he replayed it in his mind. When he pulled the spinner out of the water for another cast, it came to him. It might not be anything, but it was something he should have checked at once. Not that it was hard to overlook, but he hadn't been thinking clearly or he'd have seen that something was wrong.

He drew back the rod and sailed the spinner as far as he could over the water of the rock pit. The wind caught it and took it a bit farther than Rhodes had thought he could cast, at least halfway across the pit, maybe more. This time he was bound to get a strike.

He didn't, but the spinner that was trolling through his mind hooked something else that he'd seen, something that had meant nothing to him at the time, but it was something he should have paid more attention to. Once again, it might be nothing, but it was one more thing he'd have to check out.

This time when Rhodes lifted the spinner from the water, the old moss-backed turtle floated up almost to the surface. A smaller turtle rose beside it and bobbed up from the water like a cork. Both of them looked at Rhodes, or he thought they did. They might have been looking at the sky, or they might have been looking at nothing at all. It was hard to tell with turtles.

Rhodes delayed his cast and watched the turtles that might or might not have been watching him. A minute or so passed with nothing happening, and then the turtles sank below the surface and disappeared. Rhodes wondered how they rose and sank so effortlessly. There was obviously more to a turtle than met the eye.

He cast the spinner, wondering what else he'd overlooked in his investigation. His biggest mistake had been asking Seepy Benton for help. What had happened with Qualls wasn't entirely Benton's fault. Rhodes should never have involved an amateur, though of course Benton didn't consider himself an amateur. He thought of himself as a seasoned crime fighter, something on the order of Batman.

Thinking of Benton's amateur approach, Rhodes realized he'd made another mistake, or maybe two mistakes, both of them involving Jennifer Loam. He reeled in the spinner as quickly as he could, buzzing it across the top of the water. He didn't want a strike this time.

Rhodes pulled the spinner out of the water and used a pair of nail clippers from the tackle box to snip it off the line. He shook some of the water out of the skirt. The spinner clinked as water droplets glittered in the sun. Rhodes put the spinner and nail clip-pers back in the tackle box. After he stowed the rod and tackle box in the car, he headed back to town.

Rhodes had just passed the Clearview city limit sign when Hack came on the radio.

"You need to get out to the college," Hack said.

"Another riot?" Rhodes asked.

"Nothin' like that. It's that Seepy Benton. He says he's got to talk to you. Says it's urgent. That's the very word he used. Urgent."

"Did he say why it was so urgent?"

"Nope. Just said it was something you'd want to know about."

Rhodes hoped Benton wasn't being held hostage in his office by Qualls.

"Did he sound all right?"

"Sounded fine to me."

"Not nervous or anything?"

"That fella never sounded nervous in his life," Hack said.

Rhodes didn't want to take a detour, but when Benton said something was urgent, it probably was, even if Benton wasn't ner-vous about it. Rhodes told Hack he'd drop by the college and see what was up.

"Ruth told me about what happened while ago. You think she oughta be seein' a fella like Benton?"

"He's okay," Rhodes said.

"Hah," Hack said.

The college campus was calm when Rhodes arrived. It was three thirty, the afternoon lull between the majority of the daytime classes and the ones held in the evenings. Rhodes parked and went inside. He didn't see the dean, which was just as well.

Benton sat in his second-floor office. Qualls was there, too. They were talking quietly when Rhodes got to the door. He stood outside until they noticed him.

"Come on in, Sheriff," Benton said. "I'd ask you to have a seat, but as you can see there's not another one."

"I'm used to standing," Rhodes said.

He shoved some papers away with his foot and noticed something on the floor. He bent to pick it up and saw that it was a small ceramic turtle. He held it up and asked Benton if it belonged to him.

"Yes," Benton said. "I'm glad you found it. I've been looking for it. Did you know that turtles are considered sacred in a lot of cultures, including Native American culture?"

"No," Rhodes said, handing Benton the turtle.

"Well, they are," Benton said.

Benton held up the turtle for Qualls and Rhodes to admire. Qualls didn't look at it. He sat looking down at his feet or at something on the floor.

"Turtles figure in a lot of creation myths," Benton said, "and they carry a lot of wisdom. Turtles have been around for a long time, maybe forever. They've seen hundreds, thousands, of other animal species come and go. They know patience and how to wait. They can teach us a lot if we'll just open ourselves up and listen."

Benton set the turtle on his desk amid the clutter, and Rhodes thought about seeing the turtles at the rock pit. He didn't think it would be wise to mention them to Benton, who'd just go off on some tangent about how they were mystical visitors sent to give him insight. Rhodes didn't think that was at all likely, though Benton would have certainly disagreed.

"Hack told me you'd called," Rhodes said to Benton. "What can I do for you?"

"Ask not what you can do for me," Benton said. "Ask what I can do for you."

"I'll play along. What can you do for me?"

Benton looked at Qualls, who was still contemplating the floor.

"Dr. Qualls has something to tell you," Benton said. "You might want to close the door first."

Rhodes wasn't sure he wanted to be shut in the office with Benton and Qualls, but maybe the turtle would protect him in case of emergency. He closed the door. It locked automatically with a click.

"Your turn, Dr. Qualls," Benton said.

Qualls raised his head, but he didn't say anything. Rhodes looked at his hands, but the left one was concealed under the right.

"Let me help out," Benton said. "Dr. Qualls is having a little trouble with phrasing what he wants to tell you. It's sort of a confession."

"Sort of?" Rhodes asked, thinking of how he'd told Burns that he'd "not exactly" made an arrest.

"It's not a confession," Qualls said, speaking up at last. "It's more in the nature of a question about the law."

"I can handle questions," Rhodes said. "Ask me."

"It's not exactly a question, either."

"Just start talking, then," Rhodes said. "Sometimes that's the best way."

Qualls hesitated, thinking it over. Finally he got the words out.

"I came down here to apologize to Dr. Benton," Qualls said. "I'm the one who started our little . . . tussle. I overreacted. I admit it." He paused. "At any rate, Dr. Benton and I started talking, and he told me about his undercover work as a citizen deputy."

Rhodes hoped he didn't wince. If he did, Qualls didn't notice.

"Dr. Benton said that if I talked to you about . . . certain things, I might not have to go to jail, which was certain to happen otherwise because you were 'onto me.' "

"I didn't make him any promises," Benton said. "I know better than that."

"Can we talk about this as a hypothetical situation?" Qualls said, ignoring Benton.

"Sure," Rhodes said. "Let me help you out. If someone in this office right now was, hypothetically, the fella we've been calling Robin Hood, he really wouldn't have much to worry about. Misdemeanors only, unless one of the county commissioners gets too carried away. I think I can help out there. It wasn't the joke that bothered him, by the way. It was the tire. Robin Hood really shouldn't have shot the tire."

"He couldn't help himself," Qualls said. "Hypothetically. He hadn't planned to do it, but the car just looked so smug sitting there that he couldn't resist."

"I can see how that would happen."

"It shouldn't have. Robin Hood would be glad to apologize."

"That might do him some good. Let's say Robin Hood decides to admit what he's been doing. What would be the reason for the change of heart?"

"Dr. Benton's very persuasive," Qualls said.

Benton sat up straighter and seemed to swell a little in his chair, but Rhodes figured he was just imagining it.

"He told me that you knew what I'd been doing," Qualls continued. "He said that you were just biding your time and that you'd asked him to help out so I could get off as lightly as possible."

Rhodes had, of course, said no such thing. He looked at Benton, who had assumed an expression of what he probably thought was bland innocence.

"Then there's the fact that I seem to be the new owner of the chicken farm," Qualls continued. "Or I will be when Lester Hamilton's will is probated. That's going to take a while, according to the attorney."

"Randy Lawless," Rhodes said.

"Yes. Odd name for an attorney. At any rate, I'll eventually be the owner of the chicken farm, and I'll have a responsibility to the community. I don't want to have the possibility of a jail sentence hanging over me."

"We don't seem to be talking hypothetically anymore," Rhodes said.

"No, I suppose we aren't. I want to do the right thing. I've been childish, and it hasn't paid off. I need to clear my conscience."

"Just a minute," Benton said. "You shouldn't be so hard on yourself. The Robin Hood bit helped call attention to the problem, and the state needs to come in and get that place cleaned up now. We can't wait until you're the owner in six months or a year."

"I might have helped call attention to the problem," Qualls said, "but I went about it in the wrong way. It wasn't just the Robin Hood thing, Sheriff. I was rude to you and your deputy when you questioned me, and that was wrong, too. I'm sorry about that. What do you think will happen if I make a formal confession?"

"You'll have to pay a fine," Rhodes said. "I don't think it will go any farther than that."

"The publicity will be embarrassing," Qualls said, "but I can handle it. I can even handle making a public apology to Commissioner Burns if that will help."

"I think it will," Rhodes said, thinking that Burns might be a little disappointed that terrorists hadn't shot his tire. There went the grant for the M-16. "I can't make any promises, though, any more than Dr. Benton could."

"I wouldn't expect you to." Qualls stood up. "Let's get started."

Benton stood up, too.

"Book 'im, Dan-o," he said.

28

▼

"I'M ARMED, YOU KNOW," RHODES TOLD BENTON. "I COULD shoot you right now and claim self-defense."

"There's a witness," Benton said, indicating Qualls.

"I can't see a thing," Qualls said. "There's something in my eye."

Benton held up his hands in a gesture of surrender. "I was just making a joke. I wasn't even sure you were old enough to remember that TV show."

"I saw it in reruns," Rhodes said, "and I've heard the joke before. Not since I was a deputy, though. Even then it was old."

"I promise not to say it again."

"Good," Rhodes said. "Dr. Qualls, you can turn yourself in tomorrow. Right now I have some other business to take care of. I'll have the dispatcher give you a call."

"Whatever you say."

Rhodes left the two instructors in Benton's office and drove to the building that housed the *Clearview Herald*, Blacklin County's only newspaper. For over a hundred years, it had been a daily. Rhodes had been a paperboy there in his youth, but the newspaper industry had fallen on hard times in recent years, and the *Herald* was no exception. There were no more paperboys, just a couple of guys who drove around town throwing the paper from their cars.

Even sadder to Rhodes was the fact that the paper was now going to a three-days-a-week schedule in a couple of months, and the staff, which had consisted of the editor and two reporters, had been cut back. The editor had retired, and Nelson "Goober" Vance, who had done all the sports reporting, along with a number of other things, had become editor. Vance was about fifty, mostly bald, and about forty pounds overweight. Besides being the editor, he still had all his other duties, and he wasn't too happy about it.

He also didn't know where Jennifer Loam was.

"She told me she had to get some information," Vance said. "Then she left. She's kind of independent, in case you hadn't noticed."

"I've noticed," Rhodes said.

They were in Vance's little office, which looked out on the empty newsroom. The furnishings consisted of three desks with computer monitors on them. The computer monitors were dark. No one sat at any of the desks. The secretary had left for the day, and Jennifer had disappeared.

"She didn't give you any idea of where she was going?" Rhodes asked, though he thought he knew the answer already.

"No, she didn't say. I think it had something to do with the story she was working on, but she was pretty close-mouthed about that. It was her story, and she wasn't going to let anybody else in on it."

"So you don't know what she was looking for?"

"Nope. She thinks this chicken farm reporting is the big series of stories that's going to win her the Pulitzer." Vance wheezed a laugh. "Or if not that, get her a job on a bigger paper than this one. She doesn't seem to realize that in ten years there won't even be any more papers."

"There'll always be newspapers," Rhodes said.

"Don't kid yourself, Sheriff. Loam's just a youngster, but she's a dying breed. My advice to her would be to get herself a blog and forget the print media. It's over for us. Look around. Nobody here but me, and before long they'll get rid of me, too. That'll leave Loam, if she's lucky. If she's not, they'll just fold the paper around her and toss her in the trash."

"You're a real ray of sunshine," Rhodes said.

"Just a realist. It's not just newspapers. Won't be any books around in ten years, either. Everybody'll have those little handheld deals that you can download books into."

Rhodes thought about Clyde Ballinger. Rhodes was sure the books that Ballinger liked to read wouldn't be available on the handheld machines.

"I'm playing out the string here at the *Herald*," Vance said, "and I hope I make it to retirement before they cut me loose."

"Have the Robin Hood stories and the chicken farm stories helped the circulation?"

"Sure, but in a town this size even a fifty percent increase is no big deal. Forget it, Sheriff. Loam and me, newspaper reporters, we're history."

Rhodes didn't want to think about it, though he'd had similar thoughts of his own earlier.

"You think Loam might be at the chicken farm?" he asked.

"If I knew, I'd tell you. But I don't know."

"Thanks anyway," Rhodes said.

"You didn't say why you wanted to see her. She's not under arrest, I hope. I have too much to do around here as it is. I don't want the paper to fold today."

"Don't worry," Rhodes said. "I don't plan to arrest her."

"Good," Vance said. "I need the help."

Rhodes didn't tell him that Jennifer might be in more trouble than a mere arrest would mean. He didn't want to scare the man and have a heart attack on his conscience.

"If I see her," he said, "I'll tell her how much you appreciate her."

"I tell her that all the time myself," Vance said.

"How long has she been gone?"

"Not long. That story might be important to her, but it's not the only thing we have going on around here. If the story's another day late, who cares?"

"The readers?" Rhodes asked.

"Yeah," Vance said. "The readers. Right."

Rhodes's mistake with Jennifer Loam had been in not asking her about the evidence Gillis was supposed to produce. She probably wouldn't have told him for ethical reasons, but he should have asked. Maybe Jennifer hadn't known what it was herself, but if she had, she might have gone looking for it.

That might turn out to be trouble if Rhodes's latest assumptions turned out to be true.

One thing he should have considered more carefully was Hamilton's cell phone. It had no record of any calls. Rhodes didn't use a cell, but nearly everybody else in the county had one, and nearly everybody used them.

Hamilton shouldn't have been the exception. He was in business, and he needed to be in touch with people all the time, especially the one who was managing his business. Rhodes now believed that someone had erased all the calls from the phone, and that it hadn't been Hamilton. Someone hadn't wanted anybody to know who Hamilton had called or received calls from.

Why? The only reason Rhodes could think of was that Hamilton had talked to his killer. Maybe even told him that he was going noodling and where he'd be. The record of the call wouldn't really matter, but it would have been something that might have pointed the sheriff at a particular person. The timing of the calls could have been important.

Rhodes didn't know much about cell phone technology, but he knew that some phones had a SIM card that stored information. He'd have to ask Ruth Grady to check Hamilton's phone. Even if it had a card, the information might have been erased from it. Maybe not, however. If it was there, it wouldn't prove anything, but it would be suggestive.

The other thing Rhodes had remembered while fishing at the rock pit was something he'd seen on his trip out to the chicken farm to talk to Jared Crockett. A pickup with an aluminum boat in the bed had been parked behind the building where Crockett worked. That tied in with Rhodes's theory about the killer using a boat to get to the bridge. Crockett could even have planted the boat there days in advance and gone to the site with Hamilton. It might not have happened that way, but Rhodes thought it possible, even likely.

If Crockett suspected that Gillis was spying on him and feeding information to Jennifer, he could easily have walked to where Gillis was fishing, killed him, and walked back to the chicken farm in well under an hour.

Rhodes couldn't prove any of his assumptions, but if the evidence Jennifer was looking for had to do with Crockett, things didn't look good for the foreman. The evidence might have been anything, might have been about Terrall or Garrett or Qualls, but Rhodes didn't think so. He thought Crockett was the man. Now he had to find Jennifer and make sure.

Rhodes thought the reporter might be at the chicken farm, though he didn't know how she planned to get the evidence she was hoping for. He'd just have to go out there and look around to find out if he was right.

Rhodes didn't see anyone when he parked in front of the headquarters building. It was as if the place were deserted. Rhodes wondered where everyone was.

The smell of the barns rolled over him like a wave of noisome water when he got out of the car. It had been bad enough when he was inside, but outside it was even worse. He waded through it, taking shallow breaths through his mouth. He reached the door of the headquarters and knocked.

Nobody answered. Rhodes tried the knob. The door was locked.

It was only around four in the afternoon, too early for everyone to have left work unless Crockett had just decided to close the place down, now that Hamilton was dead. That didn't seem likely. Someone had to take care of the chickens until at least the next pickup from the processing plant.

Rhodes walked around the headquarters. He heard the raucous sound of the chickens as they squawked and cackled and scratched and flapped in their confinement, but he didn't see any humans around.

He did, however, see Crockett's pickup. It was parked behind the headquarters in the same spot it had been when Rhodes saw the boat in it, but the boat was gone now. Rhodes wondered where it was and if Crockett had managed somehow to dispose of it completely.

He went over to the pickup and looked in the bed. He didn't see any trace of the boat, no telltale paint scrapings on the sides, no oars left around by accident.

Rhodes took a breath and wished he had a respirator mask. The stink was so bad that his eyes watered, and the constant noise of the chickens didn't help matters.

Strolling along past the ends of the buildings, Rhodes looked for some indication that Jennifer Loam had been there. He didn't find anything. He'd thought her car would be parked in front, but there was no sign of it.

Crockett's pickup was there, though, and that must mean Crockett was somewhere nearby. Rhodes just couldn't figure out where.

The only thing Rhodes saw other than the buildings was the tall gray metal chimneys of the incinerators. On the chance that Crockett was doing some burning, Rhodes decided to go take a look.

Crockett was nowhere around.

Jennifer Loam, however, was there. Rhodes saw her when he passed the last of the farm buildings. She was bound with duct tape and propped up against the side of the last building. Across from her were the incinerators.

Rhodes ran to her and knelt down. He got out his pocketknife and started to cut the tape.

"What's going on?" he asked as he worked.

"It's Crockett," Jennifer said. "He was going to kill me and feed me to the incinerator."

She sounded calm about it, a lot calmer than Rhodes would have been in her situation.

"Where is he now?" Rhodes asked as he started to peel the tape away.

Jennifer helped him as soon as her hands were free. "He's taken my car somewhere to get rid of it. He didn't want anyone to know I'd been here."

"You should have told someone what you were doing."

"I didn't think Crockett would go crazy on me."

"Did you confront him about anything?"

Jennifer peeled off the rest of the tape and stood up. She was a little unsteady and put a hand on the side of the building to get her balance.

"I didn't confront him." She shook her head as if to clear it. "Well, maybe a little. He came across the desk and hit me. Then he taped me up and carried me here."

"What did you ask him about?"

"Hal Gillis told me that the workers were abusing the chickens, killing them for fun. Sometimes they get out of the barns, you know."

Rhodes recalled the chicken he'd seen perched on the boat.

"They catch them and wring their necks," Jennifer said.

Rhodes thought of his grandfather with a twinge of guilt.

"Or they stomp them," Jennifer went on.

At least Rhodes hadn't seen his grandfather do anything like that.

"Mr. Gillis was going to get pictures," Jennifer said. "I don't know if he did."

"If he did, they're gone now," Rhodes said. "Are you sure Crockett was letting things like that that go on?"

"No, I wasn't sure. I tried to be subtle about asking him, but I don't think it worked."

"Me, neither," Rhodes said, eyeing the sticky residue on her clothes.

Rhodes had wondered about a motive for Hamilton's murder. Now he had one, if the story Gillis had told was true.

"We need to get you out of here," he told Jennifer.

"Too late," a man said in a metallic voice as he came around the end of the building.

Rhodes couldn't see the man's face because he wore a respirator mask, but it was Crockett, all right. He held a revolver in his right hand.

"You didn't mention the pistol," Rhodes said.

"I thought you'd take it for granted," Jennifer said.

"This is a real mess," Crockett said. "I sure wish you'd stayed out of it, Sheriff."

"Just doing my job."

"Maybe so. Too bad about that, then."

Rhodes glanced over at the incinerators. "You'd have to chop us up mighty fine to get us in those things."

"The girl's no problem," Crockett said. "You're a little hefty, though."

"I've been planning to exercise more."

"Ho, ho, ho." The fake laugh sounded sinister through the tinny speaker. "Joking won't help you any, Sheriff."

Crockett was nerving himself up to shoot, and Rhodes didn't think it would take him long to get to it. Rhodes shoved Jennifer as hard as he could, so hard that she bounced off the wall of the building as he threw himself in the opposite direction.

Crockett fired off some shots, two or three, Rhodes wasn't sure.

Rhodes could have rolled to the incinerators for cover, but he didn't have time. Crockett would shoot him before he got there.

Rhodes twisted around, pulled up his pants leg, and grabbed his .32. This was far from the ideal situation for the little pistol, but Rhodes had to use what he had.

He looked for Crockett, but the big man wasn't where he'd been. He'd grabbed Jennifer Loam and held her in front of himself as a shield.

"Drop your gun, Sheriff," he said.

Rhodes hadn't heard that line since watching an old B-Western on television years ago. He'd forgotten what the response was in the movie, but he didn't have to use it because Jennifer raised her leg and stomped Crockett's foot right on top of the arch.

Crockett cried out and let go of Jennifer, who dived to the side. Rhodes fired his pistol, missing Crockett by a good two feet.

Crockett shot back, coming a lot closer than Rhodes had, but not close enough to hit anything. Before Rhodes could get off another shot, Crockett turned and ran. Rhodes got to his feet and went after him.

"You stay here," he called to Jennifer, not waiting to see if she heard.

Rhodes almost made a rookie mistake by running around the end of the building without checking, but he stopped just in time. It was a good thing he did, because when he took a peek, he saw Crockett waiting about twenty yards away.

The foreman stood in a crouch and held the revolver in a two-handed grip. As soon as he saw Rhodes's head poke out, he pulled the trigger. The bullet clanged through the corner, taking out a chunk of metal just above Rhodes's head, but Rhodes had already ducked back.

He waited a second, then took another look.

Crockett was gone.

29

▼

RHODES KNEW OF ONLY ONE PLACE WHERE CROCKETT COULD go, and, sure enough, chickens exploded out the door of one of the big buildings, fluttering, skreaking, and scattering feathers.

Crockett probably hoped Rhodes wouldn't follow him inside, and Rhodes wished he didn't have to do it, but it was all part of the job.

Some of the chickens squatted on the ground, dazed and confused by their sudden freedom and all the commotion. Others flapped past Rhodes, not even seeing him, brushing him as he entered the building.

The stench was incredible, like a spongy wall that Rhodes had to push through. Chickens swirled and danced around him, their loose feathers flying in all directions as his feet sank into the fetid litter.

Rhodes brushed away feathers and tried not to think of lice, ticks, mites, E. coli, and worms. It was too bad he didn't have a respirator mask. The only good thing he could think of was that Crockett couldn't possibly shoot him, not with all the beating wings and the swirling dust.

Crockett wasn't reading off the same page, however. A boom sounded over the racket of the chickens, and one of them only inches from Rhodes flew apart in a haze of blood and feathers.

Rhodes peered down the length of the building and saw a bulky shape that had to be Crockett plowing through the panicked birds, swinging his arms and swatting them out of his way like volleyballs as he made for the far exit.

Rhodes crooked his left arm in front of his face to protect his eyes from errant beaks and slogged through the litter, trying to breathe shallowly through his mouth. The smell was still overwhelming, and it was made even worse because Rhodes and Crockett were agitating the litter and bringing up odors from its depths. Rhodes wondered if it had ever been cleaned out and changed and suspected that it hadn't. No wonder the stink reeked all over the countryside. He was afraid he was inhaling toxins and airborne parasites of all kinds, but there was nothing he could do about it.

Crockett burst out the door well ahead of Rhodes, who was having more and more trouble fighting his way through the chickens. Crockett got them stirred up, and Rhodes had to blunder through them as best he could as he tried not to get pecked to death. Fending off the mass of chickens was like fighting through a jungle of living plants with beaks and claws.

It seemed to take an eternity for Rhodes to get to the exit, and then he had to stop and wait. He couldn't just run outside and let Crockett pick him off.

He knew he couldn't stay inside for much longer. The foulness was too much for him. He counted to ten and stuck his head out.

Crockett wasn't interested in shooting him. He was headed for his pickup.

Jennifer Loam was running after him. She hadn't heard, or hadn't paid any attention, when Rhodes told her to stay where she was.

Crockett either heard her coming or sensed that she was behind him. He didn't shoot her. He turned and batted her away with a fist to her head.

She fell hard and rolled over. Instead of looking down at her, Crockett looked back toward Rhodes. He brought up his pistol and fired.

The bullet twanged through metal. Rhodes calculated that was Crockett's fifth shot, maybe his sixth.

Crockett kicked Jennifer in the side and got into his pickup. Rhodes was running as hard as he could, but he saw he wasn't going to get to Crockett in time to stop him, and the little .32 wouldn't do much damage at the distance Rhodes was from the pickup. Crockett was going to get away.

Except that he wasn't planning to try. He started the truck, backed it up, and headed for Rhodes.

To get to the sheriff, he'd have to drive right over Jennifer, but that didn't bother him.

Rhodes yelled. He didn't know if the reporter heard him, but she rolled away just as Crockett got to her. He missed her by less than a foot and directed the pickup at Rhodes.

Rhodes had several choices.

He could try evasive action, but Crockett would catch him eventually.

He could try to get back into the chicken barn, but he didn't think he could make it in time. He didn't want to go back in there anyway.

Or he could try shooting. He didn't have much firepower, and he wished briefly for the M-16 that Burns wanted to buy. An M-16 would have chewed the little truck up like a toy.

Rhodes had only his .32, however, and that would have to do.

He stood his ground, brought up the pistol, and steadied his right wrist with his left hand.

As Crockett bore down on him, Rhodes could see the big man's masked face through the windshield. He looked like some kind of demented spaceman out of a bad 1950s science fiction movie, flying his rocketship on a suicide mission as if it weren't a job he wanted to do but one he had to finish.

Rhodes didn't want to be finished. He pulled the trigger three times. The .32 popped in his hand with no noticeable recoil.

The bullets starred the windshield. Crockett's head jerked to the left and slammed against the window. It bounced back to the right. Crockett's hands lost their grip on the steering wheel, and the pickup careened off course, passing by Rhodes and crashing into the building behind him. It put a considerable dent in the building, but it didn't break through. Chickens poured out the door beside it in a white avalanche.

Rhodes checked on Jennifer first. She had gained her feet and stared at him, a little dazed.

"Are you all right?" Rhodes asked when he reached her.

"I think so," she said. "My head's buzzing. He hit me pretty hard."

"At least he didn't run over you."

"He tried. You look worse than I do, though."

Chicken feathers clung to Rhodes's clothing and hair. His shoes and his pants down from just above the ankles were covered with muck. Besides that, the inside of his mouth tasted as if a dozen chickens had nested in it.

There wasn't anything he could do about it. He turned to the truck. Steam hissed from its radiator. The driver's door was sprung open, and the air bag had exploded. Crocket lay half in and half out of the pickup.

"Did you kill him?" Jennifer asked.

"I don't think so," Rhodes said.

"It wouldn't be any great loss if you did."

"We need him to tell us what he did with your car."

"Oh. I can tell you that. He said he was going to drive it into a tank."

"I hope you have good insurance."

"Right now I don't care. Shouldn't you go check on Crockett?"

"I might as well," Rhodes said.

"What if he's faking?"

"I still have my pistol," Rhodes said.

Crockett wasn't faking. He wasn't dead, either, just unconscious. Rhodes pulled him all the way out of the pickup and laid him on the ground.

"Do you have a cell phone?" Rhodes asked Jennifer.

"It's in my purse. My purse is in my car. My car . . . is probably at the bottom of a tank."

"Never mind," Rhodes said.

He looked around inside the pickup and found a roll of duct tape. He turned Crockett over on his stomach and taped his hands behind his back.

"Should you be moving him around like that?" Jennifer asked.

"I don't think he's hurt badly," Rhodes said.

"What if you're wrong?"

"We'll worry about that later." Rhodes handed her the pistol. "If he wakes up and tries to escape, shoot him. In the knee would be best."

Jennifer held the pistol as if she'd never seen one before. Maybe she hadn't.

"I don't know how to use this," she said.

"Just threaten him. That should do it. I'll be back in a minute."

Rhodes left her standing there and walked around the headquarters building to the county car. He got Hack on the radio and told him to send a deputy and an ambulance to the Hamilton place.

"You okay?" Hack asked.

"Sure," Rhodes said.

"Somebody's not, though."

"Right."

"You gonna tell me who?"

Rhodes smiled. "Later," he said.

Ruth Grady arrived just before the ambulance. The first thing she did after seeing Rhodes was to hand him a bottle of water from her county car. Rhodes thanked her and washed out his mouth. He spit the water out but didn't look at it. He didn't want to know what it looked like.

Crockett was conscious and sitting up, but he wouldn't say anything. Rhodes told Ruth to check the nearby stock tanks to see if anyone had driven a car into one of them.

"That wouldn't be easy to do," she said.

"No. He might have been lying, so look around and see if you can find the car."

Jennifer described it for her, and Ruth left.

The EMTs loaded Crockett into the ambulance and took him away.

"What about the chickens?" Jennifer asked.

"They're free-range chickens now," Rhodes said.

"Aren't there coyotes in the county?"

"Sure are," Rhodes said, "but the chickens will just have to take their chances. With freedom comes great responsibility."

"I don't think that's exactly the right wording."

"Me neither, but it'll have to do. Unless you want to round them up."

"I don't think so."

"I don't blame you a bit," Rhodes said.

Rhodes drove home and removed his shoes and pants in the backyard. Ivy came out to see what he was doing. Yancey yapped along after her.

"Good grief," she said, keeping her distance. "You smell awful. And look at all those feathers. What happened? Was there an explosion in a pillow factory?"

"I had a run-in with some chickens," Rhodes told her. "I'm going to hose myself down before I come inside."

Ivy nodded. "Good idea. You know, the county's going to get tired of paying to have the cars cleaned up after you use them."

"It's not so bad this time," Rhodes said.

Yancey stopped barking and stared at Rhodes. Speedo had kept his distance so far, but now he came over, too. He was careful not to get too close.

"Even the dogs don't like me," Rhodes said.

Ivy laughed. "I'll get the soap."

"Bring some mouthwash, too," Rhodes said.

* * *

Ruth found Jennifer's car in a mesquite thicket the next day. The cell phone was just fine, and so was everything else in the purse and car.

Crockett hadn't talked, but things weren't looking good for him. As executor of Hamilton's estate, Randy Lawless ordered an audit of the chicken farm's books. He told Rhodes that it was obvious from even a cursory check that Crockett had been cutting corners and cooking the books, pocketing the money he saved.

"Lester talked to me about things last week," Lawless said. "He was suspicious that something was going on. All the talk had finally convinced him. As it turned out, there was more going on than either of us thought."

"Do you think that's why he was killed?" Qualls asked.

Qualls was at the jail to confess formally to his crimes. Seepy Benton was with him for some reason, and so, of course, was Lawless, as Qualls's attorney.

"Could be," Rhodes said. "Crockett must have figured out something was going on. He decided to make sure he didn't get found out."

"So Crockett's crookedness explains why the litter was never changed and the incinerators weren't being used properly," Qualls said. "I'll see that things are handled better when I take over."

"Things will be better before then," Lawless said. "I'll see to that. I'll have the state come in and make recommendations whether they want to or not, and we'll do everything right. Everything will be better than standard."

"What about the employees?" Rhodes asked.

"They're fired," Lawless said. "We're starting over. Nobody's going to admit to anything, but Crockett had to have help in covering up what he was doing. Maybe the stories about the abuse aren't true, but I'm not taking any chances."

Rhodes didn't think they'd ever get any evidence about the abuse, not unless Gillis had taken photographs. So far he hadn't found a camera at Gillis's house. One might turn up, but Rhodes doubted it would happen. Crockett might have taken it, or there might never have been one.

So far there was no evidence that Crockett had killed either Gillis or Hamilton, but Rhodes was convinced of Crockett's guilt. He'd find someone who'd seen Crockett's boat, or they'd find traces of the riverbank on the bottom of the boat.

Even more likely, they'd find out where Crockett had bought the bow and arrows he'd planted in Gillis's house to throw suspicion on him as Robin Hood. They'd already faxed Crockett's mug shot to sporting goods stores around the state, and Ruth was going to search the chicken farm's computers to see if Crockett had placed an online order. Crockett had been planning to frame Gillis for a while, though maybe not to murder him.

Crockett would eventually confess when confronted with the facts. Rhodes had no doubt of it. He believed that Crockett had known in advance that Hamilton would be noodling in Murdock's rock pit and had positioned the boat days earlier. The cell phone's SIM card might even give some information about phone calls to Crockett that would help Rhodes figure out the timing. When the case came to trial, Rhodes would have plenty of evidence. He hoped.

"I guess I've proved what an asset I am to the department," Seepy Benton said. "You'd never have cracked this case without me. I've ensured your reelection."

"Right," Rhodes said, not mentioning that he was running unopposed.

"You don't sound convinced," Benton said.

"No wonder," Ruth Grady said. She'd come into the jail just in time to hear Benton's remark. "You didn't exactly distinguish yourself."

"That's not fair," Benton said. "Dr. Qualls has admitted that our little fracas was his doing. You can't keep blaming me for that."

Rhodes had a feeling things weren't going smoothly with Benton's love life, but it was none of Rhodes's business.

On the other side of the room, Hack was laughing silently. Rhodes tried not to look in that direction.

"It's kind of sad when you think about it," Lawless said.

"What is?" Benton asked.

"All this time when people were saying bad things about Lester Hamilton, he wasn't really the one responsible for the conditions at his place. Crockett was the cause of all the trouble, not Lester. Lester was going to get to the root of the problem, and Crockett killed him before he could do anything."

"Hamilton has to take some of the blame," Qualls said. "He was the owner, and that made him responsible. He should have been the one who oversaw the employees to make sure they were doing the right thing."

"He was doing that," Lawless said. "He would have taken steps within the week."

"If he'd been around," Rhodes said. "Crockett saw to it that he wasn't."

"That's just speculation at this point," Lawless said.

"Spoken like a lawyer," Ruth said.

"We do know one thing for sure," Benton said.

"What?" Ruth asked.

Rhodes put up a hand for silence, but he wasn't in time.

"No Les," Benton said, "no more."